INGRESS

An Alaska Iconoclast Mystery

Mary Ann Poll

PO Box 221974 Anchorage, Alaska 99522-1974
books@publicationconsultants.com
www.publicationconsultants.com

ISBN 978-1-59433-253-1
ebook 978-1-59433-254-8
Library of Congress Catalog Card Number: 2011940274

Manufactured in the United States of America.

Dedication

To Elaine Crabtree. Your courage and tenacity are a constant inspiration. God bless you, my friend.

Acknowledgements

I am grateful to have this opportunity to offer my thanks to those that have helped make this book possible.

Chevonne Clark for tutoring this novice on the differences between heavy equipment and the uses for each.

Buzz Kyllonen for giving me an "up close and personal" lesson in the operation of heavy equipment. I now understand the difference between a loader and a bulldozer. I will never forget the ride on the loader and watching how you operate such complicated machines with ease.

James Keri of the Alaska Native Language Center and Alan Boraas of the Kenai Peninsula College who are the editors of "*A Dena'ina Legacy, K'TL'EGH'I SUKDU, The Collected Writings of Peter Kalifornsky*. Without this complete collection, the rich heritage of Alaska would be missing from *Ingress*.

Wikipedia, that amazing online encyclopedia.

John Lohff for keeping me on the straight and narrow where law enforcement titles are concerned.

Nancy Blunck for dropping everything in her very busy schedule as an investment manager to discuss any concerns and help me clear the way for *Ingress* to be the best it can be.

And to my much-loved and sometimes neglected family and friends for their continued support and love.

Contents

The Legend of the Forgotten Place

Young James Clarke sprinted through the summerwoods of Southcentral Alaska. The day was hot so he had no need for long sleeves or the heavy squirrel parka his mother forced him to wear in winter. He reveled in the sweet smell of the birch and alder and the songs of the summer birds as he glided effortlessly through the forest.

His only goal on this rare summer day was to remain the village's hide-and-seek champion. When Smith Jonas almost caught him, James made a decision to run farther into the woods than he dared venture in his young life.

James slowed to a walk then crept forward when the birch and willow gave way to an open field. He tiptoed beside the riverbank, the gurgling and rushing water covering the occasional snap of a twig that could reveal his hiding place. He peeked through the low underbrush to the right of the stream.

"The Forgotten Place." His eyes took in the back of an old, two-story house. Five spires jutted skyward from the roof. They reminded him of bony, wooden arms straining to touch the heavens. He could almost hear the creaks and groans as they toiled to be free of the bondage of the roof.

It was forbidden to come here or speak of this place. An excited shiver coursed through his young frame. He tiptoed from the safety of the bushes, eyes focused on the five spires on the mansion's roof.

"Today, I will be a man. Men aren't cowards," he whispered. He scampered to a narrow footpath between the old house and a decaying leanto. The air turned midwinter cold. His breath came out in short bursts of fog. He shivered. *I'll never argue with momma about wearing that heavy squirrel parka again.*

He wheeled around when a deafening *bang* made the earth vibrate beneath him. A dust cloud framed a rotted board in the pathway behind him.

He squared his shoulders and turned back around. *Today I am a man.* He forced his driftwood-heavy feet to step onto a hard-packed dirt trail that had been taken over by alders and tall grass.

The summer birds did not sing here. The hair on the back of his neck came to attention right before an ear-piercing *clap* broke the deathlike calm. James jogged to the center of the bushes, tripped and landed on his backside, legs sprawled in front of him, hands behind. Between his left and right feet was a human skull. He screamed and pushed backward with both feet. Something stopped him from retreating. He turned and came face to face with the bleached-white bones of a rib cage. He felt his dazed inner being fly out of his body. It hovered above the alders like a curious bystander at one of the town's blanket tosses.

"Welcome." A voice full of gravel growled from his right.

James flew back to his body. His heart pounded and his mind screamed *run*. He willed his body to hold still.

"Your name." The voice demanded.

"J-j-james. Clark." He croaked.

"You are intruding, J-j-james Clark." The voice mocked his stutter. Fear rose in his gut. His legs tensed, ready to run again.

"You are not yet a man, James Clark."

"Tomorrow I will be thirteen." The pride of being an adult made him forget the terror that had clouded his mind.

"You are not yet a man." The disappointed voice, which had been on his right, now had moved directly in front of him.

"Leave here. *Now.*" The command issued from an inky specter that drifted up and out of the tall grass that blocked James' escape. James followed the entity's growth with saucer-size eyes while it drifted skyward until it blocked the sunlight. He dropped to the ground and covered his head when he saw the empty eye sockets and oozing hole of a mouth.

"Leave. Because you are not a man, I will let you go but you must go now. Or, the one I serve will take you and you will be damned with me in this place forever."

James nodded up and down in a frantic motion.

"*Go!*"

James jumped and ran for the clearing. He located the spires of the old house and ran for the safety of the woods. He no longer cared who might see him or that he remained the village's hide-and-seek champion. He didn't stop running until he reached his home. He slammed the door and dove onto his bed.

Elder Clark, James' grandfather, walked to the side of James' bed. "Tell me."

"James turned tear-filled eyes to his grandfather. He shook his head.

"Tell me." Shaman Clark lowered himself to the edge of James' bed.

Terror paralyzed the young James Clark's tongue.

"Did you go where you were told not to go?"

James nodded.

Grandpa Clark looked long and hard at James. "Did you see something?"

James nodded again.

"You will never be young again. You have seen what no human should see. There are things hidden from us for our good. That, James, is why I told you never to go there. That is why no one in our village can ever go there."

The older man's shoulders slumped under the heavy weight of sadness. "What's done is done. You have been noticed and that will never change. For your life, you must be vigilant. When you put the ways of a child behind you, that being will work to lure you back for his master. For this reason, I will tell you about the Forgotten Place. You must remember. Do you understand?"

James nodded, eyes wide, curiosity calming his terror.

"So be it."

"Our people do not wander. We have been blessed by abundant food here." Grandpa spread his arms wide.

"But one winter, the snow came early and it covered the willow and late-autumn grass. The moose went inland in search of food. So did we. We returned to the camp at the Tikat River when the warm summer winds began to blow and the late snows of winter melted into the earth. The shaman, a good man who cared deeply for our people, blessed the river and it was bountiful. The summer harvest was good and our people were happy.

"While some of our men were scouting the territory that surrounded our village, they discovered a beautiful child, very ill and close to death. She was brought to the village elders. The child had no memory of her people.

"The good shaman told his wife about the young girl. She begged him to take her into their home. She had never been blessed with children and longed to be a mother. Seeing his wife's unhappiness, he agreed. The young girl grew into a young woman. She had no interest in the chores bestowed on the village women. She wanted to learn the ways of the shaman.

"As you know, only the men of our clan are trained in the ways of the shamans. The old shaman had grown to love this girl as his own child and could deny her nothing. So he allowed her to help him and showed her the healing and protection rituals. She was not content. The spoiled young woman craved the respect and awe the good shaman commanded from the people. So, she practiced the rituals in private. And, in secret, she used her gift and cured many.

"The good shaman found out. His heart broke because he had to go the clan's elders. He knew the girl would be banned from the village. His wife begged him to overlook the girl's treachery. But, in the end, the good shaman's loyalty to the village came above his loyalty to his family.

"The wife took her case to the village, to those that had been cured by the girl. The village was divided—some for the old way of life and some for the girl.

"During that same season, a group of white settlers came upon the village. They were in search of gold. The clan's warriors took them captive until the elders decided if they would live or die.

"The young woman, always curious and rebellious, went to their jail and was bewitched by one of the settlers. He was a tall, strong man. He mesmerized her with his stories about books with spells and ways to get anything you want in life. She fell in love with the man and his beliefs. She went to her mother and confessed her love for the tall stranger. She told her mother that she wanted to wed this man. The wife convinced the shaman to come to the young girl's defense.

"The elders listened to the shaman and saw a way to appease the whole village and be rid of the girl, too. They agreed to spare her love but not the others. The woman only cared for that man and his beliefs so she was content with the edict."

Grandpa Clark looked at James. "You see, that was the beginning of a curse. The white settlers had done nothing to harm our clan, but the fear that those strangers could bring further division to the clan overcame their need to do what is just."

"So, the innocent men were sacrificed and buried. And, the girl married the white stranger. Afterward a wolf with yellow eyes came to the good shaman and spoke to him.

'Your clan is cursed, good shaman. The woman married the one man the elders would have been wise to destroy. They are two halves that, once together, form a powerful evil bond. Together they will destroy your home and it will be abandoned for all time.'

"The shaman went to the council with his vision. They laughed at him.

"You see, the white man had already begun to trap our clan. He taught them to build wood houses that kept out the cold. They taught him to fish and hunt. He accepted the rituals of our clan. He prospered when he sold dried fish to the inland villages. And, as he received payment, he gave half of it to the clan. So it prospered because of him. The elders rebuked the good shaman and did not heed the white wolf's words.

"Our people felt indebted to the white man for teaching them his way and sharing the bounty he received from other clans. They agreed to build a special home. That is the five-pointed house you saw there. In return he promised to teach them how to talk to the spirits so they could forever prosper.

"The village believed him and turned away from the good shaman. The white man became the spiritual leader and counsel to the elders. So, when he demanded the villagers allow white men to come in safety to the village, the elders agreed. He told them to build a structure to make the fish ready for those settlers. He convinced them to build a store and hotel, too. They built each structure as directed. The next summer, our people sold and bartered with all who came into the town. The clan became rich.

"Over that same year, the man taught his new wife to practice the evil arts of his religion. She mastered the rituals with ease.

"When he and the woman joined together to cast the spells, his power over the village increased. He shared his religious book with her. It was called *The Book of Fallen Angels* and instructed them on how to bring demons to our world. The buildings he had our people build were to be homes. Not human homes, but spirit homes. He and his mate went from house to house, one per day, to prepare them. Each house was a door that, once opened, let the evil ones come into our world.

"The good shaman discovered what they were doing, but too late. He was lured by his daughter to the big house, for a truce dinner. There he was taken as the final sacrifice. The demons were released and the town was theirs. On that day, they murdered all who were in the village. Some of our men had been hunting for moose and returned to find all of their loved ones dead—decaying and stinking. They ran for their lives."

"Grandpa, why can't you get rid of those demons? Aren't you the strongest shaman in our clan?"

"I am. I am no match for those demons. The Great and Good Spirit is the only one who can destroy them and He did not

15

come to do that—not yet. I do not know why. Until He does, we must not step foot in that cursed place. It is theirs."

James Clark guarded the story of the Forgotten Place in his heart. He followed his grandfather and became a strong and respected shaman of the clan. One summer day he left the village in search of the healing plants. It is said that on that day he ventured too far into the woods and lost his way. And that the Forgotten Place called to him and he answered. The clan knew that if they uttered his name it would call him out of the Forgotten Place to take the man or woman to her doom. No one spoke of him again.

Prologue
One Man's Soul

Grandma watched in horror as Josiah disappeared. She heard him say, "I have come to slay you, slayer of my family." The laughter rose, then a growl. Then silence. "Ravens Cove: An Alaska Iconoclast Mystery"

Josiah Williams spun on his heel to face his adversary. Instead, he confronted complete darkness. The snarl still reverberated off the ravine walls, each echo less audible than the last. Josiah took a tentative step forward and slid. An agility fueled by adrenaline saved him before he belly-flopped into the slick, squishing earth beneath him. He heaved as the stench of sewage assaulted his senses.

He squinted toward a rhythmic *plop-plop* that echoed through the unsettling silence. An effervescent green fluid stretched, then snapped, and dropped from rocks to the ravine floor. Behind the liquid, thousands of floating, red eyes focused on Josiah.

Josiah's head snapped forward. An enormous entity—as solid in form as Josiah—blocked his view. Black, coriaceous skin hung from wiry arms and legs. Herculean hands and feet jutted from the emaciated appendages. The sight was so macabre it was almost laughable. But, the long, fungus-yellow, razor-sharp talons that capped the fingers and toes dispelled any sense of the comical.

"You are Iconoclast." Josiah glared into the eyes of his enemy.

"And you are a gormless little mortal," it sneered. The wrinkled face widened into a sickening grin. "I hunger for a soul from God. And since you found it necessary to deny me my prize, I'll consider it even when I take you." Iconoclast moved forward.

Shrieks of laughter assaulted Josiah's ears. The opaque demons had solidified and descended from the ravine walls. They formed a tight circle around Josiah and Iconoclast. Josiah's heart raced and his legs trembled with the adrenaline that pumped through his body. *Don't show your fear man. Steady and slow.* Josiah turned to his enemy.

"You are wrong, Iconoclast. You cannot dine on me—my soul is God's. You can't take me from Him—now or ever."

At the mention of God, Iconoclast snapped to attention, growled and lunged. A claw whizzed by Josiah's face, so close he heard it slice the air. Josiah jumped backward, only to be pushed forward again by the ghastly spectators.

"Lord, strengthen me." He appealed in silent prayer. The truth whispered into his mind. He straightened. "You murdered my physical family, Iconoclast, but you could not kill their souls. Not satisfying to one with such an insatiable appetite."

A cold, hard smile met maroon glowing eyes. "You are a mortal. How would you know where their souls reside?" Iconoclast lifted his emaciated limbs. The ebony wings creaked in protest as they fanned up and out until they rested in full expanse behind his arms. The disfigured arms rose as if to conduct a macabre orchestra. In response, a frothy, grey mist snaked up from the ground.

Two small shapes took form first. A taller shape followed.

"Daddy." The small ones cried in an ethereal voice. "Daddy, help us."

"Joe. I'm so cold. It's dark and I'm afraid. Someone means me harm; I hear footsteps behind me. I don't know where to run because I can't see." Bonnie wailed.

The first blow of hopelessness struck Josiah in the stomach. He doubled over, gasping for breath.

"Why didn't you save us? Why didn't you protect us?" Thick, fluid voices splattered into Josiah's ears.

Josiah Williams fell on his knees. Tears bathed his cheeks as anguish and guilt flooded him.

"Oh, Bonnie, you are right to hate me, all of you are right to hate me. I failed you. I sinned and in that sin you perished." His voice broke into deep sobs and groans that echoed off the ravine walls in a melancholy tune.

"And you think your God will save you?" The smell of decay and sulfur stormed Josiah's senses. He managed to control the bile rising to his throat. His shoulders sagged in defeat.

"I don't deserve to be saved."

"Then you agree with me and I can take your soul, is that correct, Josiah Williams?"

Bonnie and the children walked forward, their gazes penetrating his mind. He lifted his shame-filled eyes to meet their rage-filled ones. He tilted his head and leaned closer to his family.

Tiny pinpricks of light glinted in the vacant black orbs. He squeezed his eyes shut and opened them again. The pinpricks still sparkled with colors. He compelled himself to overcome the horror of the empty sockets.

Multi-hued patterns swirled in the small holes. Reds, blacks, yellows, and purples moved in a kaleidoscope fashion. The unorganized motif took shape. In his young son's eyes, a small

19

child was ripped from its mother's arms on some sandy dune in a hot land. Screaming then silent as it was beheaded to stop the advance of a newborn king. He shivered and turned.

Bonnie's eyes revealed a man running for his life only to be caught by a mob, held down and stoned until his head was unrecognizable. The end to the silent movie revealed a crowd, mouths open and hands in the air, mutely cheering in approval.

In Martha's eyes, a woman was bound at the waist to a small tree trunk. Flames licked at her midsection, already having consumed her legs. A stone castle towered above her. She, too, was surrounded by a crowd that cheered each time she cried out.

Josiah continued to study his late family's eyes. When one vision ended another morbid movie swirled into view. Each scene more recent in history than the last. Each scene more graphic than the last.

"This is not my wife. These are not my children." The tremor in Josiah's voice betrayed the firm statement.

"They are, foolish man. Look again."

Josiah looked back to the vacant orbs and was met by Bonnie's eyes of robin's egg blue. The children's eyes were clear and wide. He fell to his knees again. Confusion saturated his tired mind.

"Again, mortal, do you agree that I can take your soul? Your *GOD*," Iconoclast spat the word at Josiah like he had a mouthful of rotten meat, "has forgotten you. You were a fool to believe He would forgive you for murdering your own family." The three apparitions floated forward and came to rest between Josiah and Iconoclast.

Josiah dropped his gaze to the ravine floor. "I am..." His defeated eyes came to an abrupt stop at the feet of his children and wife. He studied their ankles. He straightened to full height, jaw set, body tense.

"You are a thief *and* a liar. This is not my family!"

"They are!"

"Deluder! My wife had a birthmark on her front right ankle. A perfect circle. The mole on this thing is shaped like a knife." He turned to the family of three. "In the name of Jesus, show yourselves!"

The woman and children stretched and contorted, snapping and popping as their shapes changed. Hisses and cries replaced ethereal voices as the entities struggled to maintain their human forms.

Three brickdust-colored demons covered in coarse hair balanced on three-toed feet. The torsos were human. The demons' mouths, stretched in a permanent, joker-like grin, revealed the dagger-sharp teeth that had become so familiar to Josiah during the recent battle in Ravens Cove. Their cheeks were deeply creased by the fixed upended mouth. A palpable hatred shot from bloody eyes.

Clawed hands strained toward Josiah. Six feet stomped forward in a gruesome march. The ghastly mouths opened wider to reveal eight-inch canines. Yellow mucus dripped off the teeth. The ground sizzled every time the venom made contact.

"Stop!" Iconoclast thundered.

The trio ignored the commander and marched toward their target. One of the shapeshifters spat yellow venom at the commander. Iconoclast batted it back at the demon. The acid sizzled then disappeared into the red-brown skin.

Josiah faced the trio. *If it's my time, I'll look death in the eye before I'll run.*

"You impertinent insects." Iconoclast swiftly gathered the threesome into his arms and held them in a firm grip away from his torso. They clawed and bit the air, stretching to reach Iconoclast's midsection.

Four demons jumped onto Iconoclast's back. He pushed his wings backward, wedged them underneath the ghouls then snapped them open. All four flew upward in the force of the thrust. They screeched in surprise, snapped their wings open as they tumbled toward the ravine floor and dove at Iconoclast.

Iconoclast slashed two in mid-dive with his left talons. Their wings dropped to their sides and they plummeted to the earth. The lesser spirits, looking to move up the evil chain of command, took courage from those that had attacked the great warrior of the evil one. They jumped on Iconoclast. He managed to fend them off with his free hand, and hold onto the howling shapeshifters with the other.

All out war erupted between the loyal and disloyal hellhounds. As talon met demon flesh, a red haze crystallized overhead and fell to the ravine floor in a putrid-smelling rain. The wounds shut as quickly as they were opened and the battle continued.

Iconoclast flung the threesome to the ground and swiped at the mutinous crowd. He reeled away from the rebellious trio, splayed his fingers, pointed at the ravine floor and rotated his arms in a counterclockwise rhythm. The earth rumbled. A small crack appeared in the ravine floor and grew wider with each shake and groan. The cries of battle ceased.

Iconoclast spun, grabbed the shapeshifters and threw them into the narrow chasm. He widened his arms from left to right. The earth responded and opened until a gaping hole was all that remained of the ravine floor. The demons stared at him—some in fright, some in vindication.

"Be gone from my sight. I *am* Iconoclast. You will remember that forever!" He bent his leathery forelimbs then brought his hands forward. Every demon glided forward, an invisible belt-way moving them toward the yawning fissure.

"We fought for you, Iconoclast!" one demon screamed over his shoulder, as he ran in place trying to get to the ravine wall.

Iconoclast snorted. "Loyalty? An overused lie, Tartuffe." He continued to motion them in. Orange flames licked the sides of the crevice. Demons, not unlike the lemmings of old, began falling one row at a time into the fire. Each screamed then cursed Iconoclast as it hit the flames.

When the last of the demon scavengers fell, Iconoclast reversed his arms. Perfect puzzle pieces of earth came together. Atramentous, Gambogian, Prevaricator, Caitiff, Venenose, Bruit, Trepaner and Profligacy—Iconoclast's captains—stood in a semicircle behind him. All had watched, with horror, as the demons went into the abyss. All knelt behind him and fell to the ground in worship. Iconoclast smiled in pride as he sucked in the fear he had inflicted on his commanders. He turned his attention to Josiah.

"I have it on the best authority that you are not worth saving. You are up for grabs, you know, you and all other mortals of this earth. And, from what the most popular religions of this world say, you have to do something spectacular to get your God's attention.

"And, really, what have you done to be saved by your God? Have you died on a cross recently?" He sniggered at the memory. "Have you fought and been martyred for Him?" He held up a bony hand. "You don't need to say anything; I already know. Just wanted to make sure that you know how very inconsequential you are."

"No one can know the mind of God."

"The one you worship lives in the heavens far from this measly planet. There is only one god of this earth. Don't you remember what Saul of Tarsus said?" Iconoclast grinned, revealing the teeth that had killed so many in body and soul.

"Your struggle, old man, is not against humans but against the authorities, against the powers of this dark world and against the spiritual forces of evil that are not only on this dark world but in the heavenly realms. Your God is far too busy fighting my compatriots to worry about your rotten soul. Your pride and self-centeredness deceive you."

"Your boss quoted scripture to the Holy One, to try and trick the One that can never be deceived. As you well know, the verse begins with instruction. And, so I say: 'Finally, be strong in the Lord and in His mighty power. Put on the full armor of God so that you can take your stand against the devil's schemes.' I believe that verse is more than appropriate. Don't you?"

The release from the hopelessness came with a lightning bolt of truth. Each word strengthened Josiah. His back straightened and he held his head high. In contrast, Iconoclast shrank in size and pain wracked his gruesome features.

"If you have nothing better, be gone, Iconoclast. Join your fellows in the pit of hell."

Iconoclast lunged and caught Josiah square in the stomach with his talons. Josiah wailed and doubled over. Iconoclast released and lunged again. He dragged razor-sharp claws over Josiah's back. Skin gave way to red tissue, white bone, then gushing blood. The sickening-sweet smell of the life fluid strengthened Iconoclast. The mouth gave way to yellow teeth. He leaned over Josiah's injury and bit down. Josiah yelled as he straightened and turned to his left. Iconoclast grabbed the right arm.

"Oh you are going to taste good, worm of God." He chomped down.

Fiery pain shot up the arm and Josiah's mind went numb. Hopelessness and weakness replaced the strength of moments ago. He fell to the ground. The demons came closer, emboldened by the man of God's weakened state.

"Stay back. This one is mine. It has been ordained." They scurried back, fear of the abyss still fresh in their minds.

New pain wracked Josiah's body with each breath. When he tried to speak, the pain stopped him. Iconoclast smiled with the knowledge of a close victory. He bit down again.

Josiah rasped out between gurgled breaths, "God help your servant."

"I told you. Your God doesn't care about you. He is the great deceiver, not I. I told you the truth."

Iconoclast was so close, the stench of his breath caught in Josiah's throat. Josiah used the last of his strength to fight the cloud of hopelessness seeping into his mind from the rank breath of his attacker.

"You do not ever tell the truth. Again I say, God help me, for your Son's sake." Josiah fell to the ground and lost consciousness.

"Wake up you filthy mortal! I want to eat your fear, too. Wake up, I say!" Iconoclast swiped at Josiah again. Josiah's eyes shot open, fresh pain brought stinging tears to his eyes.

"Good. You're brain is first on my menu of delicacies." Iconoclast lunged at Josiah's head and stopped short of ripping the right eye out of its socket.

What he saw mirrored in those clear blue eyes sent terror through his black heart. Josiah's irises reflected a dazzling blue star that pulsed with life. With each pulse it grew until it filled the entire eye.

Iconoclast swung around. This light hailed from white blue to white hot. It surrounded the warrior angel of the Most High.

Iconoclast fell to his knees and covered his eyes to protect them against the blinding light.

Flames shot from the righteous eyes of the angel. He was clothed in brilliant gold. His hair moved in a nonexistent wind.

"This one is God's," the angel thundered.

Iconoclast dared to lift his eyes in challenge.

"He is in my home."

"This place is no longer yours to call home. And this one is God's. Has always been and will always be." The voice of thunder and clear running water ran through the ravine and touched Josiah.

Josiah dared not look up and focused on the ravine floor instead. He watched with wonder as it turned to glass. The walls below the glass were lined in lava-red fire then died out into bottomless space. He heard growling and wailing and malevolent laughter. Josiah shivered.

"Be gone, back to your true home. The Son of Man and the Father in heaven command it."

The clang of sword against claw filled the ravine. Josiah kept his head low, both arms over his ears because the noise was louder than an explosion.

Josiah watched as Iconoclast and all his army dropped through the glass floor and became small, dark specks in the lava-red light. The vision disappeared and dark, fragrant earth covered the glass floor.

Josiah raised his head. The walls of the ravine had been cleansed in the hot light that had come with the angel. The outcropping of rocks making up the chasm walls glistened as if they had been scrubbed. The aroma of spring flowers drifted in on a fresh breeze. The smell of rain after a cloudburst could be detected on that same wind.

Josiah stayed prone, "O God, please spare me. I am not worthy."

The angel walked to Josiah and touched him. Josiah caught his breath, and then realized it had not hurt to inhale.

"Rise, friend. Do not bow before me. We are both servants of the Most High. The Lord says to you, "even in your darkest hour and battle, you did not waver. I am proud to call you friend. Rest, Josiah. It is a season of rest for you."

As quickly as the angel had descended, he was gone and Josiah was alone in the ravine.

"Am I imagining these things, God? Would you care so much about this one sinner that you would send a warrior?" The calm and joy that were in Josiah testified to the truth he had seen. The physical change in the ravine confirmed it.

Josiah sat up, grabbed a handful of dirt and reveled in the velvet softness of the warm, wet soil as it ran through his fingers. The rich smell permeated his senses. The beauty and peace of the ravine reminded Josiah of the innocence of a newborn child.

"I could live out my life here and die a happy man," he uttered aloud.

"Rest. Your battle for now is over but there is war to come." Josiah's head shot upward in the direction of the voice. He saw nothing but trees silhouetted by a full moon. His inner peace and well-being scattered like a bird flushed from hiding.

"Be of good cheer, Josiah, God is with you and leaves you His peace."

The warmth of the voice acted as a balm on Josiah's troubled spirit. He relaxed. His attention was drawn to the sound of running water. Josiah spied a small waterfall and a pond at the far end of the ravine.

"I am thirsty." The water was sweet and cold. Energy surged

through him. To the left of the pond sat a bush covered in red berries. Josiah pulled a berry free to examine the fruit.

"High bush cranberries." He popped the berry into his mouth. The tart juice refreshed him further and satisfied his hunger. A blanket of weariness floated over Josiah's mind and body.

"I'll just sit for a minute before I head into Ravens Cove," he muttered, a slur to his speech. He plopped down by the waterfall. The cadence of the water urged him to lower his head to the soft earth.

"A short nap, then." His breathing became steady, a slight snore escaping his lips. Josiah's body went into an unnatural state for a human—hibernation. He would awaken but only by the Lord's signal to rise and fight again.

Chapter 1
A Tragic Accident

Kat Tovslosky stared at the black winter sky. Stars danced overhead, their clear white light sizzling against the frigid cold. *Come on, Kat. You've seen death before. Come on.* She willed her head down and trained her eyes on a morbid scene.

A foot in front of her chocolate brown leather boot sat a pool of coagulating blood. Tendrils of the brown-red liquid snaked out from its source beneath a large boulder. The now-deceased foreman of the construction project known as Old Town lay beneath the rock.

As if to emphasize the cold reality that pounded her consciousness, a bitter wind tunneled from the mountains to the north and rushed up and under the unbuttoned coat. It flew open, exposing Kat's torso to the zero chill-factor. She tugged her army-issue coat closer to her body, zipped it, and crossed her arms. She tuned into the droning voices behind her.

"Tell me again how this happened. And please go slow. I need to write," Police Chief Bart Andersen directed this request to the mayor of Ravens Cove.

Mayor Orthell stuffed his hands deep into the pockets of his black parka. "I told you, Bart, that excavator," he pulled one hand free of a snug pocket and pointed in the direction of a large vehicle, "malfunctioned."

Bart followed the mayor's gloved hand. The arm of the dirt-digger hung like a broken limb and flopped left to right in the wind. The attached bucket swayed and groaned with each move.

"Gordy there," he pointed at the body beneath the boulder, "was directing placement. He was standing two feet away from the cursed thing when the bucket broke. The rock lurched outward and landed square on him. Damn bad luck if you ask me."

Bart rubbed his forehead with his free hand, dragged it down his cheek, and let it drop to his side. *Please let this be a bad dream.* He thought.

"So, what you think we have here is an industrial accident?"

"That's what I've been trying to tell you. And I need your report in a hurry. I've got to get this project back on schedule and that pest of an insurance company will want all the I's dotted and T's crossed before it will give the okay to continue."

"Tommy, you've got a body here that isn't even cold yet, and you're worrying about this blasted tourist attraction?"

"Of course I'm sorry for the loss."

"Could you at least sound like you mean it?" Kat spat out in a disgusted tone. "When did you start caring more about money than people?"

"Enough. Kat, call Doc Billings, would you? We'll need his professional opinion." Bart's firm tone was the pin needed to deflate Kat's anger.

"What?" You gonna do an autopsy? I have at least five witnesses to the whole thing, man. We know what killed him—a two-ton boulder is sitting on his body. This isn't rocket science, you know."

Bart ignored the barb. "What was Gordy doing out here tonight?"

"Old Town opens tomorrow. Finishing touches."

"Right."

"Doc's on his way." Kat stuck her phone back in a pocket and glared at Orthell. Orthell held her gaze, then broke and focused on Bart.

"I'm sure Doc Billings will hurry the autopsy along. You'll be back on track in no time." He snapped the notebook closed and whipped around to face Kat. "Call Amos Thralling, will you? See if he or his brother has a piece of equipment that'll get this thing off Gordy."

Kat looked at her watch. Four o'clock. She let out a frustrated sigh, grabbed her phone and dialed. Her ability to memorize phone numbers made it unnecessary to use speed dial.

"It's ringing. Hey Amos ... no, no, this is Kat. Yes, I know it's four in the morning. No, I'm not drunk. *Listen. Please.* We have a bad situation and need your help." Kat rushed through a small summary and what they needed, and then went silent, phone to her ear.

"Thanks, Amos." She turned to Bart. "He doesn't have anything ... but, he knows someone."

"Great. The whole town's gonna know before seven," the mayor's voice reminded Kat of a bleating sheep. "A death on the property is not the way I wanted to introduce Old Town! Call him back; tell him to keep his trap shut."

Kat pushed her phone into the mayor's hand. "Be my guest."

The mayor's eyes shot daggers in her direction. He hit redial. A begrudging, "thanks," escaped his lips as he pushed the phone back at Kat.

"Welcome." Artificial warmth laced her sing-song tone.

He turned to Bart. "Get this taken care of—by tomorrow afternoon. We have a ceremony to hold and it *will* go on. My investor is counting on it!" Orthell whirled and walked off into the darkness.

"You think Amos'll keep his mouth closed?"

"Does water flow uphill?"

"Not last time I checked. The mayor is going to be one mad papa bear."

Studded tires grabbing ice announced Doc Billings' arrival. He eased out of his Audi, reached in and grabbed his old-fashioned doctor's bag and made his way toward Old Town's courtyard.

Billings walked to the boulder. "How am I going to do an initial review?"

"One of the Thralling brothers is rounding up some equipment."

Billings circled the body, careful to avoid the blood. "Seems pretty cut and dried, Bart."

"Yeah, I know, Doc. But, procedure is procedure. While you're confirming a huge rock killed him, I'll be looking to find out what caused the boom to let loose that way. Then we can close this as a tragic accident."

Doc shook his head from side to side. "Sorry shame. Gordy was a decent sort. Always there with a helping hand. Sorry, sorry shame."

"Where's the hearse, Doc?"

"I'll call the boys at the funeral home when we can move him. No need for them to be standing around in this cold."

The unmistakable whine of a large diesel engine echoed off the buildings of Old Town. The sound grew deafening as a rusty loader crawled closer. Arnie Thralling maneuvered the machine to the right of two rough-cut birch columns. The birch arms reached upward and held an equally rough-hewn birch board. The words *Welcome to Old Town—Where Time Stands Still* were carved into the wood, then scorched to a deep brown.

The ground vibrated as the loader pulled within three feet of the boulder. Arnie jumped down and jogged to the small group.

Bart handed Doc his phone. "Call the boys. The cavalry has arrived."

"Glad to see you, Arnie." Kat peeked around Arnie's right shoulder. "No Amos?"

"Nope. I'm the one with the heavy equipment and I don't let him drive it."

"Can you get the boulder off without taking part of Gordy with it?"

Arnie took a few reluctant steps forward. Bart noted the telltale sign of green that heralds the onset of losing all the contents in one's stomach. He grabbed Arnie by the elbow and led him to the woods.

"Too bad we don't have a professional staff for this kind of stuff. Arnie's gonna have nightmares for sure."

Doc Billings' concerned eyes met Kat's emerald-green ones. "I'll have him come by the office later today. See if he needs something to settle his nerves. Most likely, work will be the best treatment and he loves to work on those old boats."

Bart and Arnie rejoined Kat and Doc. Green, with a blush of embarrassment, did nothing for Arnie's long, thin face.

"Arnie's agreed to let me work the loader. He's going to wait in the truck." Bart held out the keys and Arnie snatched them from Bart's hand like a kid grabbing the all-coveted brass ring at the carousel. He nodded to Kat, turned and walked out the entrance to Old Town.

"You sure you remember how, Bartster? Your construction gig was years, well decades, ago."

"Like riding a bike, cuz." He sounded none too convincing. Bart looked at the loader, then the boulder and back to the loader.

"No time like the present, *cuz?*" Kat snapped back.

Bart nodded, marched to the loader and jumped in. As it lurched forward, Kat's survival instinct kicked in and she took several steps away from the boulder. So did Doc Billings.

After a couple of rough beginnings, Bart bounced the cumbersome machine forward at a slow, steady pace. He stopped and inched the bucket lower until it was in line with the bottom of the massive stone. The hydraulics groaned as he wormed the bucket forward. After what felt like an eternity to Kat, the boulder was up and off Gordy Zimms and sat in the middle of a tarp that Arnie had had the foresight to lie out before his unexpected illness.

Bart sprang off the dozer and jogged over to Gordy's body.

"That thing did a job," Kat said.

Gordy's stomach was too flat for a human being. The force of the rock had splintered a rib like a rotted stick. It poked through a rip in the shirt. His legs were untouched. If the rest of the body hadn't been so disfigured, Kat would have expected Gordy to jump up and say, "Gotcha!" with a big grin. But, the blood trickling from his mouth shouted that this was no joke.

"Bart!"

"What?" Kat was pointing to Gordy's face. It was a deep purple, almost bruised.

"Yeah, he's black and blue. I'd expect that."

Kat shook her index finger in the direction of the eyes.

Bart walked to the head and bent down for a closer look. His body blocked any light from the giant floods. Bart released the flashlight for his belt and clicked it on. There were no eyes. A dark and light liquid ran from the empty orbs. He turned a stricken and sick-looking face to Kat.

Doc had joined them, holding Bart's phone in midair to return it, then dropped it to his side. He studied Gordy's face in the blue light. "I don't like the looks of that one bit." He walked around Gordy to get a better look.

"Only saw this during the siege." Doc turned to Bart. "I won't know for sure until I have him in better light. I'll call you as soon as I can get a good look in the sockets." Doc bit his lip and contemplated Gordy's fluid filled orbs. "Maybe there's a scientific explanation. The force of the crush may have caused his eyes to dislodge and allow brain matter through."

"You don't sound too convincing."

"I'm not convinced. I'm hoping. I'll let you know if I find those pinpricks."

"I pray you don't, Doc."

Kat's anxiety reached boiling and she couldn't stand silent and listen anymore. "How could he be back? He was locked in the ravine. His curse was broken because he didn't get a fifth victim. How?" Kat's nightmares came crushing in on her until she felt she couldn't breathe. Tears sprang into her emerald eyes and she turned toward the darkness of the woods to hide the emotions from Bart and Doc.

"Don't know, but if this is what it looks like, we're in for the fight of our lives–again."

"Iconoclast."

"As I said, it could be a result of the accident. Don't want to jump to that conclusion, at least not yet."

Bart shook his head and sighed. "I have to locate Gordy's next of kin. I hate this part of the job."

Kat hastily brushed the tears from her eyes. She turned, placed a hand on Bart's arm and gave it a gentle squeeze.

Bart smiled down at his favorite cousin. "And I need you to get to the office."

"Now?" Kat released his arm.

"Yes, now. Not like you have anything else to do. You got a hot date with your feline?"

"No. But we've been here since midnight and I was hoping for something that might pass as sleep before the grand opening." Kat shot Bart a guarded look.

"I don't know how that opening's gonna happen today. But to even have a chance to appease my boss," the distaste was evident at the title, "I need you get the incident report typed up and call the troopers as soon as they open to get them out here to look at that excavator. Seems real odd that the boom just broke that way."

"Okay, I give. The office it is."

The hearse pulled up the curb outside the Old Town sign. Two attendants headed for the back of the vehicle, grabbed a long, white board and hurried to Doctor Billings.

"Thanks for making it fast."

"Anything for you, doc," Eric Smotherly said. His brother Jonas nodded in agreement. Doc Billings had gotten their dad through a bout of pneumonia that, they felt, would have killed him if Doc hadn't been there.

"How old are these guys?" Kat whispered to Bart.

"Early twenties."

"You sure? They look like they're fifteen if a day. And, they're skinny as rails. How are they gonna lift Gordy? He must outweigh them both put together by at least 100 pounds."

The zip of the body bag echoed against the buildings of Old Town, amplifying the finality of the sound. Kat watched in amazement as the thin young men lifted the late Gordy Zimms with the ease of a twenty-pound bag of flour. Eric and Jonas Smotherly shuffled in a united step to the back of the hearse, managing to avoid falling on the ice that covered most of Old Town's courtyard.

"I'll call you when I've got the report." Doc Billings waved over his shoulder as he, too, shuffled into the night.

An uneasy quiet replaced the hubbub of the hours before. Kat looked at the Old Town buildings, black shadows outlined by the silver light of the wintry moon and stars. The ghostly contours gave the buildings an unwelcoming feel. Kat shivered and turned to watch her cousin return from a last investigation of the scene.

"What's in your hand?"

Bart stood in front of Kat and kept his hand closed tight.

"Bart?"

"Probably nothing."

Kat planted her feet in front of Bart. "Then why don't you let me see?"

Bart hesitated then opened his hand. A small arrowhead came into view.

"There's hundreds of those around here," Kat said.

The dismay in Bart's eyes made her lean in and take a good look at the stone. Something was etched into its surface.

You belong to my Master, Katrina Tovslosky. Pet

Kat's eyes shot to Bart's, the terror forcing tears to brim over her eyes and fall down her cheeks.

Bart grabbed Kat and pulled her to him. "It's a sick, sick joke, Kat. I'll find the crazy son of a dog that did this. You can take that to the bank." Kat's sobs became uncontrollable and Bart stood helpless, waiting for them to subside. After what felt like an eternity, Kat calmed.

"I've had dreams," she whispered into Bart's chest.

"I have, too. Who wouldn't after the ordeal we went through?" He pushed Kat back and looked deep into her eyes.

"We watched them go back into the ravine and it closed. Pet, Iconoclast, and his demon commanders are back in hell."

Kat searched Bart's eyes and saw the conviction that matched his words. She drew her shoulders up and back, letting out a deep sigh. "You're right. Let's go find that creep."

Bart gave her one last squeeze and they trudged into the darkness toward the truck. Neither of them saw the small, hooved creature that had been watching their every move. It galloped off into the woods, taking the news of the battle's beginning to Pet.

Kat unlocked the door to the storefront on Main Street that housed the police station. She flicked the switch. The hum of the fluorescents broke the silence. The musty smell of old paper and baseboard heat greeted her nose. Bart came in behind her, stomped his feet, and closed the door to the cold February morning.

"I'll find the number for Gordy's next-of-kin. You get to the report." Bart handed her his notebook and continued toward his office.

The clock on the wall read six-thirty. *Still too early to get a cup of coffee from Jo's.* Kat headed toward the break room—which doubled as the interrogation room in the rare instances that it was needed—and filled the old percolator with Folger's. The phone started ringing before she made it back to the desk.

"Good morning. This is Kat, can I help you?"

"Is it true?"

Kat dropped into her chair. "Is what true, Wendy?"

"Is Gordy dead?"

Kat's last bit of hope that news of this tragedy would not spread like wildfire throughout the town evaporated like smoke. "Yes."

"How awful. How did it happen?"

"If you know he's dead, Wendy, you know how." Wendy

loved a good drama and loved even more being the first one to spread fresh gossip.

"I want to make sure Arnie got it right."

"Arnie was there. He got it right. Why were you talking to him anyway?"

"A certain large piece of equipment lumbered past my house this morning and scared me out of a dead sleep. When a loader rumbles down the streets of Ravens Cove in the early hours of a winter morning, it raises some questions. So, I jumped out of bed and peeked through the curtain and saw Arnie driving it. I gave him a call and he just called me back."

Kat hoped to divert Wendy's need to be in the middle of a drama. "Do me a favor, would you? I haven't slept and need food. Would you go by Jo's and bring me something? Bart wants this report done."

"But what about the murder?"

"No one said it was murder. We'll talk when you get here." Kat hung up before Wendy could ask anymore questions.

"Things are heating up."

Bart sighed in defeat. "Why would I even hope that this could have been kept quiet? This is going to make my life miserable."

Bart punched the phone pad. "Tommy, we have a problem ..."

The insistent ring of Kat's desk phone drowned out the rest of Bart's sentence.

"Good morning, Mrs. Tellamoot. Yes, Gordy has passed. No one said it was murder ..." The old chime clanged over the door. Pastor Lucas came in followed by Grandma Bricken.

"I just heard the news. Has Gordy's family been notified?"

"Bart's working on that, Paul. He could use your help, though. Very hard for him to share such bad news. Go on in, you'll make a bad day better."

Grandma Bricken came around behind Kat's chair. "You okay, dear one?"

Kat leaned back against her grandma. Alese Bricken wrapped her arms around Kat's upper chest and squeezed. Kat relaxed.

"Better now. It's horrible, Grandma."

"Death always is, my sweet. For us. But, he's in heaven now. For him, the battle is over and all is wonderful."

"I wish I had your faith."

"You do. Just don't know it." Grandma gave her another squeeze.

The door clanged again. Wendy whooshed in, bag in one hand, large cup of coffee in the other. "Danish and mocha." She gave Grandma a quick kiss, then shot a large pixie grin to her best friend. "Got anything else you'd like me to do so I'll quit asking questions?"

Kat's face broke into a wide smile, the first it felt like in an eternity. "I'll think of something, Winsome." Kat grabbed for the bag. Wendy pulled it just out of reach.

"First, some news."

"Blackmailer. There is no news–except that the Old Town ceremony is probably going to be postponed."

"It sure is." Bart had walked up unnoticed. He grabbed the bag from Wendy and dropped it beside Kat.

"Just got off the phone with Tommy. He's as mad as a cornered porcupine. But the grand opening is officially postponed until next week." Bart's tone was victorious.

"So, Winsome, I bet Mayor Orthell could use some help getting the word out. Town Hall is always asking for volunteers and they are really going to need it. That ceremony," Kat looked at the clock that now read seven-thirty, "is supposed to start in less than five hours."

Wendy's eyes lit up like small flares. "On my way."

"I'll call Jenny and let her know you're coming over." The mayor's assistant would be very grateful for any help—Orthell was probably on the warpath by now and she always got the brunt of it.

A closing door finished the conversation with Wendy.

"I'll leave you to your work. Come over later, child, and I will feed you a decent meal. You need to keep your strength up."

Phone at her ear, Kat smiled up at Alese Bricken. "Will do, Gram." Kat dialed.

"Morning, Jenny. Just a heads-up. Wendy's on her way to help with the cancellation of Old Town's ceremony."

Silence greeted Kat. "Jenny?"

"Sorry. I'm here. Wendy you say?" A rhythmic ticky-tap sounded in the background as Jenny continued to type furiously.

"You okay?"

"No. The mayor's in a rage and the town council has called an emergency meeting to reschedule the ceremony. Ouch!"

"What's going on?"

"Nasty paper cut. Need to get a Band-Aid on it before I bleed on everything. I'll watch for Wendy." The phone went dead.

"Glad we can help," Kat said to the dial tone.

She picked up the notebook. A *thump, thump* caught her attention. Terror thundered up her back and overtook her brain. *You belong to my Master, Katrina Tovslosky* might as well have been in neon lights as she read it again on the dark tan arrowhead. *I'll find you, creep, I'll find you.* She dug in her desk drawer and found an evidence bag. She grabbed a Kleenex from the box on her desk, picked up the rock, deposited it in the bag and zipped it closed.

"Thought you'd bagged that rock, Bart," she yelled out.

"I did," he yelled back, then came out of his office.

41

"No, you didn't. It just fell out of your notebook." Kat shoved the evidence bag at him.

"I was sure I did." Bart grabbed the bag. "You won't see it again." He hustled off to his office and back to Pastor Lucas.

Kat took a shaky breath and turned to the computer. A sharp ding announced the arrival of a new email. No subject. No return email address. It simply read, "He did bag it. Looking forward to seeing you soon. Pet."

Kat screamed and jumped up. The momentum sent her chair sailing backward. It came to a stop when it bounced off the railing at the front of the office.

Bart and Paul flew out of the office and rounded the desk. "What the hell?"

Kat pointed at the screen.

Bart turned red with rage.

"I came to see you for something else." Paul Lucas pulled a lettersize sheet of paper out of his jacket and handed it to Bart. "Read it."

> *I will have what is mine, Man of God. You won the battle. You will not win the war. You will taste hell before I am finished with Ravens Cove.*
>
> *Soon to be your master.*
> *Iconoclast."*

Kat's email dinged again. A shaky finger touched the mouse.

> *I am at your door. Prepare for war.*
> *This time, you die.*

Chapter 2
Old Town

Kat snaked her head side to side, cobra fashion, in an effort to catch a reading of the small thermometer outside the ice-covered kitchen window. She stopped, head tilted to the left and slightly bent forward. "Ten below. Factor in the wind forecast for today and we're looking at 40 below," she fumed to her feline companion.

BC fixed uninterested eyes on hers, turned, and sauntered past a cheery red couch centered in front of a small wood-burning stove. He sprung onto the deep ledge of the large picture window. He moved to the center to take full advantage of an anemic sunbeam that managed to filter through another frosted window.

BC turned his head left and back and began to bathe his side, coarse tongue catching glistening fur. He went statue-still as a raven glided past his view. His elongated back leg stretched out and up above the windowsill while he considered a way to get at the small chickadee that landed on the other side of the glass. The feline ballerina resumed bathing when the small bird took flight and became a speck in the blue morning sky.

"Great day for a dedication of the Old Town Village," Kat

grumbled at an uncaring BC, then turned and trudged to her bedroom. One resolved but frustrated sigh escaped her lips before she began rummaging through her antique oak dresser. The old drawers squeaked in protest as she yanked each one open. All nine drawers became a pyramid of jumbled color as she frantically searched for her thermals.

"Where are those stupid things?" She stomped to the closet, the floor quaking in protest. She yanked open the rickety bifold door and succeeding in pulling it off the track. There, on the top shelf, underneath old wool socks and pants, a piece of winter-white waffle-style fabric peeked through. Kat grabbed the small pile, almost pelting herself with a mound of sock snowballs.

"I do wish I'd remember where I put things when I start organizing." She smiled in relief, and then turned toward a soft noise in the doorway. BC stared open-eyed at Kat, anticipating a good romp.

"Sorry, guy. No time." BC's tail swished and his eyes narrowed. One bare leg had his full attention.

Kat's cell phone chirped from across the room. She took a hasty step forward, in part to get the phone and in part to avoid BC's wrath. The hem of her thermals, halfway up the right leg, snaked in front of both feet throwing her into a freefall. Kat grabbed the bedpost and hopped on one foot to the nightstand.

"Hello." She switched the phone to her left ear, plopped onto the bed and managed to get her left leg in the close-fitting underclothes.

"You ready?"

"Five minutes."

"Better be. We don't want to be late for this *all-important* dedication." Bart Andersen didn't even try to hide the sarcasm from his cousin.

"Just show up in five minutes ... did you happen to grab a coffee for me?"

"Indeed. And, if you hurry, it might still have enough warmth to call it hot coffee instead of iced."

"Hah-hah. I don't know why I put up with you at all."

"Because I'm only one of a few who have wheels in this town and I'm family."

"Wheels, yes. Family? That doesn't gain you as many points. See you in five." She pressed end before Bart could retort.

Kat rushed through her routine, turning off the electronic toothbrush at one minute instead of two. She ran a brush through her untamed, tangled mahogany hair.

"Good enough. I'll be back soon, BC. Don't tear anything up."

BC walked to a small, plastic inset in the front door and pushed it with his head. It held tight against the lock. He plopped down in front of it, turned his head toward his back and looked up expectantly at Kat.

"Not today, fella. It is way too cold for you to be out and you know it." The tail flipped back and forth across the wood flooring.

Snow tires cracked ice on her drive. Kat glanced through the living room window and caught the front of Bart's old truck.

She sneaked around BC, still fixated on the "cat door," and got out before he could follow. A bitter north wind slapped her unprotected face, turning it rosy red. Kat took the three front steps in one leap, and dashed to the vehicle. Her parka sung a winter melody every time the arm fabric rubbed her side. One yank and the truck door groaned open. She jumped in.

"Never remember this old truck's heat being so wonderful." She leaned toward the vent.

A smirk played around Bart's lips until it broke into a toothy grin.

"What?"

"You look like a homeless but well-fed snow girl."

Kat looked down. She had on ivory bunny boots compliments of the Army Navy Surplus in Anchorage. They reminded her of a clown's idea of fashion footwear. Her faded blue jeans stretched and strained because the thermals beneath added a good inch to her figure. Her army-green parka, fake-fur ruff and all, made her round as a pumpkin from her torso to her thighs. She grabbed the rearview mirror. The military-issue green hood framed her face, clashing with her emerald-green eyes and giving her bronze skin a jaundiced undertone.

"We thank you for your support, smart-mouth."

"Welcome." Bart gave a quick nod in her direction, then put the truck in reverse.

"Haven't seen this kind of cold in ten years. Seems a bad omen that it would come on the same day as this event." Kat sounded more serious that jovial. "Whose idea was it anyway to hold a dedication in February?"

"That would be our esteemed mayor. Orthell convinced the Ravens Cove council that it had to be done now so they'd be able to fix any problems before April and the beginning of the tourist season."

"I really don't understand Orthell or the council for that matter. Is it the power of holding office that nullifies common sense?"

Bart snorted. "Maybe. No matter when this dedication were held, I'd have to be there and so would you. I have been *ordered* to attend. And, I've been ordered to make sure that you, grandma, and Paul Lucas are also there. Seems we are the guests of honor."

"Since when has Orthell ever made anyone else the center of attention?"

"Yep. It's fishy to me, too, but I do want to keep my job."

"If anyone deserved thanks it was Josiah. I didn't do anything. I almost caused the whole town to be destroyed," Kat said sadly.

"I wish Josiah were here, too. And you didn't almost cause the town to be destroyed Kat—our apathy and unbelief did that. There is one other person who should have been on the VIP list and is noticeably absent." Bart kept his body straight and sent a sideways glance toward Kat.

"If you mean Kenneth Melbourne, why would you be surprised? He just wanted to make a name for himself and since Ravens Cove provided that for him, I don't ever expect to see his sour face here again. He doesn't care about anything—or anyone else for that matter."

"To be fair, he asked you to go with him, Kat."

Kat jerked upright, turned and glared at Bart's profile.

"And, what would I have been? A fish out of water, that's what! Worse, I'd have been dependent on him. What can I do in the big city to make a living, huh? And, I'm surely not cut out to be someone's arm candy." She whipped forward and stared at the white road ahead.

Bart hated seeing Kat this way. She had withdrawn every day since Kenneth Melbourne left, and become more sullen with each day that she hadn't received a phone call. That outburst was the closest thing he'd seen to passion in Kat since November. *Some people really are jerks.*

"I know you're hurt Kat. I really wish you'd forget about him. You're anger isn't hurting him. It's killing you."

Kat stayed stoic, concentrating even harder on the barren landscape of ice and snow.

Bart sighed. "Well, what do you think of the new, old, village?"

"One word—weird. I can't wrap my mind around the expense and effort it took to bring in all those buildings. Ravens Cove's not rich. Those fund-raisers in December and January couldn't have brought in the thousands needed to bring those five old buildings to the Cove. How did we pay for it, anyway?"

"Seems Orthell has some pull. Called in some favors and with the fund-raising efforts, that did the trick."

"Still seems weird."

"You're preaching to the choir. Weird or not, we now have two towns in one."

The ice-packed road passed through Kat's line of sight in slow motion. The winter winds had stripped the trees of snow and frost, emphasizing their bony limbs. Something small and dark darted into view. Kat leaned forward to get a better look. It bolted behind a stand of spruce and out again, following the truck. She squinted toward the forest trying to put a name to the shape. All she saw was bare trees and bushes. *Stop it, Kat. Your imagination is running again. Just stop it.*

No matter how she tried, Kat couldn't shake the feeling that they were being followed. The road she had traveled hundreds of times took on a menacing look and feel—like she had been transported to an odd fun-house version of the Cove.

Bart maneuvered the old red pickup through an icy lane bordered by cars and trucks all the way to the entrance of Old Town.

"Looks like the whole darned town's here." He peered ahead, then threw the old gears into reverse. His wheels spun as he hit the gas a little too hard.

Kat shot him a disapproving look. Bart gave her a quick, "Sorry" smile, then backed up to an open spot.

"This is as close as we get."

"I suppose I need the exercise."

"I suppose we both do."

They walked in silence until they reached the entrance to Old Town. The quiet of a block away gave way to a din of voices. People milled between the buildings, scrutinizing the outside of each. Groups of locals huddled closer than usual while discussing the features of the town.

"Okay, it's impressive. Like stepping back into another century," Kat said.

"Mmmm."

Five houses, all from the early 1900s, stood in a semicircle. Each faced a large ring-shaped courtyard.

"Isn't that the abandoned log cabin from Peri-Fay Fjord?" She pointed to the small structure on the left.

Yeah, I think so. Why is that here? Remember, we were told it was haunted and never to go near it without an adult?"

"Bart, we were kids. Grandma would say anything to keep us out of that place for fear we'd break our necks."

Bart laughed. "Funny how stuff sticks, huh?"

"Yeah it is. But you know what's creepy? It looks like it did twenty years ago. Shouldn't it be more weathered?" Kat started toward it. Bart jogged to catch up. His cousin was on a mission. Before he could stop her, Kat had dropped to all fours and was feeling for something under the porch.

"What in the name of all that's good are you doing? We'll get thrown in jail and I'm the sheriff!" Bart looped his large hand around Kat's elbow and pulled her to a standing position. Something was dangling from her right hand.

"It is that old cabin!" She held up a dirty dog-tag chain with two rusty bottle caps dangling from it.

"What the ... ?"

"Remember? We promised that we'd go back one day—just

you and me—before we found out that first cousins don't get married." She smiled up Bart, a twinkle in her eye. "Remember?"

"I'll be," was all he could muster. They had been eight if that. Grandma Bricken had taken them to the fjord on one of their history trips. Peri-Fay was one of the many areas across from the Cove rumored to be bewitched. They had listened to stories of fairies—not so nice ones—the night they stayed in the old cabin. The next morning, Kat and Bart had made a pact to return when they were older and sealed the pact by nailing the old necklace under the front door threshold.

"That thing's seventy-five years old, if it's a day. How did it survive all these years and look like it was just built?"

"Don't know. Curiouser and curiouser."

"That hotel looks like the one in the pictures of the Forgotten Place."

"Kat ..." Bart said. What he meant and didn't say was *Don't start with the legends coming to life again.*

"That's the old cannery, too, and the mercantile. And, that's the old house." She pointed to a two-story frame building. Its front porch had columns—not seen in these parts at the turn of the century—that spanned the entire house. The large windows were separated into six smaller panes. Two elongated windows flanked a small balcony on the second floor. Kat imagined a face with dark, empty eyes glaring at her. She shivered and turned to the courtyard. Kat jumped backward to avoid walking into the large boulder in the center of the town.

"Why is that still here?" She pointed a shaky finger at the huge rock.

"The mayor insisted," Bart said.

"You know what that represents, KittyKat?" Kat spun to her right at the unexpected voice.

50

"A little edgy, are we?" Wendy ignored the cold glare. "By the way, I haven't seen you much this week. How you doing, girlfriend?" The concern in Wendy's voice shook Kat's being.

Kat shrugged. "Same old, same old."

Wendy stared into what felt like Kat's soul, as only a best friend can do. She opened her mouth, then thought better of it, shrugged and turned to the boulder. "That, my friends, is the Rock of Fallen Angels."

"Do tell."

"Don't remember your local stories, huh, smarty."

"Maybe I blocked them—I've had enough for a lifetime."

"Amen," said Bart.

"Well, it goes like this. Raven and Bear were arguing over a rock that had fallen from the sky into their drinking pond. It was so large it displaced most of the water and caused a drought. The angels in heaven had been fighting. The bad angels were tied to the boulder and thrown out of heaven—a sinking stone, as it were. Bear told Raven he could save all of them because he could change into anything he liked and move the rock. Raven laughed. 'Who cares about a stupid drought? Who cares about others? No one cares about me. Leave it there.' The argument became a moral one. And, as moral ones usually go, they came to an impasse.

'I'll move it as Bear. I can't trust you if I change my shape, Joker of the world.' Bear lumbered toward the rock. He reached to give it a shove but a man, with a bright light surrounding him that frightened Bear spoke. 'Do not touch that. It will kill you. It is an evil one that destroys any who disturb its rest.

"Who are you? You look human but are not."

"You do not need to know me. But believe the Great Spirit that sent me." Bear and Raven believed the shining man and left the rock. And, there it stayed for centuries. But then two miners came. The rock blocked the spring where they laid claim. They had been warned by our ancestors to let the rock sleep. They called our ancestors fools for believing such tales. The miners rigged a pulley and moved it away from the mouth. They waited for the stream to run strong and they began to pan and dig. It was a rich claim alright but neither of them ever claimed the money. They were dead within a week. The rock stayed on the beach near the Forgotten Place. Everyone died there, too. And, against our customs, Mayor Orthell has moved it here along with that old house."

"Wow, Wendy. Great storytelling."

"Not a story. Was Iconoclast a story?"

"Iconoclast is gone. Case closed. This is just a big rock!"

Kat walked to the boulder. It was light brown with a rounded top. From the back it looked like a man's head. She ambled around the other side.

"Oh my! No wonder Orthell wanted it as a centerpiece."

Bart and Wendy joined Kat.

"That's downright awful. But Orthell is banking on that to keep the tourists coming. They'll love it."

They all stared, transfixed by the skull, which glared back at them from huge empty brown orbs. A small, sharp protrusion of a nose was set directly above a squiggly line of a mouth.

"That looks like a beak." Wendy reached out to touch the sharp spur.

"Don't." Kat grabbed Wendy's hand.

"What's wrong with you?"

Kat had no idea what prompted her to stop Wendy. The feeling was strong and right. "Don't know. Just don't touch it, okay?"

Wendy gave a slow nod, a look of both confusion and trust on her face.

"It will be a crowd pleaser. These days people just love the spooky stuff—look at all the reality shows chasing ghosts," Bart said.

"This is a curse to Ravens Cove," Wendy whispered.

"For heaven's sake, it's a rock. A creepy rock, for sure, but it's just a rock."

"You know the truth. You know the custom."

"Good morning." Kat's and Wendy's heads whipped to the hastily built stage. A dark brown podium stood in the center of the platform. The stage was surrounded by shaky wooden shutters on three sides to block the unrelenting wind. The shutters creaked and bent inward, threatening to take out the lectern, and possibly the mayor, with each strong gust.

Mayor Orthell stood square in the middle of the shutters, oblivious to the possible catastrophe. He wore a black parka, trimmed in red fox fur which only served to heighten the coloring of his crimson cheeks to neon pink. Ice laced the bottom of his ruff.

He tapped the microphone. A dead thud indicated the device had malfunctioned. He tapped again. Same. Orthell cleared his throat and raised his voice to get the crowd's attention.

"Good morning." Not hearing, the crowd continued to hum with conversation.

"GOOD MORNING." The throng quieted.

"If he doesn't watch it, his face'll freeze in that fake smile," Wendy whispered to Kat.

"Shhh."

"Thank you all for coming. I will make this quick, so we can begin the tour of Old Town. They buildings are warm."

"Now's good, Mayor." Laughter rippled through the crowd.

"Well, Arnie, soon. I want to take this opportunity to thank those that helped to save our community last October. Without them, Ravens Cove would be a much different place now."

Grandma Bricken walked up behind Kat and placed her hands on Kat's shoulders. Kat grabbed Grandma's left hand with her right and squeezed, her eyes never leaving the mayor.

"Ah, our esteemed leader is in his element, I see. Why are we really here? He doesn't like to share credit," Grandma whispered into Kat's ear.

"Don't know, but here we are."

"Two of the most special women I know, together in one place. I am a blessed man," Paul Lucas said as he stepped up beside Grandma and gave her a quick kiss on her brown cheek. Tanya Lucas came up beside and gave Kat and Grandma a bright smile then grabbed Paul's hand.

"Welcome, you two. Nice weather for a grand opening, huh?" Wendy said.

"Oh, yeah. Just what you'd expect in our town in February," Paul answered.

"… so, in closing, please help me welcome a surprise visitor home. At least for today. Agent Kenneth Melbourne." Mayor Orthell backed up, clapping. The crowd clapped and whooped.

"My day just went from bad to worse," Kat breathed.

Grandma grabbed her hand. "That man's ego knows no bounds."

"He can't resist the spotlight, that's all." Kat's heart fell as she looked at the man who had betrayed her.

"Never know what the north wind will blow in. Usually something bitter-cold. Looks like it didn't fail us," Wendy said with venom dripping from each word.

"Down, girl. I'll keep him busy until he leaves. He won't have a chance to get to Kat." Bart thought a moment. "Or, you. I still can't allow murder on my watch—and your eyes are shouting homicide."

"Shhh. Let's at least hear what he has to say," Tanya said.

"Right. I enjoy a good yarn just like the next guy."

"Mayor Orthell called me last week and asked if I could attend this gathering," Ken was saying. "I made every effort to get here." He scanned the crowd until he located the object of his search.

"So many of you in this town are the closest thing I have to family." He spoke directly to Kat.

Kat looked daggers at him and then forced herself to avert her eyes to the old cannery. *Right, you jerk. Fool me once but not again.*

Bart stepped up to Kat's left; Wendy moved closer on her right. They both leaned toward her. She could feel the heat of their breath and the loyalty she was so blessed to have in her life.

"He'll wish he was never born if I have anything to do with it," Wendy hissed in Kat's ear. "How dare he!"

Kat turned her green eyes, slightly misted toward her friend. "I love you."

"Don't go all mushy, KittyKat." Wendy smiled through her own hazy eyes.

"Mayor Orthell asked that I speak to you about the events of last October. But we agreed to nix that part of the speech so we can get out of the weather. If any of you have questions, I'd be happy to answer them in the mercantile." As if to affirm the decision, the brisk breeze switched directions and whipped Ken square in the face.

"Here's the mayor." Ken stepped back from the podium.

"Let's get going. There's hot chocolate and hot coffee inside. Courtesy of Jo." He turned and smiled.

Jo waved to the crowd. Josephina Latrell owned the town's bakery. Most of the citizens could be found there at one time or other for coffee, great food, and of course, the day's gossip.

"I believe it would also be prudent to put off the ceremony honoring those that so helped Ravens Cove until we have warmed up a little."

Ken shot down the stage. He pushed his way through the crowd, like a salmon battling its way upstream, on a direct path for Kat. He reached out to grab her shoulder. Bart caught Ken's wrist in midair.

"Don't think that's such a good idea, friend."

"Didn't ask for your opinion, *friend*." Ken jerked his hand free. "Do that again, I'll break your nose."

A threatening smile came over Bart's face. He pinned Ken's wrist. "I want to see you try, Agent Melbourne. I'll have you locked up and a call into your supervisor before you know what hit you."

Ken looked into Bart's eyes. The sheriff was not joking and it would be too close to call in a physical fight. However, Ken was sure that most of the town would come to Bart's defense and he would end up right where Bart said he would.

"Come on, Bart."

"Not now; and maybe never. You've done enough damage."

Ken sighed. He knew Bart was right. Kat looked awful. Dark circles under those gorgeous green eyes, but worse, he thought those eyes looked empty. Their smile and fire were buried.

"I know I have and I want to make things right. I need to explain why she hasn't heard from me." When Ken arrived back at the FBI in Anchorage, his world has been torn apart. He was dubbed a failure for not finding the serial killer and, worse, he was dubbed a possible lunatic when he tried to make Chief Binning understand what had really happened in Ravens Cove. *"I'd suggest you dive back into your work, Agent, and forget this ever happened. Maybe you can save whatever's left of your reputation."* Binning's tone made it an order, not a suggestion.

Ken had done just that. He contacted no one from the Cove knowing if Binning found out, his job was on the line. *No matter. My reputation is still on the line.* He thought.

"You listening, Melbourne?" Ken focused all his attention on Bart.

"Looks like that's a big no. I said if you have something to say, say it to me and I'll tell Kat. That's as close as you need to get."

"Enough dallying, you two. You can catch up later," Mayor Orthell's intuition was off, as always.

"Right," Bart turned to the mayor. "Sorry for the holdup. We'll catch up later, right Ken?"

"Sure enough. Let's see this new old town." A forced smile crossed his face but never made it to his eyes.

Kat watched the interchange between Bart and Ken from a distance. She knew her cousin well. He stood feet planted slightly apart and had unconsciously placed his hand over his gun holster. His way of saying, "I mean business."

Bart turned, strode over and rejoined Kat, Grandma, Wendy, and the Lucas'.

Kat tiptoed and whispered into Bart's ear, "I can take care of myself."

"I know that but all of us can use some help once in a while," He whispered back.

The February sun hung low in the sky. It had peeked out above the clouds around ten that morning, and at noon its light was casting long lines of shade from the south buildings onto the courtyard. The shadows thrown from the buildings on the north stretched into the surrounding trees and danced among the windblown limbs.

The old mercantile was sided in whitewashed planks. Oblong and more narrow than long, its two-story structure looked sterile against its backdrop of wintery birch and spruce. The small front porch seemed more like an afterthought, a corrugated roof over it to keep out the snow. The two-by-fours that held the small roof in place looked too fragile for the task. Two miniature windows flanked a larger one on the upper floor. Kat thought she saw movement in the small left window but the curtain that framed the window was undisturbed.

The small troop walked up the four masonry grey steps to the wood-plank porch. The boards creaked beneath the weight.

"Don't like that sound."

"Old building. Gonna creak."

The front door was new and made of solid wood. It was stained mahogany. Two small square windows were set into the door and mirrored the larger ones set on each side of the entry.

Paul opened the door and was greeted with laughter from those who had already managed to make it inside. The dark, rough-cut flooring was original. It had been refinished but deep scratches and nicks still screamed of a time gone by. The yellow light from the theme lanterns overhead drenched the room in a welcoming glow. The antique counter reflected the same dark finish as the floors.

"It's like going back in time," Kat said.

"Yeah, I feel like I should be wearing long skirts." Wendy pinched her jeans, creating an imaginary skirt and curtsied.

Kat watched Jo lead the first tour out and away. Amos Thralling followed her to the courtyard with another small group. This assembly was abnormally quiet, almost anxious. Kat noted the sour expression on Amos' face, which seemed to be the root of the tension.

"Amos is here?" Kat said.

"Amazing, isn't it? Not even Amos wants to fish with a forty-below chill factor, I guess."

"Still don't know how the mayor got him here. Amos loves people about as much as a feline loves a bath."

"I want to be on his tour. He's got to be old enough to know the history of these buildings personally."

"Wendy Hareling, mind your manners," Grandma chided.

Wendy's shoulders slumped and her chin dropped low.

"Sorry, Grandma," she muttered.

"You know I love you like one of my own. I wouldn't say something like that otherwise."

Wendy brightened, "I love you too."

Kat and Bart brought up the rear of the small group as it made its way to the main room. Kat skidded to a stop causing Bart to bounce into her back. She jerked her head to the right, peering into the blackness of the adjacent room. A lonely window allowed the late-winter light to throw a grey veil on anything in front of it. Otherwise, the room was lost in blackness.

"A little warning next time?"

"Do you see someone in there?"

Bart squinted into the darkness. "Maybe. I might have seen some movement."

A large sign sat on an easel blocking the room beyond. Its tall, black lettering said, "Do not enter. Under construction."

They walked around the sign and headed toward the darkness.

"Whoa, you two. That room's not on the tour." Mayor Orthell had appeared from nowhere. Bart peered over the mayor's shoulder, craning his neck for a better look.

"Kat thought she saw someone in there."

"I'll go have a look then." He disappeared and returned a minute later. "All clear." He waved them toward the bar.

"Maybe they're hiding." Kat was not convinced.

"Think your eyes are playing tricks on you, young lady."

An uneasiness that had been whispering to her gut since she stepped in the door of the mercantile started to yell. The lights snapped then flickered and steadied. Kat watched as the flames in an antique oil lantern waved in a ghost-wind. Kat turned saucer eyes to Bart.

"What?" Bart seemed oblivious to the movement of the fire.

Kat looked back at the now steady flame. "Nothing."

The mayor had lost some color but managed a quick recovery and an even quicker smile. "Seems you're not quite over our little adventure from last fall."

And you act like it never happened. Why is that mayor? She managed a thin smile.

Orthell held her gaze briefly, searching her face.

"We're still getting the bugs worked out. Always the way with a project this size. See you up front." The mayor made his way toward the counter, stopping and shaking hands as he went.

Kat did an about-face to follow the mayor and was almost drenched in a steaming cup of hot chocolate. She jumped back before the liquid sloshed out of its mug and onto her coat. She looked up into those blue eyes that had mesmerized her not so long ago.

Ken managed to steady the slopping liquid before it swam over the brim and onto the rich, dark floor. He smiled down at Kat.

"Are you okay?"

"You missed." Kat managed to steady her voice and rubbery legs. She took a graceful step around Ken, made it to the front counter and grabbed the edge to steady herself. She inhaled in a deep, slow rhythm to calm her racing heart.

"Did you get a mocha?" Kat shot a look to her right and gazed into the handsome face of Ravens Cove's new librarian.

"No, no, I didn't. That is not on today's refreshment list." She smiled up at Brandon McGill.

Gary Wenfred, the librarian's assistant, stood beside him. Ever since Brandon had taken the job, Gary had made it his personal mission to protect Mr. McGill. Seems the death of the lovely Anita Conner last October had made Gary a bit edgy where his supervisor was concerned.

"And, how are you, Gary? Heard from the family?" Gary's family had chosen to leave for Anchorage to find work.

"Nope." Kat got the distinct impression that Gary was reveling in his independence.

"Going wild with this newfound freedom, right?" Brandon said.

"Yep. Only problem is I don't make enough money."

"Well, if you didn't eat at Jo's every night, you'd be surprised how far your money might go."

Gary's eyes narrowed to slits, and then he recovered and smiled. "You're probably right, Mr. McGill. I guess I should get some cooking lessons."

"Grandma would be happy to give you some tips. She or Jo, either one." Kat offered.

Gary grunted a reply, and tensed his jaw before he focused on her. Gary's hostility gave her a strong feeling that he blamed her for everything that had happened in Ravens Cove, not the demons that had come to destroy and dine on its good citizens.

Kat turned her attention back to Brandon. "How are you doing? Settling in?"

"Can't complain. No matter what else Ms. Conner is known for, her reputation as an organized librarian is pristine. Didn't have much to do when I got the job except make sure everything stayed business as usual."

Kat shuddered at the memory. Anita Conner had been murdered during the demon siege. She and Reverend Martin Plotno had died at the hands of Mrs. Plotno when she discovered them in a compromising position at the church altar. She, too, had been murdered, but her death remained a mystery. Ransom Plotno had been found at the top of Ravens Ravine but her body was not like those lost to Iconoclast.

Kat's eyes wandered to Ken's six-foot-something, athletic body as he passed through the door and out into the cold day.

"Hello?"

"Sorry." She willed her eyes back to Brandon.

"I'd love to discuss your work with Police Chief Andersen."

Kat grinned. No one who had lived in Ravens Cove for any length of time called Bart by his formal title. Somehow, with his Wild West ways and old-fashioned attitude, *Sheriff* had been bestowed on him and it stuck.

"Sure. Sometime sounds great."

"How about tomorrow afternoon?"

Kat's left eyebrow shot up and she turned her full gaze to Brandon. "Tomorrow?"

"I'm an aspiring writer. Unsolved mysteries are my passion." His eyes glittered as he spoke. "This town is steeped in mysteries. One of the reasons I took the job."

"Well, Bart has the facts and background information on any of our unsolved mysteries. I'm just the administrative help. Part-time at that."

"You don't give yourself enough credit. I find someone in your position not only knows the entire story, he or she also brings a unique perspective to the case."

"Well, then, I guess we could meet tomorrow. But, I still think you need Bart's insight. How about if I get him to come along?"

Brandon deflated. "Suppose you could do that."

"Okay, then. I'll find him and let you know. Oh look, there's Wendy. Need to catch her before she leaves for a tour."

Wendy watched Kat beelining in her direction at an unusually fast clip.

"What's up?" Wendy scouted the area Kat had left and found her answer.

"Just wanted to make sure we got on the tour together."

"Right, and I was born an hour ago. That cute new librarian make you uncomfortable?"

Kat sighed. "I think he was asking me on a date. Said something about writing mysteries and wanted to interview me about the cases in Ravens Cove."

"Well, that was lame but I'll give him an A for creativity. I think you should go."

"I have no desire to get into anything that even hints at a romantic relationship. Besides, Bart's the real expert and I want to invite him along."

"Bruck, bruck, chicken little! Where is that friend I knew—you know, self-confident, spunky, and willing to take risks?"

"I think you are mistaking me for someone else. I don't remember being that kind of person."

"Well, you were and I miss you."

Amos Thralling threw open the door and stomped into the mercantile. "That forsaken old house at the end has no heat."

Mayor Orthell came over in a flap. "Of course it has heat, Amos. All the buildings have heat."

"Not that one, Tommy."

"Where's your group?"

"Left them at the house."

"Go back. Now! They could wander and cause all kinds of problems."

"Doubtful. Frozen humans don't wander too far."

Orthell moved forward. Amos threw his hands in the air.

"Okay, I'm going. Just thought you'd want to get that heat fixed." Amos rushed back out the door, walked at a rapid clip across the courtyard, and disappeared into the house.

Mayor Orthell hesitated and then hastily retrieved his coat from behind the counter.

"I'll be right back, folks. Enjoy yourself. Jo should be here in a moment to take the next group around. Until then, please don't wander. The mercantile is still under construction and I don't want any of you hurt." He bounced toward and out the door.

"How refreshing to see Tommy lose a little of his arrogance. Adds a bit of reality to this fantasy of his."

"Grandma! That doesn't sound like you at all."

"Well, you have to admit almost anything would be more appealing than watching the mayor hold court in his new town." She looked past Kat and saw Kenneth in a group coming out from the old hotel and heading for the cannery.

"Then, of course, I forgot that your day has been full of surprises." Sadness overwhelmed Grandma as she remembered the first days of Kat's heartbreak over Ken and their inability to agree on how their relationship should move forward.

"Yep. That was sure a shocker I could have done without."

Jo swept into the mercantile and threw a warm smile to Kat and Grandma. "Bundle up you two. It's getting nastier out."

"Us, too." Paul, Tanya, and Bart stepped forward. Brandon joined the group.

"Where's Gary?" Kat asked.

"Phone rang. Said he'd catch the next tour."

"Well, looks like we are almost complete." Jo motioned for a couple of others to join them and they headed for the door.

"On second thought, I'll wait. Gary looked pretty concerned when he answered the phone."

"You want us to wait with you?"

"Sure he does." Wendy answered.

Brandon gave Wendy a quizzical look then glanced at Kat. "Let me see if I can get hold of him."

Kat pulled Wendy close and whispered, "thanks a lot, you brat."

"No problem," Wendy murmured.

Brandon turned off the cell phone. "He joined Amos' tour group. Said he'd catch up with me later."

"Then we're off." Jo pushed the door. It held tight. She leaned in and shoved it with her shoulder. The door opened a few inches before it was ripped out of her hand by a gust of wind. Jo managed to catch the heavy wood entry before it slammed into the outside wall.

The trees surrounding Old Town moaned and swayed in the rising wind. Icy fingers of snow twisted sideways across the courtyard. The short walk to the small cabin became a test of endurance.

They toured the one-room domicile. A large rock fireplace in the corner dwarfed the cabin. Rough-hewn log walls glinted in electric candlelight from a fresh coat of shellac.

"Pretty impressive. Looks move-in ready." Wendy joked.

"Yep. It must have been refurbished. Wonder if Arnie had anything to do with it?" Bart said.

"Maybe. He's the only one I can think of who'd have the knowledge. Still seems a huge project for just one man." Kat took in the gleaming wood beams and timbers.

"Wasn't Arnie. The mayor called in outside help for this one." Wendy remarked.

"Of course you'd have the inside scoop, Winsome." Kat squeezed Wendy's arm.

The group lingered at the cabin, none of them willing to take on the biting wind for a second time.

"Gotta move. We're on the mayor's schedule." Jo smiled, opened the cabin door and motioned them through.

The hotel had the same dark plank flooring as the mercantile, finished to a high gloss that emphasized the deep brown grain. A natural-oak counter glistened from a fresh oiling. A brass kickstand ran from one end of the counter to the other. Behind the reception counter, numbered boxes waited for a note to a ghostly patron.

"Sorry we can't do much more of a tour here. Still finishing the upstairs and dining room. Off limits, per the mayor." She lifted her nose in distaste.

"That's disappointing. I was hoping to get a feel for this old hotel." Brandon said.

"Really? Why?" Wendy asked.

"Research." He smiled and winked at Kat.

"He's an aspiring writer, Winsome. Likes mysteries. This one probably holds a few, or so you hope."

"Exactly."

"If it were up to me, I'd send you all up to take a gander. As it is, the mayor doesn't think people know how to take care of themselves. And, then there is that insurance liability. I told him that this is Ravens Cove, not Boston, and people don't sue on a whim here. I didn't win that argument."

Paul sighed. "It seems that even our fair town isn't immune to the heavy hand of bureaucracy." They started toward the cannery. Amos intercepted them.

"Have you seen that guy Gary? I can't find him anywhere. He was with my tour group …" Amos bent over and gasped for breath.

"He can't be far. Maybe he just went home." Worry crept over Jo's face.

"The mayor'll kill me if someone got loose in that house he's so proud of."

"How about I help you look? Two sets of eyes are better than one."

Amos mulled it over. "You're the sheriff. Mayor won't get too mad, will he?"

"'Course not."

Bart followed Amos as the rest of the tour continued into the old cannery building.

The inside of the building was a weathered grey. A foot below the roof, a row of ten transoms ran the length of the building on both sides. The floor's weathered grey appearance matched the walls. Support beams were exposed to the inside. Any piping or electric wiring was also exposed, although running through large conduits to make it safer and slightly more appealing.

The smell of long-dead fish mixed with stale salt water assaulted Kat's nose. "This place needs an air freshener."

"Guess the mayor wants it to be real. That smell sure makes it that way." Tanya Lucas spoke through the wool scarf she'd pulled up over her mouth and nose.

An anemic natural light illuminated the building. Its pale glow threw shadows into the corners that swayed in a ghoulish breeze. Kat crossed her arms in a protective hug.

A temporary railing of rough timbers nailed to two-by-fours flanked the metal steps leading to the second floor. The stairs ended prematurely in pitch-dark. The light from the small, high casements glinted off darkened glass on the upper floor. Again, a sign warned them off the upper floor.

"Hope this place will be ready by April," Kat said to Wendy.

"No kidding. Why are we here, really?"

Kat shrugged. "I wish I'd followed my first inclination to stay in bed under the warm covers."

"Me, too."

"Are we done in here yet?" The bunny boots and wool socks

were setting Kat's feet on fire. The discomfort intensified her desire to run from the day's spooky events and chance meeting with Ken.

"Indeed," Jo answered a sly smile on her face.

Kat sighed in relief then gave Jo a sheepish grin before they stepped out the old double doors. Bart met them at the bottom of the ramp.

"Find Gary?" Jo asked.

"No. I told Amos I'm sure he went home and I'd take a run out there later, just to make sure."

"You think he's okay, right?"

"No reason to think he's not. He's a young kid, first time on his own. Probably makes him feel good not to be accountable for his comings and goings."

"Makes sense." Jo sounded relieved.

"I've seen the old house, top to bottom. Think I'll get back to the office and get some work done. I've had about all I can take of this place for one day."

"Now?"

"I need to talk to Doc about Gordy and then I'm going out for some welfare visits to our more remote citizens."

"Want me to come with?"

"You bet. Mrs. Tellamoot has me concerned. That old dog of hers passed and she's all alone now."

"I'd be happy to." *Anything to not run into Ken and Mrs. Tellamoot is far from town and a good excuse to be gone from home.*

"I'll give you a ride to the office, Kat, when we're done here. Told Grandma I'd drop her home, too."

"Aren't you the good Samaritan today, Winsome."

Wendy gave her a weak smile. "Gotta help out when and where I can."

"Right."

An illogical dread hit the pit of Kat's stomach as they climbed the porch stairs of the old house. It grew stronger as she approached the large front door. The door latch clicked and the door opened by itself. Kat jumped back. Wendy caught her and they both almost tumbled backward off the stoop.

"What is with you today?" Wendy grabbed the post to stop them both.

"Don't know. Sorry." Kat climbed the second step and onto the decking just as Ken Melbourne walked onto the porch. She hopped backward to avoid contact. Ken caught her before she took a hard tumble through the rickety railing.

"We need to stop meeting like this." He had stopped her from a concussion-producing fall a few months back. That time on Bart Andersen's front porch when they had gone and found him precariously pointing a Magnum .357 at his own face.

"We have to stop meeting at all." Kat jerked her arms free and moved toward the door.

"Well, if it isn't Mr. Fibber," said Wendy. "Trying for that knight-in-shining-armor thing again? Been working on it, maybe? In case you don't know, the last time you failed—miserably."

Ken stood silent, not taking his eyes off Kat. Wendy stepped in front of Kat, breaking the stare down.

"I really would like to talk to you, Kat," he said around Wendy's statue stance.

"Nothing to talk about."

"Yes there is. Please talk to me."

"No."

Kat walked through the door of the house, leaving Wendy squared off against Ken.

"You are a real piece of work." Was all Wendy could manage to say before she followed Kat into the house.

Ken faced the closed door. He took a step toward it, hesitated and turned to go down the steps. Mayor Orthell blocked his descent.

"Did anyone find Gary?"

"Who's Gary? Oh wait, the kid from the library? Is he lost?"

"Amos says he can't find him."

"Well, did you look inside?"

"Bart did. No sign of him."

"Why so concerned? Don't you think he just left and went to work or home?"

"Yeah, probably did." The mayor's eyes darted left and right, tension pursing his upper lip.

Ken felt a nagging concern; instincts shot to the surface.

"You have reason to think something else might have happened?"

"No, no." A line of a smile met Ken's concerned face. "Just trying to make sure everyone's okay—the construction and all."

"Well, I'll tell him to come find you if I see him."

"Thanks and have a good time visiting the Cove today. You're going back tomorrow, right?"

"Don't think so. I put in for some time off and may hang around for a while."

"Really? Well, that's good, Mr. Melbourne. We'll be glad to have you as our guest." He hurried off toward the cannery.

"Why do I think you didn't mean that?" Ken asked under his breath.

Ken decided to make his way to the Ravens Cove Inn. He had not felt like telling the mayor that his career was on shaky ground right now and his chief, Andy Binning, had ordered him to take administrative leave the night before Ken left for the Cove.

Binning began with, "I am very concerned about you, my friend," before diving into the real reason he'd summoned Ken to his office. When Andy leaned forward and laced his hands in front of him on the desk, Ken knew what was coming.

"I haven't been able to get a straight answer out of you since you returned from Ravens Cove. There is a serial killer on the loose and you don't seem the least bit interested in finding him or her. Your report was sketchy and unbelievable. I've given you every chance to correct it and put this thing to bed. Times up. Consider yourself on a leave until I contact you."

Ken still felt the sting of those words. "So, here I am. Back in that same small town where I lost my credibility and reputation—in more ways than one," he said, thinking of the mess he and Kat had made of their would-be relationship.

Well, I'm here to fix my part. We'll see if the Ice Queen will melt a little.

Chapter 3
Of Thieves and Liars

Hesitant steps broke the tomb-like silence of Old Town. Mayor Thomas Orthell cringed with each new sound, fearful of alerting any straggler or intruder to his arrival. He made his way through the darkness of an early night that cloaked Old Town in blackness. Large, black spruce announced the beginning of the deep woods that held the town in a tight grip. The needled nightshades blocked any evening light from touching the town. Orthell jumped when a great horned owl hooted from the forest beyond.

The short, round figure of the man broke into a trot. Once he reached the cannery door, he looked back over his shoulder to convince himself he had avoided detection. The door latch gave a satisfying *click* as it released. He slipped inside and headed up the stairs to the second floor. He wove in and out of the adjacent rooms, one last check to satisfy his fear of detection.

In the last office, Orthell strode to the back corner closet and yanked the wood plank door open. He ran his right fingers under a subtle lip on the left side of the back wall and pressed down when his fingers came to a slight bump. The hidden latch released with a loud clack. The false divider flew open, revealing a small, stuffy room. Orthell pushed the partition closed and scanned the back wall with a flashlight. The yellow light shone on grey, weathered planks covered in dusty cobwebs and held together by rusty nails. He stopped scanning when the light revealed several blood-red candles on a low, rectangular table. He took a disposable lighter from his parka, lit the candles and knelt.

"O great ones. I have brought you deserted human dwellings of wood and stone. Dwellings that hold horror in their walls. Make them your homes." He kissed the table and blew out the candles.

Orthell performed the same ritual in each building of Old Town. He saved the large, five-spire house for last. Once over its threshold, he fell to his knees and kissed the wood floor.

"My home of homes. You are no longer an outcast to be inhabited by vermin. You will again know the glory bestowed on you by my father's father. Because of you, my ancestors and my friends will be avenged."

Orthell rose and admired the wide, flared staircase, and rich, dark walls of the entry hall. Before heading to the next floor, he stopped to caress the hard, cold banister. He searched the three bedrooms on the second floor before continuing up the next flight to the attic.

A small storage trunk, as old as the house itself, sat beneath the diminutive attic dormer. The trunk had been in the house when the Forgotten Place was a thriving town and home to his Denali Indian grandmother and his Scottish grandfather.

"Theirs was a love I only dream about. Only the spirits knew what their love could do."

His grandmother had been a healer, but chose to practice the dark arts of his grandfather's people when the village had shunned and humiliated her. His grandfather had come to

Alaska and told all that would hear that it was in search of gold. Orthell's father had told Tommy the real reason. The man had escaped Scotland before he was to be tried as a warlock. Grandpa Orthell believed in the forces of nature—what some called elementals—and their masters. He melded Christianity with the practice of nature. To Grandpa, all elementals, their masters, and the God of the Christians were related. He wrote the *Book of Fallen Angels* for his new religion. Together, he and his wife developed a new sect. The Forgotten Place was rumored to be destroyed by disease. Orthell knew it had been an act of punishment because the villagers had angered the elementals and their masters.

"I'm going to change all that. Ravens Cove will become your new home and place of worship. They destroyed my friends and my church and I will resurrect them all. I swear by my ancestors that I will set this wrong to right."

Orthell opened the trunk and removed the various pictures, vintage dresses, and toys that dated back to the early 1900s. He searched with his fingers and found a latch underneath the old chest's lining. It popped open, revealing an old, leather bound volume.

He smiled, sat down cross-legged on the floor of the attic, opened the book and began to read.

Kat reached over the Subaru's front seat, kissed her grandmother, and turned to Wendy.

"Thanks for everything. You are a true friend."

"I try."

"And you succeed."

Kat jumped out and made her way to the police station. The old brass bell chimed her arrival.

"'Bout time."

"Hey, give me a break. I'm supposed to be home cuddled under the covers reading a good book or something. Instead I'm joining you on a manhunt."

"Not quite a manhunt. More like a scouting mission to satisfy our esteemed mayor that no one has managed to hide away in one of his prized buildings."

Bart strode to meet Kat at the door. "The sooner we leave, the sooner we can get back."

"I'm beginning to feel like I live in this truck," Kat said as she hoisted herself into the passenger seat.

"Today you do." Bart turned the key and it roared to life.

Main Street was empty except for a few hardy souls who had ventured out for some shopping or a cup of coffee. Forty-below zero didn't deter the residents of Ravens Cove from finding human companionship to offset the loneliness of a small town in a remote place, far from big-city entertainment.

Bart made a U-turn and headed north on Main. "First stop, the library. If Gary's shown up, we can go on to Mrs. Tellamoot's." They rolled to a stop.

Dread hit Kat's stomach. The last thing she wanted to do right now was to make nice with Brandon McGill. "I'll wait here."

"No you won't." Bart turned off the truck. The cold seeped through the metal in seconds.

Kat huffed and jumped out. They strode up the concrete steps and entered one of the town's more ornate buildings.

Brandon stood behind the counter, concentrating on a large computer screen. He looked up and brightened.

"Good evening, Kat—and sheriff." His smile lost its zeal.

"Gary show up?"

"No. Think he took off for home after the event."

"Doesn't he usually work 'til six?"

"Usually. But, today being an impromptu holiday, I did tell him to take the rest of the day off. Usually, he doesn't do what I say. Today he did. Go figure."

"Well, since the mayor seemed mighty concerned, guess we'll go check the house. Thanks."

"We still on for coffee tomorrow, Kat?"

Kat thought. She had no other appointments and maybe Wendy was right. "Sure. See you at three?"

"Great."

Kat and Bart walked back to the truck in silence.

"You're having coffee with *Brandon?*" The way Bart said it brought back Kat's original doubts.

"Guess so. Why?" Somewhere in the last few hours, Kat had decided against inviting Bart to join them.

"Why? He's new to town and awfully slick. Not to mention, you don't know anything about that man."

"Well, coffee seems to be a good way to find out. For heaven's sake, Bart, I'm not taking him to meet Grandma or marrying the guy. And he is cute."

That got Bart. "Cute doesn't mean a thing, and you know it. You're doing it to tick off Melbourne."

"Mr. FBI will be gone tomorrow afternoon. I am just trying to get on with my life."

"Don't like it, cousin."

"I promise I won't take him home to Grandma. And, if he becomes too bothersome, I will take him home to meet BC. Feel better?"

Bart smiled. "How about you have him to your house for coffee first? Then I won't have to worry at all." He smiled wider at the thought of BC. That cat was the best bodyguard Bart could hope for where his cousin was concerned. He attacked any man who had an eye on Kat. And he had run off all but one. That one being the man he had called a friend. Bart frowned. He had accepted that Ken Melbourne would be part of their family and Ken had surprised them all when he broke things off and ran for Anchorage.

"You know you're overprotective, right?"

"Right, and I plan to stay that way."

They had started north on Main again. As they left the lights of town behind, darkness enveloped them. The headlights shown a few feet ahead on the one-lane road.

Bart stopped the truck. He and Kat both looked to the burnt out shell of a house that had once been the church of Paul Lucas. The reminder put them both in a sober mood.

"It really did happen, didn't it?"

"Yep, KittyKat. I have a hard time remembering the events of last October. Do you?"

"Yes. I don't think I want to."

They sat in silence, each lost in the memory of the fight with Iconoclast and his legion of demons that had come to take Ravens Cove. Iconoclast had not succeeded but still had taken several members of their town and had left the Cove scarred and scared. The innocence of Ravens Cove had been replaced by an underlying distrust.

"We won."

"God won," Kat said.

"True."

"I still miss Josiah." A tear spilled onto Kat's cheek. "He died for me. Why would he do that, Bart?" Kat turned innocent, confused eyes to him.

"Don't know but I will always be grateful that he did." He grabbed her hand.

Kat smiled at the love she so often took for granted. "My life is blessed and I don't even know it most of the time. Drive on, and let's make sure Gary is where he's supposed to be."

Bart turned west onto Alder Way—a small, dimly lit hole of a drive. The only house on it was Gary's. It had been part of his family's homestead. The small, rundown log cabin popped out from the surrounding woods. The windows were dark. Bart stepped onto the porch and looked through the window beside the door. A large, black shape hit the window so hard it shook. Bart jumped back. The muffled barks and growls kept coming.

"Gary's got a dog."

"You think?" Kat's heart still thumped in her chest.

Bart glared at Kat. Her glib tongue was getting on his last nerve right now.

"Sorry." Kat gave Bart an apologetic smile.

Bart knocked. "Gary?" Only silence greeted him. He knocked again.

"Odd."

"Yeah, it is. Gary has no life outside work and guarding Brandon. If I hadn't told Mrs. Tellamoot we'd be there today, I'd go on a search. On second thought, I'm concerned that he might be out in this cold somewhere. Will you call Mrs. Tellamoot and tell her we'll be there as soon as we can?"

Kat returned the phone to her coat pocket. "She's okay. Already been visited by Pastor Paul and Tanya. Says she's kind of tuckered out and she'd see you tomorrow."

"Thank you, Pastor Paul."

"I'm starving. Can we stop and grab a sandwich before we go on this search?"

"Really, Kat? There's someone missing and you want food?" Frustration laced Bart's urgent tone.

An all too familiar guilt chomped into Kat's conscience. "Maybe Jo or someone there has seen him. Seems like as good a place to start as any."

Bart couldn't argue with the logic. "Okay. Five minutes is all we have."

———

Mayor Orthell opened the *Book of Fallen Angels*. The yellow pages and black ink jumped into view. He hesitated, half closing the old book. *I can turn back and no one would know the difference.*

"Who says I want to turn back?" His voice sounded unconvincing even to himself in the dark silent attic. Visions of the Right Reverend Plotno and Anita Conner swam into his sight. He had gone to the funeral home that doubled as the town's mortuary. He had seen firsthand the bloody bodies of his friends.

"If Paul Lucas had stayed away from this place they'd still be alive." Resolve straightened his spine. He closed the chest, reopened the book and gently placed the old volume on the lid. He clicked the flashlight. Dead. He turned and looked around the room, located an antique oil lamp and lit the wick.

At the center of the first page were four symbols. Several lines topped by a cloud—like a puff of smoke drifting on the wind. A lizard with large feet and a line of symbols down its back breathed fire. A small, malevolent dwarf and a spout of water rising from the middle of a large pond completed the symbols.

Orthell read aloud, "as my ancestors before me, I am calling you to come. Make my home your home. Make my life your life and make all that I see your domain. Destroy those that would do me harm. Destroy those that are my enemies. I will serve you and you alone if you will do as I ask. I await your greatness."

An odd glow filled the darkened room. Shapes and colors

took form in the sphere of light. A vision of Gary Wenfred floated in the light and a real-life play unfolded before the Mayor's eyes.

Orthell saw Gary crouching inside the built-in clapboard of the darkened room of the mercantile. Gary released the latch and brought his lanky frame to its full height. He spent a moment shaking each leg to get the feeling back and then he started to trot, afraid he would get caught. He made it to the front counter and grabbed the silver candlesticks that had been on display.

Mayor Orthell jumped at the sound of Gary's voice. He turned; sure he'd see the young man at the rear of the room. He realized the voice was also coming from the misty ball.

"Sorry, mayor. A man's gotta eat."

Gary sneaked to the top of the stairs, each step groaning in protest under his weight. At the top he looked around the gutted apartment. His nose wrinkled at the musty odor that permeated the upper floor.

"Yuck. Definitely needs a new coat of paint," he whispered aloud.

He jumped and whirled around when a board creaked behind him. "Stupid nerves," he chided.

Gary ended up face-to-face with the white wall that separated the hallway from other parts of the living quarters. He methodically checked all the rooms. He kicked the wall of the last room when he found nothing of value to line his pockets. He headed back into the hallway.

Gary smiled when his eyes lit on a small black latch at the end of the corridor. He walked over and gave it a yank. The wall popped open, revealing a narrow staircase, flanked by white painted walls. It disappeared into the darkness above. He pulled out his flashlight and turned it on. He reached the top and gasped. "I knew he had to have hidden the stuff."

He ran to a table full of antique lanterns, old snowshoes made of softened birch and dried leather, even some odds and ends of ivory carvings. He grabbed the ivory and began shoving it in his coat pockets. One of the carvings caught his attention. It was just like the rock in the courtyard of Old Town. It was so old the ivory had turned brown. The eyes and beak were perfect imitations of the one on the boulder.

"I can make a fortune on this ugly thing alone." He grinned. "Especially once the town's a famous tourist attraction."

Gary stuffed it in his pocket and began scouring the room for other items that were lightweight and easy to turn into quick cash. The sound of someone sweeping with an old straw broom caught his attention. "Who's there?" Gary headed toward the sound, forgetting his treasure hunt.

He examined the corner and found no one. He swung the flashlight left to the right and back. He stopped the light on a small, round table holding a maroon candle. The wax was still soft. Gary leaned in. A five-pointed star had been etched into the table beside the candle. On four points were odd creatures. The only one he recognized was a lizard.

"What the heck is this? You're not part of this old building, that's for sure," he said to the pentagram.

"What are you hiding Mayor? And, how much would you pay me so I won't let on?" He thought hard. Understanding dawned.

"I'll be rich! I'll keep my job, though, just to keep up appearances. Wouldn't want to let anyone know."

Something moved in a far corner of the room. He turned and saw a large shadow and ran for the narrow stairs. Halfway there, he was sure he heard a hiss and a growl.

"What'd he do, bring in snakes, too?" Gary laughed at his own silliness.

"No, he brought in something even more amazing," a voice answered from behind him.

Gary whirled, heart pounding, and came face to face with the black shadow. The dark mist grabbed and swept Gary into the air before his feet hit the first stair.

"Welcome to my world. A thief and liar you are and a thief and liar you will continue to be."

Gary opened his mouth in a silent scream. His vocal chords were paralyzed, along with his mind and body. He could not comprehend what was in front of him. His mind screamed, *fight,* but he stayed still instead.

He found his voice and croaked. "I'm so sorry. I didn't know anyone was here. I will put everything back."

"No, I'll put it all back. Hand me the skull."

Gary frantically searched his pocket, trinkets bouncing off the attic floor. He found it.

"Here." He shoved it at the being.

The creature smiled, which made it all the more terrifying. The razor-sharp teeth were red.

"I am just a humble herald of the one who is coming. But you will make a good meal and sacrifice *for me.*" Atramentous tightened his black mist around Gary and squeezed. The candle on the table burst into flame and a small crack broke through the wall behind the pentagram. It widened to the size of Gary's frame. Atramentous flew through, Gary in tow. Gary's screams diminished when the wall closed.

Mayor Orthell dropped the *Book of Fallen Angels.*

"That didn't just happen, did it?" He asked aloud. He jumped up and raced into the night.

———

Josiah Williams awoke to the sound of running water. He

rubbed his eyes like a child and looked around. A cranberry bush, full of ripe berries, stood beside the water.

The memory of battle flooded his conscious mind. He searched his own body, first with his left hand, then rolled over and searched with the right. No pain. No sign of the deep wounds and torn flesh that had resulted from the attack. He felt his face. He had a full beard where before it had been clean shaven.

The rivulet of water gurgling beside his ear made his dry mouth water in anticipation. Josiah cupped his hands and lowered them into the cold, sparkling spring and drank deeply of the sweet liquid. He hungrily plucked the berries, and ate handfuls at a time.

"A feast like none I remember." Josiah marveled at the surge of energy he experienced. He sat up straight and really looked at his surroundings for the first time. The tall and rocky ravine walls greeted his eyes. He stood up while his eyes traced the hard surface of the ravine to its opening high above the chasm's floor. Bare trees and dark spruce bent toward the gap in an unrelenting wind.

"Why aren't I frozen or cold?" he asked aloud. "Maybe I'm dead."

"Not dead, Josiah Williams."

He spun, lost his footing and fell toward a glowing being. He waved his arms in a backward circle, managing to keep upright. Fear and awe overcame him. Josiah fell to his knees and then prone on the ground.

"Get up! I am not to be worshipped. I am a servant of the Most High, just as you are."

Josiah's shaky legs had just enough strength. He stood.

"You have seen me before, why are you afraid, Man of God? I have come to awaken you and tell you to return to Ravens Cove and your friends. It is ordained by the Lord Jesus."

Josiah could only nod agreement. He took his eyes off the blue glow to look around and up the Ravine. The original path was still blocked by a large rock that had grown up out of the ground on the night he confronted Iconoclast.

"With all due respect, how?"

The angel pointed to a bush-covered area beside the small waterfall and pond. A narrow pathway peeked through the thick shrubbery. It ran at a steep upward angle from the bottom of the chasm floor to the land above.

The angel shot skyward.

"Excuse me." The angel did not return.

"Lord, you know I am not young. And, I know I'm not supposed to question you. But, really, Lord, is that the only way?" Josiah waited. The gurgling stream was the only response.

Resigned, Josiah took in a deep breath and made his way to the trail. He grabbed a branch with his left hand and pulled himself onto the footway.

"One for the money, two for the show ..." He walked forward and tripped over an obstacle on the path. There lay his worn winter coat, the button still missing. The hood looked new. Beside it were his favorite winter boots, black, heavy, and equally worn. He had intentionally left these behind when he travelled to Ravens Cove in October because they were additional weight to an overloaded bag.

"Your ways are amazing, O Lord."

He slipped into the coat and boots and began the long and slow uphill climb.

Chapter 4
Missing No Longer

Jo's Bakery was empty except for a few good citizens that seemed reluctant to face the cold again and make their way home.

"Good evening, Kat, Bart." Jo nodded and smiled. "What can I get you?"

"Kat's starving and we're looking for Gary. So, I guess you'd say we are killing two birds with one stone."

Jo smiled wider. "How do you stay so slim, Kat. You eat, what—six times a day or more?

"I know, I know. I'm a bottomless pit, or so Grandma Bricken says. Am I known for anything else in this town?"

"Yep, there is your scathing tongue when you get riled up."

"Oh, there is that," Kat said meekly. "I'm working on cleaning that up a little—patience does not come easily for me."

"Not for any of us, sweetie. Just keep trying."

"Give her a mocha and something fast, Jo. Has Gary been in?"

"Not yet. But he should be here soon. Has made this his dinner place since the family left."

She turned and looked at the clock. "Actually, he's late." She pushed the mocha and two turkey sandwiches across the counter.

Bart gave her a questioning look.

"You need to eat, too."

"Thanks. If Gary comes in, have him call me."

"Think something's happened to him?"

"I'm more inclined to think he's playing video games at a friend's or something else."

"Gary has friends?"

"Don't know but anything's possible. Maybe he's made a few since his parents left."

Paul and Tanya walked up to the counter.

"Thanks for visiting Mrs. Tellamoot."

"We enjoy her company." Tanya said. "She has some great stories about the old days and how Ravens Cove became a town."

"Sounds like you two are settling in more and more. I'm glad. Thought we were going to lose you for a month or so."

"None more surprised than me," Paul said. "But I prayed, as I am apt to do." He smiled at Bart and Kat. "I know Ravens Cove is home."

"I'm so glad!" Kat hugged Tanya then Paul. "I'd miss you in the worst way if you left."

"We'd miss you, too. So much so, I think my heart would be shy a piece if we left." Tanya answered.

"Not to mention, that congregation of mine came together and somehow convinced the council and mayor to let us have that abandoned building south of town. They took to it and that place shines. Heat was installed this week so we are on propane now and aren't all bundled up. By the way, where have you been? I miss seeing your smiling faces."

"Oh, you know, things keep coming up even for a small-town cop like me."

Kat nodded. Not really having an excuse except that her warm bed kept her from venturing into the cold.

"Well, we'd sure love to see you again. Come by when you can." Paul and Tanya walked to the counter.

"I feel so guilty."

"Me, too."

"Gonna go?"

"You gonna go?"

"If you do, I will."

The old sibling gauntlet had been thrown. Bart sighed. He felt responsible for Kat in all ways, even spiritually. He couldn't shake his need to protect her.

"I'll pick you up Sunday."

They ventured back out into the night, back to the task at hand. Just as they reached the all-familiar truck and as Kat was steadying herself for another jolting ride out of town, the mayor ran up.

"Come quick. Someone has broken into the mercantile."

"What?"

"I said, come. I saw a light in the window."

"Go back inside." Kat, glad for the reprieve, moved toward Jo's.

She turned. "Call me later? I don't want you disappearing on me tonight."

"I do this for a living, you know."

"I know and that's what makes me worry."

"I'll call. Go."

———

The old mercantile was silent and made eerie by the darkness and shadow play from a full moon's light coming through the windows. Bart and Tommy Orthell walked into the empty room that had been off limits to Bart earlier in the day.

"There." The mayor pointed toward the left wall.

Bart squinted in the direction of the mayor's finger. He

walked to the back wall, a portion of which now protruded into the room. "Hidden clapboard?"

The mayor nodded.

Bart shone his flashlight all around the small storage space. The light unveiled footprints in the dusty cabinet. Two large shoe prints made their way into the small space, then turned and stopped at the back wall. Another distinct set of footprints led back to the main room.

Bart unsnapped his holster. "You stay down here. I'm going up to take a look around."

"You don't know the upstairs, sheriff. You could get hurt, there's still construction stuff everywhere not to mention loose floorboards." Mayor Orthell's voice sounded like he was using a megaphone.

The sheriff put a finger to his lips and motioned the mayor to follow. The old steps creaked and moaned under their weight. Bart paused on each tread and listened.

Orthell hung back in the hallway while Bart checked each room. "Haven't found anyone yet. That's a good thing, right?"

"I'd say so."

Orthell thought a moment. "There is one more place."

Bart threw Orthell a questioning look.

"The attic. It's well hidden because the original mercantile owners needed to keep valuables in a safe place." Fear gripped the mayor. "That must be where the thief is." He hurried to the end of the hallway, grabbed and pulled the latch. The small doorway popped open.

Bart heard a sickly thud, then a thump. Mayor Orthell let out a bloodcurdling scream and Bart broke from a fast walk to a run. He skidded to a halt as the mayor jumped backward, turned, and screamed again, this time in Bart's face. A large, mushy object lay at their feet. Bart shone his light on it.

Orthell threw a hand over his mouth to stifle another scream. He excused himself and ran for the stairs and out the door.

Bart turned to the corpse. It lay face up, staring at the ceiling through cloudy eyes. The arms were splayed to the side. So were the legs, but their position was unnatural, both broken from the knees down. Other than that, the body was intact. The fear in the vacant eyes sent a chill through Bart.

He squatted, bringing the flashlight closer to the body. There were definable indents around the torso and neck. He looked closer at the face. He released the cell phone from its holder on his belt and dialed.

———

"Getting ready to close up. Need a ride?" Kat was enjoying her second mocha, a real treat at the end of a busy, tiring day.

"Might. Let me give Bart a call." Bart had been gone more than two hours when it should have taken half that to look over a building.

Her phone trilled before she could dial. Bart's number was in the display.

"Where are you?"

"Found Gary."

"Good. Come get me."

"I found Gary—dead."

The color bled from Kat's face. This town was becoming a real live horror movie—again.

"Frozen?" She hoped, because the alternative was frightening.

"Nope. Body's in a bad way. I'm calling doc. I'll be staying a while. Can you get a ride?"

Kat looked at an impatient Jo.

"Yep. I got a ride." Jo nodded.

"Good." The phone went dead.

———

Doc Billings' well-known Audi slid to a stop. He hurried up the porch stairs and into the now brightly lit mercantile.

"Where?"

Bart pointed up the stairs. "I'll go before you. The floor's a little tricky."

Billings pulled on a pair of white latex gloves and removed what looked like a meat thermometer from his black bag. He placed the thermometer over the liver.

Bart could not stand watching this part. He couldn't shake the thought of how that would feel. "I'll be downstairs. The funeral home's on its way for the body."

"Good. I'll get more from there."

Bart headed out the door to his truck for his fingerprint equipment. His head popped out of the truck when he heard a car engine. His face flushed with anger when he saw Kat.

"Thanks, Jo." She gave a cheery wave to the red taillights receding down Willowbend Circle, and then headed for Bart at a fast clip.

"Going home, I thought," Bart growled.

"Didn't say that. Said I could get a ride. I thought you could use some help."

"Didn't say that."

"You never do. Changing the subject, this place is spookier in the dark."

Kat looked at the houses. Each was lit by a single spot. The skull-rock was the center of attention with two spots. Everything between the skull and the houses was pitch-black. The wind had calmed to a breeze. Instead of making it more inviting, the slight movement of the trees, highlighted by the houses' spotlights, pitched shadows left and right on the roofs. The birch limbs portraying skinny, knobbed arms bent upward and waved for help as if they were being held hostage by an invisible villain. The darkness behind the windows of the log cabin, cannery, main house, and old hotel drank up the light like a black sponge.

"Yep," said Bart. "But, then again, I think that bout last fall heightened the ole survival instincts.

Kat let out a nervous laugh. "Probably."

Bart started back toward the mercantile building. Kat jogged up beside him. Bart stopped, blocked Kat and stared a challenge at her.

"I'll stay out of the way. I won't go up or anything. I just don't want you here by yourself."

"I'm not alone. Doc Billings is here."

"Great. He can autopsy you and himself with as much help as he can give."

"How you going to stop a big, bad murderer?"

Kat reached behind her back and pulled out a small .22 caliber revolver.

"Put that thing away! Where did you get it anyway?"

"Last trip into Anchorage. Makes me feel safer."

"For the safety of us all Kat, just put it away."

Kat slipped the small gun into the holster behind her back. After another blazing-eyed reprimand, Bart turned and motioned her to follow.

Kat waited at the bottom of the mercantile stairs, perusing the rock, the courtyard, and the buildings. Movement next to the log cabin caught her eye. She looked with intent as the shadow disappeared behind the building and then appeared again between the cabin and the old hotel.

"Bart," she whispered from the left side of her mouth.

"*Bart*," louder this time.

Bart was in a crouch, working to get a good fingerprint from the brass knob on the front door. He jerked his head over his shoulder.

"This is exactly why you should have gone home. What is it!"

"Lower your voice. There's someone over there between the cabin and hotel."

Bart stood up and turned to face the direction of Kat's finger.

"Don't see anything."

"There is! Wait."

"Your eyes are playing tricks on you—I'll be a monkey's uncle, I see it." Bart watched as the shadow, definitely a two-legged one, made its way from behind the hotel to the woods. For the second time this evening, he unclasped the holster and, this time, pulled the gun and pointed it in the direction of the spruce and birch.

"Stay." Bart raised a tense outstretched hand at Kat.

He strode in giant steps toward the hotel, the crunching snow announcing his movements. He ducked behind the hotel, then headed into the woods and disappeared.

Kat stared after him, as if she could will protection over him. She heard a tussle in the woods, then saw a tall spruce shake from the weight of someone or something being thrown into it. She reached behind her back, brought out her .22 and started running. She stopped at the edge of the clearing and took careful strides, trying with all her might to silence her footsteps.

Movement caught her attention and she swung to her right. Two tall shapes came into view, one holding the other against a tree, its arm pushed up under the second person's neck.

Kat held the gun with both hands and stretched out her arms.

"Back off!" she yelled at the form. The unidentifiable head snapped around.

"Put that blasted thing away, Kat, now."

She knew that voice. She wavered and lowered the gun a slight way toward her legs, still holding it with both hands at the ready.

The shadow on the tree pushed the other off and straightened.

"Yeah, put that blasted thing away." That was Bart.

Ken and Bart sauntered to the light looking like two kids who had just had a fight in the schoolyard—disheveled, heightened color and smiling like only men do when they've just had a fight, the rules are understood, and they are best buds again. Kat continued to hold the gun in front of her, looking as if she might bring it up and shoot. She thought better of it and lowered it to her side.

"Good evening," Ken flashed a smile. Kat ignored the electric impulses that shot through her.

"What are you doing here?" she spat out.

"I was taking a walk. Why are you here? Doesn't BC need your attention?"

"Why I'm here is none of your concern. Neither is BC, for that matter."

Ken tilted his head to the right and gave a slight shrug. Always the sign that he didn't have a ready retort but didn't agree just the same. This was the same shrug he'd given Kat at the end of their last conversation. Right before he'd turned and walked out of her cabin and her life.

Ken turned to Bart. "Why are you here, my friend? Didn't get enough of Old Town in the daylight?"

Bart hesitated then launched into his explanation. "Well, seems we have another murder in Ravens Cove."

Kat shot an angry, betrayed glance his way. Bart cringed. He knew Kat felt like he had taken sides with the school bully. But he had missed Ken's insight and intelligence and friendship. It was a lonely life as a small-town police chief. There were not many who understood and shared a passion for it.

Ken's raised his eyebrows. "You don't say."

"I do say."

They all stood in silence, Kat feeling like the odd man out and wishing she'd had Jo deliver her to the cabin.

"Well, I'll be meandering on home now. You surely don't need little ole me to hold your hand. You have a big, strong man here for that." She paused. "Watch your back, cousin. This one's not good at following through."

She spun on her heel and walked toward Main before either of them could respond. Bart found his voice first.

"Hey," Bart yelled to her back. "It's cold. It's dark. There's a murderer on the loose."

Kat kept walking. She reached into her left pocket and pulled something out and a beam of light appeared. She pointed the beam at her right hand and waved the gun back and forth.

"I'll be okay. You do what you need to do. It's not like I've never walked home in the dark before." She lowered the gun and placed it in her right pocket. She tightened her hood with a firm gesture and picked up her pace.

Ken took a step toward Kat. Bart blocked him with an arm. "She is strong-willed and feisty. She's okay. Call me when you get home," he yelled after her.

Kat threw her right hand in the air and waved.

"Maybe she will, maybe she won't." Bart looked at his watch. "If she's not home in thirty minutes, I'll go find her."

A van pulled up to the curb. Black with baby-blue lettering announced, "Ravens Cove Mortuary."

"Well, the boys have arrived and that means we can get the body out and the rest of the investigation started."

Bart opened the mercantile door. "Van's here, Doc."

"Great." Billings appeared at the top of the stairs pulling latex gloves from his hands.

"My initial look-over is complete."

Bart gave him a quizzical look.

"All I know so far is that he has two broken legs and a crushed rib cage and he died within the last couple of hours. I'll know more when I can open him up."

"How soon will you have something?"

"Gordy's on his way to Anchorage. So, I'll do an initial review tonight and send Gary on for a consult, hopefully tomorrow. Soon as I hear from the Anchorage M.E., I'll call."

Doc smiled and stuck out his right hand. "Agent Melbourne. How wonderful to see you. What brings you to our small, usually uneventful, town again? Happen to know there was going to be a couple of murders?"

"No, Doc. Didn't know that. The mayor asked I come down for the opening of this place, something about a recognition ceremony. Didn't see you there."

"Little tied up." He motioned to Eric and Jonas Smotherly. "Up the stairs, to the right and watch your step, boys. Some loose floorboards."

Eric gave Doc a quick nod. He and Jonas disappeared up the stairs. The next time Bart saw Gary's corpse, it was neatly wrapped in a black body bag. The pair gently laid it in front of the entry and left to get the gurney. They were gone and back in a flash.

"Well, better get to work." Bart said.

"Feels like old times." Ken looked like a guy who'd won the lottery.

"I pray this isn't like old times."

Ken sobered. "Me, too. But for the life of me I can't shake

that *déjà vu* feeling." They climbed the staircase in silence and maneuvered the hallway's rotten boards.

"No sign of a struggle. Little or no blood. Floor's almost too clean."

"You'd think there'd be something here."

"You'd think."

Bart gloved his hands and dusted the latch for fingerprints. He took a small sample. Then he turned the knob. "No time like the present." Bart led the way and Ken followed him up the narrow stairs to the attic.

Chapter 5
A Familiar Stranger

Kat power-walked the icy streets to the edge of town. Her anger and hurt propelled her up the gentle rise that leveled at the top of Ravens Ravine. She paused to catch her breath before cutting to her left and taking the small trail that led to the road in front of her cabin.

The ravine area felt so different than it had a few months earlier. There was lightness to it. She could hear little creaks and snaps coming from a stand of alder bushes that hedged the top of the cleft. She smiled. The familiar sound of small animals settling in their winter homes made her feel warm and secure. It brought the same comfort and the same melancholy that she felt when snuggled into her old quilt from Gran Tovslosky. Gran had passed several years before and she still missed her.

"Stop it, Katrina Agnes Tovslosky," she scolded.

She turned onto the old trail and stopped short. The moon's light silhouetted the figure of a man ahead of her on the path.

"Oh for goodness sake. I've had enough scares for one evening. This guy had better be ready for a fight because I'm done with this and now!"

The figure didn't seem to notice her. She could have circled back and found Bart. *Probably the smart thing to do. But I don't feel like doing the smart thing.* That old anger surfaced when she realized she would rather take her chances with this stranger than go back and face Ken Melbourne.

Kat pulled the .22 and headed down the footpath. When she got close enough, she turned her flashlight's beam to the stranger's face. "Who the hell are you and what are you doing here?"

"Your grandmother would be none too happy with your language, Katrina Agnes Tovslosky."

The color drained from Kat's face. "What did you say?"

"Your grandmother does not allow such colorful language."

"No the other."

"Katrina Agnes Tovslosky. That is your name, I believe."

The figure turned and faced her. She was confronted by a man clothed in an old, ragged coat and even older boots. She brought her gaze slowly up to the face—a face covered by a long white beard and surrounded by a black fur ruff. The coat was missing a button but otherwise was closed all the way to the hood. What caught her attention was the crystalline blue eyes, dancing in a smile of recognition and friendship.

Kat's knees gave and she dropped to the ground, still looking at those eyes. "It can't be."

"No, child, it can't. But it is." Josiah Williams walked forward, took hold of Kat's gloved hand, and pulled her up.

Kat fell against him and sobbed. She pushed back from his chest, wet-rimmed eyes glistening in the moon's light, and then whacked him solidly on the chest in an angry blow.

"Where have you been and why didn't you come to find us earlier? I don't like you one bit, Josiah Williams. I've been grieving for months. Where have you been?"

Josiah grabbed her and pulled her into a warm, fatherly embrace. "I have been here, Katrina."

"Where?"

"In the ravine."

"The ravine? No better lie to tell?"

"I'll explain as we get you home. You are very cold. And I hope you have some hot coffee for this old man. I have an inexplicable urge for coffee."

"Start talking and, if the story is a really good one and I forgive you, then I'll find you that coffee and a blanket, too."

Kat let Josiah put his arm around her shoulder and squeeze. She was still angry but relief and joy had begun to take root. She put her arm around his waist and gave him a squeeze. He felt thin. If he got back in her good graces, he'd be at Grandma Bricken's and get fattened up in a flash.

As the two walked and Josiah began to relate his story, neither of them saw the yellow eyes glint from behind the spruce on the path. And neither of them heard the menacing growl that followed them in the night. A wolf howled and the trees went silent.

"Enjoy the reunion," the thing sneered, "It won't last long, I promise you."

———

Ken and Bart stared into the dark attic. Bart's flashlight illuminated an overturned rocking chair and an antique maple table. Drag marks through dust reminded Ken of ruts in an old dirt road.

"Looks like there has been quite a struggle here."

"And we're dealing with someone whose stronger than the average Joe." Ken pointed to the shelving on a back wall. Items on the top shelf were scattered and spilled over to the floor.

"Man, he was up high."

Ken walked over. "Hand me the flashlight. See that?"

"Sure do."

The dust in the top shelf showed a clear imprint of the front half of a shoe. The zigzag treads were so defined they might as well have been set in wet sand.

"Got the camera?"

Bart pulled a small silver rectangle from his coat pocket and handed it to Ken. A brief flash lit the room like a flare. Ken pocketed the camera.

They continued around the room.

"Nothing else seems disturbed."

More antique tables lined the walls. Some were covered with old mining gear, snowshoes, and ivory. Others held shiny nails, hammers, and miscellaneous carpentry tools. Ken stopped the beam to illuminate the far corner of the room. A small, dark puddle absorbed the light. He retrieved the camera and another flash lit the darkness.

"Looks like wax," Ken said while slipping the camera into his back pocket.

Bart took out his pocket knife and worked it around the edge of the wax until it came free. He placed it in a Baggie and continued toward the wall.

"Pretty sure this is where the attack started. I do wonder how Gary ended up at the bottom of the stairs, though. There's nothing disturbed on that end of the room."

"I'd like to come back in the daylight. May be able to see something new." Ken looked at Bart.

Bart nodded, then looked at his watch, unhooked his phone and hit speed dial. He heard Pachebel's Canon in D.

"No way."

He hurried down the stairs and followed the tune to the front door. Kat's cell phone sat on the first stair of the mercantile's porch. He picked up the instrument and stuck his head back in the door.

"Gotta go, Melbourne."

Ken came to the landing on the second floor. "What's up?"

"Kat dropped her phone out front here. She should have been home a long time ago and called from there. I shouldn't have let her go by herself."

Ken raced to the bottom of the steps. "I'm coming."

"Don't know how to tell you this, friend, but you are the last person she'd want to see—dead or alive."

"Don't remind me. Still, if there is a killer on the loose, you need backup. Besides, I'd never forgive myself if something happened to her and I could have stopped it. No matter what you all think, I do care about your obstinate, not-always-so-lovable cousin."

Bart stared into Ken's eyes and Ken returned the look. Sincerity was all over him.

"Get in. I'm already in hot water with her; this can't do much more harm. I am really praying she didn't run into whoever did that to Gary."

Terror gripped Ken. "How about you shut up and drive—fast."

Bart punched the gas, almost sending the truck into a spin. He slammed the brakes, pushed the column into park, jumped out and put the old truck in four wheel drive. They were down Main and to the dirt road in five minutes. Bart pulled into Kat's drive, pushed the door open, left the truck running with the lights on, and dashed for the door.

Bart's mind registered low lighting and two shadows on the living room curtains. He kicked the door with his right foot. It swung open. Ken lunged past Bart and grabbed a white bearded figure he was sure he saw holding a weapon on Kat.

He heard a satisfying thud as the weapon hit the floor in front of him.

"For the love of Pete, what are you two doing?" Kat screamed.

Ken felt hot liquid seeping into the front of his flannel shirt. He glanced at the floor and saw a large, now broken, coffee cup, and the weapon he'd been sure was threatening Kat—a teaspoon.

Bart had come around beside Kat, holding a gun on the stranger. He lowered the gun, his eyes grew wide, and then a shaky smile came over his flushed features.

"I'll be a donkey. Let him go, Ken. This isn't our killer but he sure has a lot of explaining to do."

Ken looked at Bart to check his crazy meter. Bart seemed sane. He twirled the perpetrator around, not quite ready to let him go. He stared into the clear blue eyes and let go, walked to the overstuffed red couch and dropped down. Ken's eyes never once broke contact with Josiah's.

"I'm already on shaky ground at the Bureau. You have some explaining to do—because now *I* really have some explaining to do."

BC, having taken shelter under the end table when the ruckus started, jumped to the arm of the couch and trotted to Ken. He walked onto the familiar lap and began kneading Ken's leg with his front claws, a loud rasp of a purr growing in volume with each knead.

"Easy, little big guy." Ken grabbed the front paws and stretched the cat gently out and down onto his knees. The purring grew louder as BC pulled the rest of himself into Ken's lap.

Ken turned his attention back to Josiah. "I saw you disappear behind a rock, actually a small mountain, into a den of demons. Why aren't you dead?"

"Sorry to disappoint you, Agent Melbourne. It is obvious the Lord did not think it was my time."

"And you've just been vacationing around Alaska, not thinking to let your friends know you're alive?"

"Not exactly. I seem to have a lot in common with Rip Van Winkle."

Bart took the other end of the couch. "Listening."

Kat escaped to the kitchen. She lifted her eyes to the ceiling, *Why did he have to show up tonight?*

She took a deep breath, willed her hands steady, and then poured a fresh cup of coffee for Josiah. She brought it to him and motioned him to sit down in the overstuffed chair.

"Thanks."

Kat shot Josiah a warm smile and returned to the kitchen to make another pot. Seeing Kenneth Melbourne and BC together flooded her with emotions—emotions she had successfully buried over the last few months.

Josiah placed the coffee on the burlwood table. The spoon clinked a gentle melody as it touched the side of the cup. "Suffice it to say, the Lord intervened."

"That is not an explanation."

"No, it is not. But, the long explanation is even hard for me to believe."

"Still listening."

"I was almost dead from Iconoclast's attack. An angel of the Lord appeared, a chasm opened and the demons fell into a bottomless pit. The floor closed and I was told to rest. I found a freshwater stream and cranberries at the far wall of the ravine. I ate; I drank; I fell asleep. I woke up this morning to a visit from the same angel who told me to return to Ravens Cove. I thought it best to see Katrina before I went into town. I met her coming down the path to her house. And here we are."

Bart and Ken stared in disbelief at Josiah.

"More coffee?" Kat broke the silence.

Josiah smiled and brought his cup up to meet the pot.

"You don't drink coffee." Bart looked at Josiah as if he'd been replaced by an alien.

Josiah shrugged. "Do now."

"Where were you really, Mr. Williams?" Ken brought them back on subject.

"That is the truth."

"If that's the truth, and I'm not saying it is, how did you get out of the ravine? The only path to it is blocked by a twenty-foot boulder."

"There is another path, across the ravine from the boulder. It was tricky."

"I've lived here all my life and never noticed another path." Bart's tone was that of an interrogator, not a friend.

"You've lived here all your life and never really looked at the ravine. And, that is understandable."

"There is one way to find out. Tomorrow we go looking for that path. If Josiah came out, someone might have gone in. It's a perfect hiding place."

"That sounds like a long shot, Bartster." Kat said, sitting on the edge of the overstuffed chair beside Josiah, taking a sip of coffee from her favorite soup mug.

"It's about the only one we have."

Ken nodded. "Tomorrow's taken care of. But, I need to know what we are going to do about you tonight, Mr. Williams."

"Do?"

"Well, you need a place to stay out of the cold, don't you?"

"Kat has offered me her couch." Josiah glanced at BC who returned the look with a cool gaze. "And BC has agreed."

"Here? Why not Bart's or my hotel room?"

"I've missed Josiah and would like to spend some more time with him. We have a lot of catching up to do." Kat's face broke into a wide grin.

Ken's face screamed, *improper.*

Bart answered Ken's silent concern. "You're kidding, right, Melbourne? Even I know that Kat is as safe with Josiah as she would be locked up and under police protection."

Ken couldn't come up with a rational argument. His hopes of getting Kat alone were dashed.

Bart gave Kat a solemn look. "Someone has to tell Grandma. Not to mention Pastor Lucas."

"I'll take Grandma if you take Pastor Paul."

"Deal." Bart had not looked forward to his great-aunt's reaction. He never dealt well with those tears he was sure would follow her shock, then belief that Josiah had returned from the dead.

Bart stood and motioned to Ken to do the same. Ken scooped BC up and lowered him into the spot he had just vacated.

"I'll ..."

"I know. You'll be here tomorrow to get me. Another rush on a report. Got it."

Bart smiled. "You willing to point out that path, Mr. Williams?"

"Happy to. Bring your climbing gear, though. This old guy almost didn't make it out."

Bart laughed then sobered. "We thought you were dead. I don't know that I believe your story but all the same I'm glad you're alive." He held his hand out. Josiah grasped it and shook.

"I'm glad to see you again, too. Didn't think that was going to happen. The Lord does work mysteriously."

"Or so someone wants us to think." Ken took one step over

the threshold, then turned. "Look forward to seeing you to-morrow, too, KittyKat."

Kat through a dishtowel at the closed door. "Not if I see you first." She gave Josiah a sheepish smile. "Sorry."

"You still have feelings for him."

"I do. And, if I follow through on them, I'd end up doing twenty-five to life." Kat sunk into the couch, grabbed BC and buried her head in his fur.

Once outside Bart turned to Ken. "I didn't want to say anything in front of Kat but I don't like how things are beginning to stack up."

"Me, either. But, why not say that in front of Kat?"

"I found an arrowhead at the first murder site. A threatening statement etched into it and addressed to Kat. Thought we had a real crazy on our hands. Later that morning she received an anonymous email that reiterated that threat. Both were signed *Pet*. I've been trying to play it down as a prank. With this second murder, I'm not so sure."

"Why didn't you mention this before?"

"I don't have the facts to back it up. And, you're leaving tomorrow so I didn't think you'd want to get involved."

"I'm not leaving tomorrow."

"That won't go over too well with the Bureau."

"Not under normal circumstances. But, I was drop kicked out the door yesterday for an extended leave. And, now that I'm back, I think that was a blessing in disguise. I have a bit of business I want to finish."

"Kat does not want and does not need a fly-by-night lover."

"I'm not looking to be that to her."

"Changed your mind?"

"I just know I have to set things right—I'm not sure what that even means."

Bart's phone chimed. "Hey, Doc. You're up late." He pulled to the side of the narrow road and watched tendrils of snow snake across the road as he listened. His forehead creased as he concentrated on Doc Billings' report.

"What?" Ken mouthed.

Bart held up a hand. "You sure?" The color is Bart's face had gone from healthy to pallid. "Not questioning your expertise, Doc. Just can't make sense of it. Send me the photos." He turned to Ken.

"And?"

"Seems Gordy has small pinpricks in both his eyes."

"Some creep copying Iconoclast."

"If so, the perp has it down pat. The brain's gone."

Ken stared into the darkness, his mind working for any reasonable explanation.

"Well consider yourself my partner—since you've got nothing better to do."

"You mean so I'll stay away from Kat?"

"That, too."

Ken scowled. His desire to solve the mystery outweighed his need to corner Kat. "See you at Jo's." He jumped out, shut the door and headed for the inn.

Kat locked the heavy door, a rare occurrence at her house.

"What happened with you and the good agent, if I might ask? I was certain there was a romantic interest—on both sides."

Kat turned defeated, sad eyes to Josiah. "I thought so, too. I was wrong."

"Not wrong, Kat. Just not time."

Kat walked to the couch and purposely sat where Bart had.

"I'm afraid that time has come and gone."

"You not only have feelings, you still love him."

"I have not even admitted it to Grandma or Bart, but, yes. And I don't like myself much because of it."

"You can't will away strong emotions anymore than you can will BC to speak. Have you prayed?"

"Not been too into that. I've been trying to forget what brought me to praying in the first place."

"Katrina, you are on dangerous ground. You are called to be God's child. You can ignore Him and make your life hard or you can accept Him and never have to face life's trials alone again—and life always has its trials."

"I know."

"You know it here." Josiah pointed to his head. "You'll believe it when it reaches here." He patted his chest.

"How do I do that?"

"You pray. God will make it happen. It happened for me."

"I'm not sure I want it to happen. My experience with God has been nothing less than terrifying and dangerous."

"That's part of the adventure."

"You think fighting demons and watching horrifying murders is an adventure?"

"No adventure is without danger and risk. Otherwise, it's a holiday.

"I can't believe you saw the siege as a learning lesson. I thought I knew you." Kat's disgust shouted through her tone.

"Oh, you know me Katrina. I was repulsed by the murders and terrified by the evil behind it. But we are assaulted by ugliness all the time. The only difference between *that* ugliness and day-to-day assaults against us was it was visible. A lesson for all of us about the subtlety of sin and the horrifying consequences of its culmination."

"Still don't buy the adventure angle but I'll think about it. And, about talking to God."

"Please do. And do it soon. I am not sure why we are all together again, but there is a reason. The Lord had me stay in Ravens Cove and kept me from freezing and dying for four months. I am concerned we are in for another battle. A more violent battle."

Kat dropped her eyes to her hands. She was rubbing them together, releasing unconscious tension. Josiah had voiced what was in the back of her mind. The events of the last week—the deaths, the odd shadows she had witnessed, even the creepy feel of Old Town had been gnawing at her subconscious. She had put it off to her overactive imagination.

"It's not your imagination."

Her head shot up.

"It's *not* your imagination. I'm not sure what is happening here or why this place is such a magnet for evil, but I feel it too."

"I don't have the strength to face whatever's coming."

"You do. But that is why it is so urgent that you go to God. His mercy and protection are the only sure way to victory."

"I can't think about this anymore." Kat pushed herself up from the couch and went to her bedroom. She returned with two sheets, a twin-size peach-colored down comforter, and a pillow.

"I don't have a guest room, so…"

"The couch looks very comfortable." Josiah patted the firm cushion. "Very comfortable."

"Well I'll be up early. BC let's go."

BC yawned, stretched and continued to lie in the spot Ken had left earlier.

"Anytime, Black Cat." Kat turned and headed into the bedroom. BC jumped down, tail in air and trotted after her.

"See you tomorrow. I'm so glad you're not dead."

"Me, too," Josiah chuckled.

The warmth of that laugh soothed Kat's nerves like a sweet balm. "You're different."

"Am I?"

"I never heard you laugh before."

"Not much to laugh about as I remember."

Kat smiled. "True, good night."

⁂

Mayor Thomas Orthell paced the floor of his ornate living room. He stopped, walked across the imported red, black, and cream wool rug, picked up the phone and dialed.

"You didn't tell me all the consequences."

"You didn't ask."

"You said only the ones responsible for the murders would be punished."

"I didn't open the door. You did. Now, things must play out the way the masters see fit."

"Gary had nothing to do with this. You promised me the masters wouldn't take an innocent."

"And they won't. But who is truly innocent?" Loathing shot over the phone line. "You'd better make up your mind whose side you're on. Otherwise, you will become another tragic victim."

Mayor Orthell stopped drumming his fingers against the rich mahogany desk.

"Do you understand?"

"I understand."

"Good. We'll talk tomorrow." The phone went dead.

Orthell rounded the desk and lowered himself into the tufted burgundy leather chair. He placed his palms on his forehead and dropped his head.

"What have I done?" he wailed into the glossy surface of the desk. "What have I done?"

Chapter 6
The White Wolf

Bart sat by the window in Jo's, taking in the brilliant starlit sky. The promise of sunlight kissed the dark horizon. The low light made Bart wish for the long days of summer.

Kenneth walked through the door. Bart noted dark circles under his eyes and an unshaven chin.

"You don't look so good."

"I don't feel so good. Didn't sleep worth a nickel. When I did manage to drift off, the dreams—actually nightmares—would start. Think being back here is bringing out the worst in me."

"Bringing out what you tried to forget, maybe."

Ken gave Bart a guarded look. "Listen …"

Bart's phone chirped. "Hold that thought."

He looked at the phone. "Yo, sunshine. What's up?"

"That dog at Gary's, did anyone take care of it?"

"No. forgot all about it. I guess that takes priority over the rest right now, huh? I'm on my way." Bart stood up, grabbed his to-go cup of coffee. "Forgot about a dog."

"A dog?"

"Yep, I double as the town animal control officer."

"You're kidding, right?" Small-town law enforcement was looking less and less like an attractive alternative to the FBI.

"Wouldn't kid about this. Come on. We can talk on the way."

They drove past frosted trees on the icy road. The narrow street was devoid of anything—human or animal.

Bart jumped out of the truck, went to the back and yanked a large kennel from the bed. He snapped the top open and grabbed a pole with a long noose.

"That necessary?"

"That animal hit the window with a full body blow last night—not taking any chances."

Bart jogged up the steps to the front stoop that ran the length of the cabin. Its brown boards creaked under his weight. He rapped sharply on the door. Ken moved in behind him.

A thud on the door, followed by a loud snarl answered Bart's knock.

"See what you mean." Ken backed down the porch. He trotted to the truck, picked up the large crate and moved it closer to the cabin.

"I'll back you up from here." Ken smiled from behind the crate.

"You're a true friend, Melbourne. Make yourself useful. There's a tranquilizer gun and darts in the truck bed. Grab them for me."

Ken retrieved the gun and dart case.

"Thanks." Bart unsnapped the case and loaded a dart into the pistol. He opened the door a couple of inches. The canine lunged with a force that slammed it closed. Bart put his shoulder to the boards and leaned in. He jiggled the knob again. The dog sprang again and Bart hit the door with his full weight. The door groaned and flew open. A white blur twirled on muscular haunches and jumped. Bart shot. The dog yelped and dropped. He stayed on all fours and headed toward his target. Bart watched as the dog's legs started shaking. It still worked to get to the object of attack. Bart backed up, drew his gun and cocked it. The white dog fell at his feet. *Thank you that I don't have to tell Kat I killed the animal.*

Bart took a deep breath—the first in an eternity by his thinking—and stuck his head out the door. "This guy is a big one. Want to help me get it to the kennel?"

Ken jogged the three stairs. They lugged the animal to the back of the crate and placed him as gently as possible through the opening.

"That looks more like a wolf than a dog."

Bart studied the sleeping animal. Its hair was snow-white and medium in length. An undercoat of grey tinged the ivory topcoat. His snout was elongated but squared. Even in sleep this dog had a regal quality.

"Maybe part wolf—some of our huskies look similar. Haven't seen him around here before, though. Afraid, with his attitude, he may not be long for this world."

A threatening scowl darkened Ken's features. "You seem awfully matter-of-fact about putting him down."

Bart shrugged. "Comes with the territory." They hefted the kennel into the truck bed.

"I'll drop him at the vet's for an evaluation. It'll ultimately be his call."

Growls and threatening barks were coming from the kennel before they were halfway to town. They pulled up in front of the veterinary clinic. Bart threw a pair of heavy leather gloves in Ken's direction.

"Watch your hands. Those only give so much protection." They rounded the back of the truck, wheedled the heavy kennel from the bed, and proceeded through the vet's door to the counter.

"Hey Bart, what you got there?" A young blonde smiled radiantly at them. She barely noticed Ken.

"Hey, Nyna. An abandoned dog. I need Carl to give him the once-over and call me with his opinion as to its health and personality. It's been aggressive and I'm concerned it could be a danger."

Nyna studied the waking animal. The growls had ceased and the dog had rolled onto its stomach, sitting like a sphinx watching them through glassy eyes. She walked through a half-glass and half-wood door behind the reception counter.

When she returned, a tall, thin man with salt-and-pepper hair came with her.

Carl Douglas took Bart's hand and gave it a firm shake. "Good to see you, sheriff." He gave a quick nod to Ken. "Welcome to town, Agent Melbourne." Carl Douglas crouched down in front of the kennel. Gold eyes met his brown ones. Douglas looked up at Bart over his right shoulder.

"Where'd he come from? I can't say for sure until I give him a good once-over, but I almost positive that's full-blooded wolf. White and rare."

"Found him at Gary's."

"Really? Wonder where he found it." Doc Douglas focused on the wolf again. "He sure didn't do this one any favors."

"He is in rough shape. Glad I ran across it. Anyway, see what you can find out about his behavior. It's a waste of life to put down a healthy animal but this one's aggressive and would have taken a chunk out of me—or worse."

"Understand. I'll call you later."

"Thanks, Carl." Bart headed for the door. Ken followed his lead.

"Hey, Bart, don't be a stranger," Nyna called after him.

Bart turned and smiled. "I'll work on that, Nyna."

"That one likes you."

"I've known Nyna since first grade. She's a good friend."

"She was screaming signals at you, buddy. Take it from me; she wants to be more than friends."

"Take it from me—it's none of your business. And you are the last person I'd ask advice from when it comes to understanding the signals of the opposite sex."

"This is about body language, not personal history."

"Drop it."

Ken took in the scowl and heightened color. "Consider it dropped."

"Good. Let's go see McGill. If he hasn't already heard about Gary, I need to let him know."

The late-morning sunrise touched the tips of the distant mountains, turning their tops a pastel pink. In all his travels, Ken had never seen a sparkling blue sky that matched the glory of this one. Black dots with wings played in the distance, on wind currents high above them.

Ken continued to watch the ravens' antics while they drove the short distance to the police station. Once parked, they walked the half block to the library.

Brandon looked up from the computer screen and smiled. "Seems I've lost my assistant. Hope he shows soon." The smile left his face when he saw the seriousness in Bart's eyes.

"You found Gary?"

"Afraid we did. He's dead, Brandon. I'm so sorry."

Brandon sat down in the secretarial chair that served as Gary's station at the library.

"I didn't know him that long but his loyalty earned mine." He sat in silence staring with unseeing eyes at the newest copy of *National Geographic*.

"Want me to call someone?"

"Not necessary. Work is my best healer and I get to see your lovely cousin this afternoon. That will help, I know."

An electric pang shot through Ken's gut. Brandon McGill now merited investigation. Ken mentally assessed this new threat. He saw a younger man, chestnut brown hair and tan skin. His eyes were almost black.

Brandon seemed to sense Ken's unspoken thoughts. His eyes moved in a smooth motion from Bart's to Ken's. His silent challenge screamed at Ken, *I want her and I am going after her with everything I have.*

Bart watched the spark in Ken's eyes flare to a bonfire. He kicked sideways, bopping Ken's foot.

"What?" Ken blinked.

Bart turned and walked toward the door.

"Take care, Mr. McGill. Give Kat my best when you see her."

Ken followed Bart outside. "Something funny about that guy."

"Yeah, like he has an eye on Kat. You're not sure you want her but then you don't want anyone else to have her either."

"Not what I said."

"Didn't have to. It's that body language thing—your actions speak volumes, even to a small-town lawman's mind. Oh, blast it all!"

"Now what?"

"Kat'll be wondering what happened with that beast. If I don't call her, she'll be at the vet's office and have taken it home before I can talk any sense into her."

Kat answered on the first ring. "I'm going to see him."

"Nothing you can do right now. Carl's evaluating him. If he's not a threat to society, we'll see where we can place him."

"He could end up dead. I'd rather bring him home than have him put to sleep. I can work with him!"

"No, No. You *do not* need that dog. If it's not a danger to society, we'll find it a good home."

"You don't know what I need. I am fully capable of assessing that for myself ..."

Bart stopped listening and rolled his eyes to Ken, motioning a "yack-yack" sign with his free hand. The talking stopped. "Kat?"

"You stopped listening."

"Why would you say that?"

"I just know. Here this loud and clear—if that animal dies and I haven't had a chance to help it, you'll be sorry you were born, Bartholomew Andersen."

"I will let you know. Yes, I promise. See you soon." He hung up before she could continue the tirade of how every animal was important and they could all be rehabilitated. She always pointed to BC as the example and he always lost that battle.

"This is one time I can truly say you are fortunate that she doesn't want to talk to you."

"She did sound like she is on a mission."

"Kat believes we can find the white beast a good home. She believes it is just scared and will be a good animal. She might be wrong this time and if she is, I'll never hear the end of it. Let's get to the office."

They passed an empty storefront. Paper covered the interior windows. A sign announcing "Grand Opening Soon," was painted in white lettering on one of the windows.

"Miggie's old place got a new tenant, I see."

"Yeah, some woman who wants a more relaxed pace, decided to open an antique store. Don't know how well that's gonna do here."

Horace Stoddard was throwing Ice Melt in front of his hardware store.

"Mornin', sheriff."

"Morning, Horace. How's business?"

"Can't complain. Winter is my best time—summer ain't too bad either." He stared at Ken.

"Sorry, this is Ken Melbourne. Visiting from Anchorage."

Horace stuck out his hand. "Welcome. How long you stayin'?"

"Not sure yet."

"Well, come on by if I can be a help on anything."

"Thanks."

"Horace is a good guy. A real salesman, though. Careful, he'll sell you that sin-ugly shirt on your back while it's still on your back."

"Sin-ugly? This is my best small-town uniform." Ken pulled on the red and black plaid flannel underneath his coat.

"Still sin-ugly."

They arrived at the small storefront that was the sheriff's domain. The brass bell over the door clanged its familiar sound. The smell of paper and dust assaulted Ken's senses.

"Still needs a cleaning."

"You offering?"

"Not in a month of Sundays."

"Then keep that opinion to yourself."

Ken took in the three-room office. Kat's desk, the sheriff's private office and the coffee/interview room looked just the same.

"Still got the jail cell in the back?"

"Yep."

Johnny Campo, the town's newspaper editor, and a member of the town council strolled in. "Been looking for you." He glanced at his watch before sending a reproachful look to the sheriff.

"Been waiting long?"

"It's well past ten."

"Had an animal-control issue this morning."

"That's not an issue. If the animal is a problem, then put it down, that's what I say. Problem solved."

Bart's neck started to flush and worked its way above his collar and to his cheeks. "What can I do for you?"

"Need an interview. Need to know about this newest murder in Ravens Cove." His excitement sickened Bart and surprised Ken.

"Well, first, I don't know how you found out and second there's no news yet. I haven't heard from Doc Billings as to the cause of death. Finally, you know I can't let out anything that could impede the investigation."

"Are you refusing to talk to the press?"

"I'm refusing to talk to the press—right now."

Johnny Campo narrowed his eyes. "Is that your final answer?"

"No. My final answer is, 'no comment.'"

"That's fine for the outside press, sheriff. Not okay for me. This town has a right to know what's going on."

"When I have the facts, I'll call. Just because you're on the council doesn't mean you have access to my files."

"Well, things could go bad for you fast, sheriff, without someone to speak up for you."

"Is that a threat, Campo?"

Campo shrugged. "Let's just say, it is fortuitous that I have a meeting with the mayor in an hour and this interchange will probably come up in our conversation."

"The answer is still no."

Johnny Campo stood his ground. Bart turned his back and walked into his office. Ken followed.

A minute later the brass bell clanged.

"Seems the esteemed councilman has left the building."

"You know you haven't heard the last of him."

"Probably not. But while I'm still police chief, I need to call

Gary's family and give them the news." He sat down behind the oak desk, flipped through a large Rolodex, found the number and dialed.

"So sorry to give you this news, Mrs. Wenfred. If there's anything I can do ..."

"Just find the guy," she said through sobs. "I knew he should have come with us." She burst into a loud wail.

"Believe me when I say I won't rest until I know who did this. You'll know as soon as I have an answer." Bart placed the phone in its cradle.

"Time to start interviewing everyone who was at the opening yesterday."

The brass bell over the door and the office phone sang out in an off-key duet.

"I'll get the phone—you find out who's here."

"Mornin', again. Yes, the dog's still at the vet's. No I don't have an idea on what's going to happen to it yet. Yes, I'll call." The phone went dead and Bart let out a heavy sigh. Kat wouldn't let it alone until that dog was safely someone's pet.

"Looks like you have your first interview." Ken stepped back and revealed Amos and Arnie Thralling.

"Thought I'd come by and get this over so I can get on my way. Today's an ice fishing day," Amos said. During the Iconoclast siege, Amos had been the first to find the bodies and had become a suspect for a short time.

Bart stared at the brothers. He was losing control of the investigation already and it had only just begun. Interviewees were seeking him out. Only in Ravens Cove.

"How about some coffee?"

Amos and Arnie followed Bart into the coffee/interview room and the process began.

"I pray that dog is okay." Kat said as she hung up with Bart. "It's such a shame for any animal to have to die because some people hurt them."

"Bart won't let that happen."

Kat smiled and returned to the small kitchen table, bathed by a southeast sun. She extended the coffeepot.

Josiah took a short sip. "I don't understand this sudden desire for coffee. But, it really does taste better than I ever remember."

The right side of Kat's mouth turned upward in a lopsided smile. "It is a curious side effect. But, then, you are a mystery of a man. It fits."

"I don't know if that's a compliment or insult. So, I'll take it as a compliment." Josiah lifted his cup in a mock salute. "You know we need to get to Alese before someone else does."

"Oh, I do indeed. If Grandma finds out you're here and hasn't been told, she'd lose her respect for me. I couldn't stand it. I'm just trying to figure out how I can be two places at once. I have to get to the office to finish the report on Gary."

"Well, since Ravens Cove is having a heat wave," Josiah had noted from the thermometer that the temperature had risen into the single digits and the wind was no longer bending the trees, "we can start by walking into town." Josiah lifted his cup again and smiled.

"When you're ready."

They stood up at the same time. Kat broke into a tinkling laugh.

"I'll run a comb through this mop and grab my coat. I'll be back in a jiff." She walked to the cupboard, grabbed two black travel mugs. "How about you make yourself useful and pour us some hot coffee into these while you're waiting."

The cups were filled and capped when Kat returned. The

blanket, pillow and sheets sat in a neat pile on one end of the couch. Josiah had settled into the big overstuffed chair with BC draped across his lap.

"What you looking at, Lazarus?" Kat said.

"Just marveling at the wonder of nature from the warmth of this lovely room."

Kat followed his gaze. A pair of eagles sat on the tall birch whose top stood ten feet above the bluff directly in front of her window.

"I forget how wonderful it all is. They are beautiful. Eagles and ravens—one so mysterious and regal; the other so mysterious and playful."

"You are a poet, missy." Josiah lowered BC to the floor.

"One could hope." Kat checked the cat's food and water supply before slipping on her boots, coat, and gloves.

The refreshing and invigorating scent of salt air was unmistakable.

"I love that smell." Kat took a deep breath and jumped from the porch.

Josiah inhaled. "Nothing quite like it."

They reached the small path in record time.

"You sure have a new spring in your step, old man." Kat teased.

"The surprising benefits of that long sleep just keep coming." The intense aches and pains of a few short months ago were but a memory. Josiah looked at the packed ice. "I'd be jogging if it were summer."

"Not me. One of the blessings of winter—one can only walk at a snail's pace."

They started up the small path. Their footprints from the night before were still clear in the snow. They had been joined by small, elongated prints zigzagging from one side of the path to the other in an upward movement.

"Snow rabbit," Kat pointed to the new prints.

"I'm impressed."

"Grandma made me memorize every animal track by the time I was nine. She wanted to make sure I was safe. This was just one of the many things I've been taught."

"She is an amazing woman." Josiah opined.

"That she is."

They trudged the rest of the way in silence. The leafless alders lining the top of Ravens Ravine were unwelcoming, even in the bright sunlight. The original path down to the ravine floor had been disturbed by several animals over the course of the winter. The hag tree stood guard at the entrance.

Kat shivered. Josiah grabbed her hand and gave it a small squeeze.

"It's funny. I don't remember anything, really. It's a blur of color and odd music. But, it scares me to look at that trail just the same."

"I know."

As they reached the end of the ravine, Kat swung around.

"What's wrong?"

"I don't know. I feel like I'm being watched—and not in a nice way." She scanned the area. The clearing was vacant.

Josiah sensed a darkness not present the day before.

"I feel it too. But, I think our imaginations are running wild. I was in the ravine. It was at peace."

"It probably is just nerves. Let's get to town."

A four-foot tall black-hooded creature left its hiding place from behind a spruce. It held a sharp, curved blade close to its right side. Another creature, the same height, joined it. "Nihilist, is that the one?"

"That's more than the one. The other was dead and is alive. They both must die."

"I'll let our comrades know."

The second dwarf slid back among the alders and disappeared into the earth.

"We need more of our brothers." Nihilist said before the other dropped into the cavern.

"Done."

Chapter 7
Interviews and Dreams

The scene in the sheriff's office made Kat think twice about staying. Wendy Hareling sat in the visitor's chair, swinging one leg impatiently while flipping in rapid motion through an old copy of *Time* magazine. A harried Bart hadn't put the phone back in its cradle before it started yelling for more attention. When Ken came out of the interview room escorting Amos and Arnie, Kat had to will her body to stay.

"Good day, Miss Tovslosky."

"Hi, Arnie. You're here early."

"Wanted to answer any questions the sheriff might have so I can get to more important things."

Kat nodded and turned her eyes to Bart. She could feel Ken's searching look.

"Good morning." Ken's resonant baritone sent an involuntary chill through her. That response put Kat in a fighting mood.

"*Was* a good morning." She raised her eyes to meet his.

Ken lifted his eyebrows, turned and strode to Bart's office.

Wendy waited until Ken was out of sight. "Good one, O barbed-tongue." Glad you finally got here." She stuck out her hand. "And good morning … ?"

"Josiah Williams." He took her hand in a firm shake.

"The dead guy?"

"Presumed dead. But, by God's grace, here I am."

"By someone's grace, anyway. Well, welcome back."

Josiah gave a slight bow. "Thanks, miss. Am I to assume you are the much-loved Wendy Hareling?"

"Much-loved doesn't ring a bell. But you got the name right."

"Oh, you are deeply loved. Not just by Kat but by God Almighty." Wendy grimaced.

"I don't go for that much. But, thanks just the same."

"Wendy really only believes in what she can see, feel, and touch."

"Sounds like another young woman I know."

"Yeah. I probably rubbed off on her," Kat smiled and poked Wendy in the side with her elbow.

"Or it's the other way around, smart a ..." She looked at Josiah, "smart aleck. Anyway, I came by to see if you have my blue shirt in your extensive wardrobe."

"You came by to get the latest gossip on the victims."

"That, too."

Kat inhaled. "I have nothing to share about the victims or the cases. You'll just have to speculate like everyone else." She placed her hand over Wendy's mouth. "And I haven't seen the blue shirt but I'll go on a search when I get back to the house."

Wendy's mouth dropped into a pout.

Bart jumped out of Kat's chair like it was on fire and motioned for her to sit. "Thanks for joining us. Late though it is."

"With that comment, I should just leave you to do your own darned report."

"But you won't."

Kat took her place behind the desk and turned on the computer. She reviewed the pink message slips while it was booting.

Bart nodded to Josiah. "Well, how about I get the interview with you over, too. You sure seem to show up at the worst times. At least times that make you look pretty bad." Bart motioned Josiah to the interview room and offered him a cup of stale caffeine. He took it eagerly.

"I was telling Kat, I can't seem to get enough of this stuff. Never used to like it. Go figure."

"Where were you yesterday afternoon?"

"Making my way up a steep path. I told you that."

"I don't suppose anyone saw you."

"I ran across a moose at the top of the ravine, does that help?" Josiah gave a wide smile, enjoying his newfound mirth. Since awakening from his deep, unexplainable hibernation, he had felt lighter than he could remember in his entire life. A battle fought on a spiritual and physical level had released his anger and darkness.

"No, it doesn't help."

"Not a time for levity, Mr. Williams." Ken had entered the room unnoticed. He pushed off the wall, took a few determined steps forward and sat down on the other side of the table.

"Well, the only person I saw was Kat and that was late in the day. It took several hours to get out of the ravine. I had ventured to Kat's house. She wasn't home. I started back up that small path and ran into her, and succeeded in scaring the living daylights out of her." He smiled again. *Most everything seems funny today. I feel like a small child who has just discovered a new world.*

Ken and Bart stared at Josiah. The change was undeniable. It showed in his mannerisms but it really showed in his face. He looked twenty years younger. He sat straighter and those bright, piercing blue eyes were even more piercing and bright—if that was possible.

129

Kat had taken up her favorite eavesdropping position by the copier. She hurried back to her desk when she heard the interview coming to an end.

"Hey, Winsome ..." Wendy crossed her arms and turned an expectant look on Kat.

"Would you drop Josiah and me at Grandma's?"

Wendy relaxed. "Sure."

"Thanks." Kat grabbed her coat and gloves. She rushed back to Bart's office and skidded to a halt. Ken and Bart were in a deep conversation, heads down, comparing notes.

"Déjà vu," Kat said.

They both looked up at her.

"You want to run off somewhere, I assume." Bart noted the coat was half up her left arm.

"Going to Grandma's—with Josiah."

Bart had forgotten completely about letting Grandma Bricken know about the murders and that Josiah was still a well-kept surprise. Relief flooded him at the thought of not having to give bad news one more time today. "Works for me. Need to get the rest of the notes together, anyway. What time you think you can get back here?"

"Couple of hours." Kat scooted toward the door. They piled into Wendy's Subaru and minutes later were deposited on Grandma Bricken's street.

"See you later, KittyKat." She waved out the driver's side window and took off.

"Here we go."

Kat and Josiah didn't get halfway up the sidewalk before the front door flew open and Grandma Bricken clomped down the stairs to meet them.

"I didn't believe it."

"Believe what, Grandma?"

"I awoke from a horrible night's sleep but there was one wonderful dream amid all the nightmares. Josiah Williams was talking to you at your home. He looked wonderful, just like now. I thought it was part of a nightmare but it was a dream come true."

She grabbed Josiah and pulled him to her. "Welcome, home, my dear friend."

He returned her bear hug, and then drew back. "I never left."

"Then where've you been and why haven't we heard from you?" Her tone of joy had turned to one of accusation.

He took Alese Bricken's elbow. "Do you have some coffee?"

"Of course."

"Well, if you'll give me the benefit of a doubt and reserve that fury for after, I'll tell you what's happened."

"I'll make time." Grandma grabbed Kat around her waist and drew her close before they walked up the covered porch and into the house.

The storm door stuck in the open position.

"I'll be right there." Kat grabbed it and gave it yank.

"Hey, Kat." She looked in the direction of the voice. Pastor Paul waved his hand in the air to catch her attention.

"Hi, Paul. What brings you here?"

"Is it true that Josiah has returned?" A familiar fear hit her gut. The last time visions were commonplace in Ravens Cove was before the battle with Iconoclast and his army. The fear turned to dread. *Stop It, Kat. Wendy probably got to him.*

"It's true. Who told you?"

"Had a dream about the ravine. Saw a beautiful waterfall with a pond and a cranberry bush close by. Saw Josiah sleeping beside the pond." He had made it to the top of the stairs, a little out of breath.

"Guess you'd better come on inside."

Grandma Bricken had moved up beside Kat. "The more the merrier. Too bad Kenneth was only here a day. We might have had a real reunion—and maybe I could have gotten a few things off my chest, too."

Kat's jaw went tight and her face flushed. The change didn't escape Grandma's attention. Grandma took all the coats and hung them on the pegs over the boot bench, then turned to Kat.

"He's still here?"

"Was when I saw Bart at the station." Her voice dropped to a simmering whisper.

"You don't say." She turned to Josiah. "Let's get you that coffee."

The four of them walked into the cheery kitchen. The impromptu reunion erupted into a good-spirited party.

Grandma went to the pantry and returned with a fresh loaf of blueberry bread. She cut it into generous slices, arranged it on a bright yellow plate and set it in the middle of the table. She motioned everyone to sit and she grabbed the coffeepot. Kat brought napkins and cups for all.

Pastor Lucas lowered his head and the others followed suit.

"Heavenly Father, thank You for every blessing You give us. Thank you that Your mercy and compassion are unending. Thank you for bringing Josiah back to us. Please bless this food and drink. In Your great Son's name. Amen."

Josiah raised his head. "May I add something?"

The banter and laughter ceased. The small group lowered their heads.

"Father and Jesus. I know You so much more personally than I ever thought possible on this side of heaven. Thank you for not leaving me abandoned. You, in Your great wisdom and understanding have given me a family again. I am forever grateful for all You have done and continue to do. Thank you again in Jesus Name."

He raised his head, tears glistening in his eyes. Kat's heart went warm and she reached over table and took Josiah's hand.

"So, about that story …"

"Getting to it." Josiah launched into a story that would have sent him to a mental hospital in most instances. In this family, everything he told them was not only believed but also made perfect sense.

Chapter 8
Servants of Evil

Mayor Orthell made his way to Old Town before dark blanketed the Cove. He went from building to building, extracting blood-colored candles from their hiding places and chanting the spells performed by his ancestors.

"Today, I can complete the ritual." He made his way to the rock skull in the middle of the courtyard. He searched the area around the buildings and the forest behind. Satisfied he was alone, he knelt. He retrieved dried blueberries, a Baggie filled with smoked salmon, and a small flask from his left pocket. He placed the offering of food and wine beneath the straight line of a mouth.

"I beseech you, O greatest one, show favor on your servant. Arise, return, and avenge me and those that still believe." He stood and kissed the rock between its eyes.

"What you doing there, Tommy?"

Mayor Orthell whirled into Johnny Campo. "You're early, Campo. How long have you been watching me?"

"Long enough to see something that brings many a question to my mind. And long enough to know there is more than a story about an old bunch of buildings here somewhere."

"I don't know what you *think* you saw. But, you better believe that if you print anything that is detrimental to me or Old Town, you'll be in court so fast you won't know what happened."

"I'll keep that in mind, mayor. Now, let's get on with the interview and a few pictures." Campo held up a thirty-five millimeter camera and took a wide-angle photo of the complex. He snapped a picture of the skull rock.

"Where next?"

"Let's start in the log cabin." They walked the short distance over the stone courtyard.

"Tell me, and by *me* I mean our readers, why this development is so important to you and what makes it of benefit to the citizens of Ravens Cove."

"As you know, our town economy is stagnant. I believe the historical draw of these buildings will start it moving again."

"Several people have asked me where the money's coming from. They are concerned the capital for school improvements and other town projects, like the upgraded water system, is the source of funding."

"Tell your readers not to be concerned. Not one dime of public funds has gone into the project."

Johnny Campo stopped and lifted his microphone to the mayor's face. "Then where did it come from?"

"As I told you and the council, I have invested my personal funds and there are other individuals interested in seeing this project succeed. These people moved the buildings from the Forgotten Place and the one cabin from the fjord for the price of gas and a few cases of beer."

"Awfully generous of them."

"Yes." The mayor smiled.

"That explains the town, but are you telling me that you had enough money available to develop this area, then run utilities to the buildings? That would cost more than you and I have put together, Tom."

Mayor Orthell hesitated. "This needs to be off the record."

Campo turned off the small recorder and stuck it in his pocket. "Done." His hand still on the recorder in his pocket, he turned it on again.

The mayor looked toward the skull, lost in thought. He turned back.

"I was approached by a person who wants to remain anonymous. A person who knew how much I wanted to save those buildings. After all, most of them come from where my ancestors originated and they have always held a special place for me."

"Most of them?"

"Yes, the one from the fjord was not in the original plan. The benefactor requested it be moved here also."

"Why?"

"Didn't say. It was a small price to pay to bring this opportunity to Ravens Cove."

"What else does this very generous patron get out of it?"

"Of course he will get some of the profits. The rest is a gift."

"He?"

Tommy Orthell flinched. "I said he's anonymous."

Campo snapped pictures of the cabin's interior before they made their way to the mercantile, hotel and cannery. The interview ended at the house.

Orthell walked Campo to his car. "The friend of Ravens Cove is dead serious about being left unnamed. And *he* gets very upset when things don't go the way he expects."

"You know me. I'm the epitome of tact and diplomacy." Campo smiled.

"I mean it. Don't try to find out who he is."

"I hear you. I'll keep it under wraps." Campo shot another smile at him over his shoulder before he drove away.

"He's a problem." A disembodied voice spoke as clearly as someone was standing next to him.

"No. He'll do as I say."

"He's a problem."

"Please. Let me take care of it."

"Who are you talking to?" Brandon McGill walked toward the mayor, holding out a book.

"Jenny told me you were here. Thought I'd deliver this to you; sounded like you wanted it as soon as it got here."

The gold lettering on a dark sand background glinted in the afternoon sun.

"The Legends of the Denali—a Comprehensive Collection," he read aloud. "Thanks for bringing it to me so late in the day."

"Who were you talking to?"

Orthell gave a small chuckle. "Me, myself and I."

Brandon seemed to accept the explanation. He looked at the old buildings. "They look much more foreboding than I remember."

"Good. That's what I'm hoping for. After all, the Forgotten Place is foreboding. Add the events of last fall and we have a real tourist attraction."

"I see what you mean. Well, then, you've done a good job."

Brandon turned and walked back out the circle to Main. He looked at his watch and picked up his pace. It was almost three and he didn't want to be late.

———

The farthest thing from Kat's mind was a meeting with Brandon McGill at three o'clock. She had been roped into the report after Bart had searched her out at Grandma's. Then the vet had called about the white wolf.

"Dr. Carl has not been able to make a decision," Bart called out from his office.

"Why not?"

"It has a skin infection. So bad he can't even be touched. When Carl tried, he almost lost a hand. He'd be treating himself for a bite if he hadn't gotten out of the way in time."

"So what's the plan?"

"Doc gave him a mild tranq so he could get intravenous fluids and antibiotics into him. Says he won't know anything until that animal starts feeling better. He also said he doesn't hold out much hope. It's really sick. Even if the infection's the cause of the aggression, it may not matter. He could die from the illness. Sorry, Kat."

"Don't condemn him yet." Kat grabbed her coat and headed for the door.

"I'm going to see Doctor Douglas. The report's done."

"Thanks and no I don't need anything else right now."

Kat managed to shrug her coat on before she stepped into the cold. Brandon McGill watched in astonishment as she sailed past Jo's.

"Be back in a few." Ken walked to the door and out. Kat was already yards ahead of him. He'd need to run to catch her. He looked at the icy sidewalk and opted for a fast walk.

"Hey, Kat."

Ken watched as Kat marched her way up the street, oblivious to whoever was calling her name. Ken followed the voice and realized with satisfaction it was Brandon standing half in and half out of Jo's door waving to Kat's back.

Ken did an about-face, stuck his hands in his pockets and started to whistle. He'd catch up with Kat later. He sauntered back into the station to wait for Bart who, after a long discussion that had turned into a battle of wills and logic, had finally agreed to take Ken to see Grandma.

Kat sailed into the vet's office and rang the bell on the front counter. Nyna popped out from the back.

"Hi, and what can we do for you today? Is BC okay?"

"He's fine. I heard about that wolf, though. Is Doc Carl here? It sounds like he's going to put him down."

"Slow down. He hasn't decided that yet."

"He can't. That creature deserves a chance."

"An animal that is a danger to people doesn't get a chance. You know that." Nyna answered.

"I don't agree."

Doc Carl walked out of the back. Bart had called with a heads-up on Kat's disposition and to let them know she was headed in their direction.

He smiled that knowing doctor smile. Kat turned to launch into her sermon on the rights of animals.

He held up both hands. "Kat, I didn't say we were putting him down. I said it didn't look good. But for the good of all, if that animal continues to lunge and snap at me, he will have to be put down."

Kat bit the inside of her bottom lip. She made a decision.

"Can I see him?"

Doc Carl sighed. "Do you promise not to get within arm's reach of the kennel?"

"Yes!"

He motioned her behind the swinging half door of the counter and escorted her to a large room full of mostly empty kennel suites. Two of Fergy Jensen's mushing dogs were in residence. At the far corner, isolated from the barking huskies, lay a hulk of a canine. His fur was glossy white. His breathing was steady. He was hooked up to an IV. Kat tiptoed to the kennel.

"He's tranquilized for his own good. He had to be in a tremendous amount of pain. I'm not sure he'll make it through the infection, Kat, even if he is a good animal. His body is ravaged."

Kat looked up into the Doctor's eyes and nodded. The animal had the appearance of one that had been wasting away for a long time. Upon closer inspection, large patches of fur were missing. Boils, red and rageful, gathered in clumps like menacing flower petals. His breathing was labored.

"I don't understand why Gary, or anyone for that matter, would let an animal go through this torture."

"I don't either, Kat, but I've seen it more than I care to. People look at animals as things. Not like living, breathing, creatures of God. Good stewardship is hard to find and, of course, I see owning an animal as a huge responsibility." He smiled at her.

"When will you know?"

"It's gonna take at least forty-eight hours to see if he can fight the infection. After that, we'll see what we shall see. I won't put him down unless I have to."

"I know. Sorry to bust in here. Just got to me that he was abandoned the way he was. If we hadn't gone out there looking for Gary that poor beast would have died from this raving infection and starvation. No living creature deserves that. I don't understand God. How can He not care and stop this stuff?"

"That's a question for Pastor Lucas and a good one at that."

"Well, enough ranting for one session."

"Anytime, anytime."

Thanks, Doc. I'll call tomorrow."

"How's Bart?" Nyna called out from behind the desk.

"He's doing okay—busy with this stuff, though."

"Bet he is. Hey, does Bart like cookies?"

"He's the original cookie monster."

"Great. Would you take him these? Fresh baked last night."

"Be happy to." She took the bag, gave Nyna a big smile and started back for the police station.

Bart was driving toward her and slowed. "Going to Grandma's. What's that?"

Kat held the package out toward the truck. "Oh, these are for you—from Nyna." She stuck the bag through the window.

Ken smiled. "Told you so."

"Told him what?"

"Never mind, you want to come along?"

Kat looked at her watch. It was three-thirty. "Oh for the love of Pete! I missed an appointment. I need to run. I'll catch up with you later." She took off toward Jo's. She scanned the small eating area.

"Seen Brandon?"

Laura Talen, the new hire, walked to the counter, wiping her hands on her apron.

"He left about fifteen minutes ago."

"Rats." Kat felt terrible, but she also felt a little relief. She had kept the appointment to prove to Wendy and more to herself that she was moving on from Kenneth.

"Thanks." Kat turned and headed to the door. She considered crossing the street to the library, then decided to call Wendy instead.

"What's up, KittyKat?"

"Want to go to Mrs. Tellamoot's for a visit?"

"Not my idea of excitement for the evening ahead. Why?"

"Well, you know she lost her dog in December."

"He lived a long, long, long life." Wendy emphasized that

A scraping sound drew his attention to the rock. A bright yellow and red glow came from underneath the skull. Four hands pushed him sideways until he fell into the hole beneath.

Mayor Orthell ran to the window of the mansion. He looked over the courtyard, silent except for the howl of the wind through the trees.

"Must have been an owl."

The mayor left the house and surveyed the quiet town square. "*I'm home for the first time in my life.* He took a satisfied breath, smiled and made his way to Main.

Orthell never saw his precious house shake with an invisible force. Nor did he see the upstairs attic begin to glow as a round portal of energy appeared in its wall. A body flew through the portal and shattered the dormer and the silence of Old Town as it tumbled with a sickly thud to the courtyard below. Johnny Campo continued to bleed, having lost his neck and heart only moments earlier. The body deflated like a balloon as all his bones melted into liquid.

Cassie Martin huddled into her coat on her way up Main. Her thoughts were on her warm apartment and a hot cup of chocolate. A loud *plop* shattered those thoughts and brought her to a stop in front of Old Town. "No Trespassing. Violators will be shot," was nailed to one birch column. Cassie heeded the sign as much because of the warning as the unwelcoming feeling created by the spotlights and the weird rock centerpiece.

Cassie squinted toward the courtyard to locate the source of the noise. A dark shape obscured the light in front of the old house. She tiptoed up to the right post and leaned in to get a better look. Sweat beaded her upper lip in spite of the freezing temperature. She reached a shaky hand into her pocket and punched the speed dial number for the sheriff.

Bart had rightly predicted the tension between Kenneth and Grandma—immediate and strong. What he had not foreseen was the backlash directed at him.

"What made you think it was alright with me for you to bring this man into my home unannounced?" Alese Bricken scolded Bart like a five-year old. Bart lowered his head and shrugged his shoulders.

"Get yourself a cup of coffee and sit!"

"Yes, ma'am." Bart looked to Josiah then Pastor Lucas. Josiah shot Bart a kid-silly smile and the pastor raised a disapproving eyebrow.

Bart used his left palm as a headrest and traced countless figure eights in the cup of coffee he'd been ordered to take to the table. A nerve-wracking *clink* sounded each time the spoon touched the edge. He studied the swirling liquid, looking for an answer like one does from a cup of tea leaves.

"Stop that noise, Bartholomew."

Bart sighed and placed his spoon in the saucer.

Grandma Bricken's green eyes focused on Ken. Ken held her gaze. The silent battle went on for an eternity.

"Nice of you to come out of hiding."

"I wasn't in hiding. I was working."

"No phones in Anchorage?"

Ken dropped his head and stared at the patterned linoleum. He had been in hiding and now he had been called on it. He raised his eyes. "You look good, Mrs. Bricken."

"Can't say the same for you. Want something to drink or eat?"

"No. Can't stay long. Just didn't want to miss seeing you." His soft voice resonated with warmth.

Well, you aren't going to leave right this minute, Kenneth Melbourne. Sit down. I have a lot to say to you."

Relief flooded Bart when his cell chirped. "Be right there."

"What's up?"

Deep lines were chiseled into Bart's young face when he turned to Ken. "Seems there's another body."

Pastor Lucas echoed, "another?"

"Well, guess I'll make it official. Gordy's death looks suspicious and Gary was definitely murdered yesterday and found at Old Town. Cassie just called saying there's another one."

"Is it the reporter?"

"I don't know but why would you ask, Paul?"

"A dream. A very troubling dream."

The smile left Josiah's face. "Are you sure it was a dream?"

"I don't know. I've been having troubling dreams since last October. In the last week, I've been having them every night. I've been fighting the thought that something wicked has entered Ravens Cove again."

Ken clicked a thumbnail across his forefinger. "That's improbable."

"That's what I've been telling myself, too."

A malicious laugh flooded Bart's mind right before terror hit hard and a foul mental picture rocketed out of Bart's subconscious. A very dead and hollow-eyed John Doe swam into view. He felt the fiery bite that shot up his arm and to his brain. He saw the barrel of a .357 Magnum inches from his face. *Remember the terror and hopelessness.* Trepaneer breathed the lies into Bart's consciousness.

Bart waved a hand past his right ear, smacked the invisible demon in the stomach and sent it flying. "I can't do this right now. Coming Melbourne?"

Ken almost jumped off the kitchen doorway he'd used for a back rest. "Definitely."

"We're not finished, Kenneth." Grandma called after him.

Bart and Ken reached the front door before Ken exhaled.

"She's a tough one. And you'll be explaining yourself. She doesn't let go."

"I know. And I feel terrible that I am grateful for a body to break me free from Grandma's interrogation."

Bart smiled. "She's tough, but she's also fair." He remembered the several talkings to he'd received from his great-aunt. The most recent of which had been about his love life—or lack thereof. "She's the only woman who can meddle in my life and get away with it."

"Let's go see what Cassie found. Maybe it's something else and just looks like a body to her. She was a bit traumatized from the last incident, too."

"True."

Grandma watched the taillights shrink to the size of confetti dots. A sense of dread had come over her since that last phone call to Bart.

"Dear God, please help our town. We are once again under siege. I prayed before they brought those awful buildings in, Lord. I prayed for Your will and Your protection. You do not fail those that rely on You. Please protect Kenneth and Bart as they go into that domain of evil. In Jesus' name. Amen."

She returned to the kitchen, oddly silent.

"God is with them, Alese."

She smiled and sat down at the table. "Josiah, I was against them bringing those old buildings here. You know Ravens Cove and my ancestors abound in legends. Well, those old buildings are another legend of the evil that has permeated this place since I can remember. I can't shake the feeling that we are going into another battle. Worse than the one we fought in Ravens Ravine."

"What is the story?" Paul asked.

"I don't know it well. The buildings came from an old mining town, several miles north on the Inlet. That mining town has been called the Forgotten Place since the day a hunting party returned to the settlement and found everyone in it dead. It was declared cursed and no one, but no one, dared go there. My people are not from that area but heeded the warning just the same. I don't know anymore about it, but there is someone in Ravens Cove who does. I just don't know how we are going to get to see her. Too cold to walk. And too old to learn to drive." She gave a quick smile.

"How about I see if Tanya'll let me go just a little longer and I'll take you where you need to go. And where is that anyway?"

"Mrs. Tellamoot. Her blood comes from the Forgotten Place."

"Can I use your phone? Sometimes it's best to give my other half a heads-up when plans are going to change."

"Of course."

Paul returned in a couple of minutes, a broad smile on his lips. "Tanya is thrilled. She's almost finished with some new curtains to dress up the very old windows at our house. She'll be busy for a couple of hours. I'll get the car. Can you be ready in thirty minutes?"

"Sure can. Thanks so much."

"Are you kidding? I should be thanking you. The culture and legends here are mesmerizing. It's a privilege to take you. I'll be back before you know it." Paul headed out the door.

"I'm going to gather a few things to take with." Alese walked into her ample pantry, came out with two paper bags full of food and set them by the front door.

"You are a thoughtful and generous woman, Alese Bricken."

"It's the least I can do."

"Hello, Gram." Kat called from the entry.

151

"In here."

"What's with the groceries in the front hall?"

"We're on our way to Bernice Tellamoot's. Want to come?"

"I just came from there. She's doing fine so maybe you can go tomorrow."

"We need to see her tonight. There's been another murder in Old Town. Bernice knows about those old buildings."

"I'm in."

The honk of a horn announced Paul's arrival.

"Right on time."

Josiah scooped the bags up into his right arm and offered the left to Alese. "You hold on."

"Always the gentleman, Josiah Williams." She looped her arm through his.

Paul smiled at them both before jumping out of the car to open the trunk. Josiah deposited Grandma into the front seat, and ducked into the back alongside Kat. The quartet set off to talk to Mrs. Tellamoot.

Bart and Ken pulled onto Willowbend Circle. Cassie ran for the passenger side before Bart cut the engine. "Can I go home now—please?"

"Not just yet, but soon." Bart stepped down from the truck.

"How exactly did you discover this body?" Ken asked as Cassie backed away from the passenger side and let him out.

Cassie shot Ken a cold glare before she turned to Bart. "I was on my way home when I heard a loud noise. I didn't go past the sign but I peeked in and saw a dark shape blocking the light—it's between the old house and that horrible rock-thing. I know I saw pants and the bottom of a shoe on one side. I just know it. Can I please go home now?"

"Did you see anyone else?"

"No. The place is as quiet as a tomb. Eerie quiet." She shuddered.

Caroline put her arm around Cassie. "If you have more questions, can't you come see us at home?"

"Were you with her when she made this discovery?"

"No, she called me and I didn't want her to be by herself. I came right over." Caroline's tone became defensive.

Bart closed his notebook and looked at Cassie. She was pale and shivering. "Take her on home. I'll come over if I need anything more."

Ken watched them disappear into the night. "Well, there goes all hope of keeping the rumors from flying. Main will be abuzz tomorrow."

"You've learned the first lesson of small town living, Grasshopper."

"And I was worried I'd never understand how you think."

"You don't but keep trying."

Ken squinted toward the buildings. "Sure enough there's something behind the rock and in front of the old house."

"And, if I'm not mistaken, I see the sole of a shoe. I was really hoping Cassie was wrong." Bart took off at a fast clip toward the boulder.

Ken came alongside and looked at the corpse. He followed an imaginary line to the top floor of the old house. "I think it's safe to assume he exited the old house through that." He pointed at the broken attic window.

Bart nodded and then turned his attention back to the corpse. "Take a look at this."

Ken scrutinized the sticky-looking puddle that used to be a human being. The legs bent away from each other at the knee. The effect was an unnatural L shape. "Okay, let me in on your secret."

"Legs are broken. So were Gary's. But that's different." Bart pointed to the torso. A deep red stain surrounded an oval-shaped chest wound. Flesh lay on either side of a gaping hole that had once been a throat.

Ken looked at the face. Purple and black oozed from the eyes. "Iconoclast *is* back."

"Or someone wants us to think he is! The legend says he was defeated and can't return."

"He can't return to Ravens *Ravine*. Nothing says he couldn't return to the area. But the question is why here and how?"

"I'm going with a copycat."

"I should follow your lead. My reputation, not to mention career, is already on shaky ground. If this is Iconoclast, I don't see Agent in my title much longer."

Doc Billings drove up and the funeral home hearse came up right behind him.

"We're going to have to hire a regular CSI unit, this keeps up." Billings knelt down beside the corpse. He slipped his right hand into a latex glove and probed the pockets.

He held up a wallet. "Jonathan Campo." He turned the ID photo toward Bart and Ken.

"Body's too degraded to confirm that by a visual ID. But we'll get what we can and have the M.E. in Anchorage confirm the identity."

"I saw Campo earlier today. In fact, he was smiling, which is unusual for him."

"You mean that newspaper guy from this morning?" Ken asked.

"Newspaper and *town council*, don't forget."

"Well, if he weren't in such a state of decomp, I'd say we need to look at a few people—he has to have made enemies. Wouldn't that be a great find!" Hope laced Ken's words.

Bart gave Ken a disbelieving look then turned. "Thanks, Doc.

Let me know when you finish your initial autopsy." Bart started for the front door. Ken followed.

"Locked up tight."

"Then, how'd he get in at all?"

"Don't know but I'm going to ask the only one with keys to this place."

The heavy sound of boots echoed through Old Town five minutes later. "Who is it?" Mayor Orthell reached into his pocket with a shaky hand.

"Haven't got a positive ID." Bart put his hand out for the key.

"Can't let you go in without me, Bart. I'm liable."

"Can't let you go in at all. It's a crime scene."

"I'm the mayor."

"I'm the police chief unless you want to fire me right now. Then you can go on in and I'll go home to a nice warm house and cozy bed."

Orthell slapped the keys into Bart's hand.

"I want them back *tonight.*"

"Will do." Bart gave a mock salute to the Tommy Orthell's back and turned on his heel.

"That didn't sound too good."

"It wasn't. Sure I'll hear more about it at the next council meeting. For now, let's get inside."

The front door gave a begrudging creak. Bart, then Ken, stepped onto a polished wood floor. A large staircase dwarfed the entry hall.

"Spared no expense on this one."

Ken walked up beside Bart while taking in the grandiosity of the main floor. "Seems out of place for small-town Alaska."

Imported wool runners in a cream background with red and blue designs, led the way to the second floor. They climbed the three steps that led to a left wing. That floor ended at one bedroom adjacent to a nursery. They backtracked to the upstairs landing and took another set of three steps to the right wing. They investigated the four smaller bedrooms and an ornate washroom—complete with a tub, sink, and toilet. At the end of the hall a narrow set of dull and well-used steps led to the third floor.

At the top and to the left of the steps was an austere-looking bedroom. A one-by-two-foot window adorned the middle of a dormer. It overlooked the forest. On the right side of the hallway was a closed door. It opened into the rest of the attic. Odds and ends greeted them behind the entry. A rusty iron headboard was still attached to a dirt-covered mattress.

Ken and Bart followed a cold draft to the front of the attic. Pieces of wood dangled from a broken window frame. Red-tinged shards of glass jutted out of the splintered wood and glinted ominously each time the breeze moved them. Blood trails ended at the windowsill.

"I don't see any large stains. With those wounds, there should be something around here."

Ken turned from the window and walked to Bart who stood in the middle of the attic. Dust, the color of sand, filtered through the flashlight beam. The smudged light illuminated an area in transition.

Unopened boxes were stacked in neat columns, while others gaped open with their insides discarded in a pile. Farther in, several had toppled onto their lids and sides. A dark liquid stained the back wall and floor. A trail of blood smeared a path to the window.

"Well, we know where he was before he went out the window," Ken said as he walked toward the wall. "But, how did he get in here? The place was locked up tight."

"Must have been in here before it got locked. There's still not enough blood to account for the wounds, though."

"Look at this."

A larger puddle of blood lay in a half circle against the wall. It crept farther into the room as it continued to seep through the wall.

"There must be another room behind this wall." Bart put his ear close to the wall, knocked and listened for any tonal differences.

"I'm heading outside to look for any sign of one."

Bart gave a quick nod, then turned back to pound the wall again.

Ken came back in shaking his head. "That wall is the outside of the house. I could hear you knocking, plain as day."

"Well, then how'd it get behind the wall?"

Ken rubbed a thumb on his chin, studying the dark pool. "You know, if the body was facing the wall when the heart was torn out, the force of the arterial blood may have been just enough to force it under the floorboards."

"Seems unlikely."

"Got a better idea as to how blood is seeping out of a one-foot thick wall?"

"Can't say as I do," Bart conceded. "So, until I do, we'll go with your scenario. Let's get this wound up. I want to return this key to the mayor."

"You really are going to return it tonight?"

"Sure." Bart smiled. "Then I'll have a good reason to talk to him about how Campo got locked up here in the first place."

When they walked back outside, the night sky had stooped so close Ken felt he could reach out and touch each fiery white star. A small green curtain shimmered in the distance.

"I've never seen the northern lights. They're almost magical."

"That's a small show. Stick around, Melbourne; you can see something much more amazing." They disappeared toward Main.

A piercing screech summoned four small beings to the court-yard. Venenose materialized at the broken window overlooking skull-rock. The four bowed.

"Dacoit needs." He pointed a knobby black finger at the skull. "You let two get away."

"Iconoclast ordered stealth. We took one tonight." Nihilist answered.

"You fool! Iconoclast ordered you to take a victim unseen—not to limit the number." He pointed again and Dacoit growled, then moved. "If you fail again, you are his next meal. Go!"

The four bowed in unison before scampering for the safety of the forest.

Nihilist stopped at the edge. "I swear by the dirt you live under that you are the fool, Venenose. When the time comes, I will destroy you and take this town for my people."

———

Ken and Bart veered to a walkway between the town hall and the library. They made their way to the leaded glass door of a large house. A plain, clear glass storm door with a brass kickplate covered the ornate one. Bart opened the storm and knocked.

A petite woman with curly brown hair greeted them.

"Hi Bart."

"Hi, Maureen. Tommy here?"

"He's down in the basement. Come on in."

Maureen disappeared through a door under the stairs.

Ken took the opportunity to get some insight into the mayor of Ravens Cove. The house was modest and yet screamed elegance. There was a cold-looking seascape to the left of the entry. A large rock protruded from the ocean and angry waves broke over it. Almost invisible seabirds flew low over the water. Ken leaned in. It was an original oil painting. He couldn't make out the name.

"Stop gawking," Bart whispered.

Maureen Orthell reappeared.

"He'll be right up. How about something to drink—wine or a beer?"

"Still working."

"A cup of coffee or tea then. It's a cold one again."

"Coffee sounds great, if it's not too much trouble."

"None; already have a pot made for Tom. How about you, Mr... .?"

"Ken Melbourne." He held his hand out. Maureen Orthell took his fingers in hers and gave them a lukewarm squeeze.

"I don't need a thing."

"Go on into the living room." She pointed to a door that stood to the left of the stairs. "I'll be right back."

The walls of the large living/dining combination were white. An oversized fireplace flanked the outside wall. Jet-black granite framed the decorative expanse of peach-colored stone that surrounded it. A cream background on the furniture was dotted with burgundy and pink roses. A dark cherry coffee table stood between the couch and two wing-back chairs. The dining room table, hutch, and chairs were in the same rich wood.

Maureen returned and set a tray with a coffeepot, three cups, sugar and fresh cream on the table.

"Thought you might change your mind, Mr. Melbourne, so if you do, help yourself."

"Got the key, Andersen?" A gruff Tommy Orthell came through the living room door, wiping his freshly washed hands on a kitchen towel. He handed the towel to his wife.

Bart dug in his pocket, located the key, and dropped it into Orthell's outstretched hand.

"Thanks." Orthell turned to leave the living room.

"Just a couple of questions."

Orthell hesitated for a moment, then turned.

"What questions?"

"Did you lock up Old Town this evening?"

"Of course. I'm the only one with a key."

"What time?"

"Actually it was early in the day—around two. Why?"

"Just routine questions."

Orthell narrowed his eyes. "They don't sound routine."

Bart ignored the statement. "Did you see anyone around before you went into the buildings?"

"No." The mayor thought. "The only people I saw today were John Campo and that new librarian."

"What time was that?"

"Don't know but Jenny would. I went right back to the office for a phone conference. I didn't think I'd need to account for my every move."

"I'll call her tomorrow."

"You aren't seriously considering me as a suspect, are you?"

"Until this is solved, everyone's a suspect. So don't leave town for a while, okay, Tommy?"

"Wasn't planning on it. Are we done here?"

"For now."

Orthell turned and headed out the door and to the basement.

"You tired of being the town sheriff?"

"Maybe I am. I'm sure tired of being the town football and Orthell is the prime kicker and works hard to make sure I don't forget it."

"Well, maybe you'd better start thinking about new career choices. If he's innocent, you're gonna be mud."

"Orthell has had a chip on his shoulder since that whole thing happened last October. He was a member in good standing with Martin Plotno and that Congregational Alliance bunch."

"He blames you for their deaths?"

"That's the only explanation that makes sense. We got along fine until then. Ever since, though, my job has been on the line. He just hasn't been able to find a way to cross me up and get me fired."

"Take it from me, you don't want to give him a reason. This life is in the blood. I miss being in the field. You would, too."

They had gotten to the truck when a silver glint caught Bart's eye. He squinted to get a better look. At the edge of the woods between the cannery and the old house was an orb of light. It flickered and disappeared. Bart started moving.

"Hey!" Ken broke into a jog, slipped on some ice, then resumed jogging.

"Looks like a flashlight beam." Bart pointed toward the area where he had seen the light. He released his gun from the holster and walked toward the artificial light of the courtyard.

Ken grabbed his arm. "We'll be sitting ducks out there. This way."

Bart nodded and they headed toward the woods beside the cabin. The crunching snow beneath their feet rang out like shotgun blasts.

Bart stopped and listened, then moved forward. They reached the area where Bart had seen the light.

"Something's been here. Looks more like an animal than a person, though." There were cloven hoof prints about two inches in diameter. Bart could make out four separate tracks.

"There are only two prints each. For that animal there should be four. Whatever made these tracks was walking on two legs."

"There's nothing like that here; in fact, I'm not sure there is anything in this world that matches the description you just gave."

"It is what it is. You have a different explanation?"

Bart thought, shook his head then looked at his watch. Just past nine. "I'll call Douglas and get him out here. If anyone knows, he will." He grabbed his cell phone and dialed, still eyeing the unmistakable marks in the snow and ice. He had not told Ken but he had been told of such creatures by his mother—he laughed at her then and told her they couldn't exist. *Please let there be another explanation.*

Doctor Douglas arrived a short time later. An amateur zoologist, he was always on the lookout for an undiscovered species. He crouched on the balls of his feet, flashlight in hand.

"I'd say it's a small goat ..."

"The way the path moves, Doc, it looks like a two-legged creature," Bart pointed to the tracks.

Doc gave him an impatient stare. "As I was saying, it looks like a small goat *but* I have never seen any goat walk on its hind legs. And I don't know of any other animal that has this track and can walk two-legged for any extended period."

"It could have jumped. That'd make it appear two-legged, right?" Ken stooped over the tracks and followed them into the woods.

"No, no, I don't think so." Doc Douglas was shaking his head while scrutinizing the tracks in a new light.

"An animal in a jump would use both hind legs to push off. This one walks with a human gait, first one foot and then the other. No. This one was on two feet."

"Maybe it was trained to do this?"

"Maybe. I sure haven't run into anyone that's been training a miniature goat. Since I'm the only vet in town, odds are I would have." He smiled up at Ken.

"I'll get some pictures and the cast of the print to some friends of mine. You'll be the first to know if I find out anything."

"Soon, right?"

"As soon as I can." Doc grabbed his tools.

"Hey, do you know any more about that wolf?"

"First, I'm not sure it's a full wolf. Second, it seems the antibiotics are doing their work. He's still sedated. But he is eating and drinking. Looks like he's going to pull through. I'll know more tomorrow afternoon. Talk to you then."

Ken turned to Bart. "You recognized those prints."

"No. Just shocked by them, that's all."

"Why don't I believe you?"

Bart dropped his eyes back to the footprints. "Another legend that our people and this town are so famous for, that's all."

"And … ?"

"My mother warned me about these creatures. Said they have been seen throughout time by different people. They aren't animal but they aren't human either. They serve the fallen angels, demons."

"That sounds crazy."

"Yep. But you know what's crazier?"

"No."

"I have a drawing by my great-grandfather. It matches those prints."

"How's that possible if they don't exist?"

"Thought it was an artist's interpretation of the story. I'm rethinking that assumption. The rest of the legend portends the same thing we went through in October but in a more devastating manner—if that's possible."

"Still crazy."

"So was the confrontation with Iconoclast. Impossible and crazy. But it happened just the same."

Bart thought about the body they had just seen. "After what we saw tonight, I'm losing hope that this is a copycat. I think

Iconoclast's found a way to work his way back and he's doing it at a fevered pace."

A branch snapped. Ken and Bart spun to face four silver-haired beings. They backed away, each drawing his gun. A guttural threat came from behind. Bart flipped to Ken's back and they stood together, looking at three more of the creatures. They started firing at the same time.

Chapter 9
The Forgotten Place

Kat, Paul, Josiah, and Grandma gathered in a semicircle around Mrs. Tellamoot's front door. The planked wood entry of the tidy older cabin obscured any view of Bernice Tellamoot making her way to the door. Kat knocked a second time.

"Hold your horses. What does it take for an elderly woman to get you people to leave her alone?" A tall, thin woman with thick, grey, shoulder-length hair opened the door.

"Oh, the wellness check now needs a committee, I see." She honed in on Kat. "You left here a couple of hours ago. I still don't want to talk about that dog." She pointed at the others. "Just 'cause I'm old doesn't mean I can't take care of myself. Tell that to all those other busybodies who believe I can't live alone." She shut the door.

"Bernice, we're here about the Forgotten Place."

Bernice Tellamoot opened the door a crack. One chocolate brown eye peeked at Alese Bricken. "Why?"

"Your mother hails from there, Bernice. Bad things are happening in those buildings Orthell brought in. Any information you could give could help us."

"Who are they?" She lifted her chin toward Paul, then Josiah.

"Friends of Ravens Cove."

Bernice snorted. "Doesn't make them friends of my people."

"They are here to help. God brought them to Ravens Cove last October to stop the Iconoclast siege. And God has reunited us now."

The door flew open. "How dare you mention God. He has abandoned me now—and He abandoned my people then."

God help her. Her hurt is so deep. Her pain so strong. Paul prayed in silence.

"Where was your mother that day?" Josiah asked.

"She took me to visit her cousin at the next village. She had a new baby and wanted me to see him. Why?" She broke eye contact with Grandma and focused on Josiah.

"Your mother was accused of being part of the destruction, wasn't she?"

"Yes. And she was a believer in God. She had encouraged all that would listen to turn back to Christ. And, how did God repay her? He abandoned her, that's how! My father was murdered. My mother and I were left alone and penniless. I have no time for this God of yours." She started to close the door.

"How did you and your mother survive?" Josiah asked.

"We moved in with that cousin I just told you about."

"Would you entertain another idea about God?" Paul asked.

Her eyes searched his. "What?"

"I do not pretend to be an expert on God's mind. But it seems to me that He honored your mother's faith. He protected her from the carnage of that day. That sounds more like a loving Father than a harsh God that abandoned you and your mother."

"How did your mother die?" Josiah had no idea why he asked this question.

"In the arms of my stepfather. Later in her life, she developed heart trouble."

"Was your stepfather a good man?"

"He was good to my mother … and to me." Hard, brown eyes softened. "He treated me as his own."

"Mrs. Tellamoot, please hear us out. We wouldn't have bothered you if we could find answers somewhere else."

"I told that stubborn mayor and his cronies not to bring them here. They don't listen."

"They don't respect our traditions. But these people do."

"People are dying. If this legend has anything to do with it, we need to know." Paul pleaded.

Bernice Tellamoot stood in the doorway, scrutinizing each member of the small party. She nodded, stood aside, and let them enter.

Josiah held out the two grocery bags. "We know you can take care of yourself. But Alese seemed to think you'd like these for your pantry."

Bernice smiled and took the bags from Josiah. "Sit down. I'll get something to drink. This will take a while." Grandma Bricken followed her to the kitchen.

The tan fabric of the Early American couch was worn but clean. A matching rocker and footstool was positioned across from the couch. Above a small fireplace, a grey and white canine with gold eyes stared at them. A gold plaque, engraved with "Benny" named the portrait.

Mrs. Tellamoot reappeared from the kitchen with a well-used teapot. Alese followed her with a tray holding matching cups and blueberry muffins. Bernice Tellamoot sat in the rocker and leaned forward.

"This is the legend of the clan. Those of the clan—she nodded to Grandma Bricken—were not involved in the story of the Forgotten Place. It is a story of shame and evil. It

167

has been passed down in our clan as a reminder and warning against greed.

"In the early years of the nineteenth century, my people were settled in a small village. They were a hardworking people and lived unto themselves. They did not welcome strangers. Those who were thought to be a danger to the clan were killed."

"That's horrible," Paul said.

Bernice shrugged. "That was the way of my ancestors. This is what my ancestors were instructed to do by the Great Wolf."

She shot a sad smile to the dog's picture. "The wolf and the dog were great companions to my people. And, up until this time, we enjoyed their protection and loyalty. They warned us against danger and alerted us in the hunt. But even these great creatures could not protect the doomed ones from the deceit that befell our village."

Bernice told the rest of the story. Of a good shaman and two bad people who came together and made a complete evil. Who succeeded in destroying the village because they tricked and murdered the good shaman. Bernice sighed and hung her head.

"As I said, this is a story of shame and evil. Because of this evil, the Great Wolf left us. It is rumored that one day he will return and fight the demons that took my people."

"If the demons are still on the loose, why haven't they been seen?"

Bernice shrugged. "Nothing to feed on and make it strong. Until now."

"There is another part of the story that was handed down by word of mouth. It is said that one of the hunters was chosen to return to the village by my mother's cousin's clan. They were afraid the demons would travel to them and they would die, too.

"That hunter returned to the village two days later. He swore he sneaked up to the edge of the village as he had been told to do. At first, he thought he saw the Great Wolf among the dead. Then, it stood on its back legs and the fur became a white robe that was on fire. A mighty warrior with a blazing gold sword stood in its place. He fought the demons and won. Then he sealed all the portals the demons had used to enter our world and buried the bodies of the dead. He said the being began to glow, like the blue of lightning during a summer storm. Then, it shot into the air."

"A mighty warrior?"

Bernice shrugged again. "This is the story; this is the truth of my people."

Kat looked at Alese Bricken, then Paul and Josiah. The story had been just a story until she heard the description of the warrior. By the look on the others' faces, they felt the same.

"Did your people know the name of this white settler?"

"I do not have the name but it would be listed among those that died in the Forgotten Place. He and his wife did not realize they, too, would die. As with all greedy and evil people, they think they are immune from the very destruction they unleash."

"No wiser words have I heard," Josiah remarked.

"That list is at the newspaper archives."

"Umm, Johnny Campo is not there right now and I wouldn't have the slightest idea of how to begin a search in those boxes of his."

"Well, there should be a copy at the library. I donated it myself less than a year ago."

"Thanks, Bernice. I know this was hard for you."

"I was rude to you, Alese. You didn't deserve that. I'm just a tired and cranky old woman." She gave Alese a weak smile.

"You're singing to the choir," Alese quipped.

"I don't understand why an angel of God would appear as a wolf," Josiah whispered under his breath.

"Why wouldn't he? A wolf to that clan would have been far easier to believe than a streaking blue blazing light of a man."

"Still don't fathom it. But, then, it is rare that I understand the workings of God."

Kat didn't enjoy where this conversation was going. It was giving her the heeby geebies. "On another note, I'll go to the library and look for that list tomorrow. I need to make an apology for a missed coffee meeting to the new librarian."

"Do they have a copier?"

"Think so."

"Then bring a copy to the house and we can have a look at it. Maybe we'll see something that sheds light on our current predicament."

Josiah got out of the car at Alese's house.

Alese leaned in the car window. "Josiah and I discussed it and he is welcome to stay with me. I have more than enough room and I could use the company."

Kat felt a bit of relief. Her tiny cabin felt crowded sometimes with just her and BC. She knew Grandma was safe with Josiah and felt good knowing she would not be alone.

Paul dropped Kat close to her front steps. She waved as she watched him pull out of the driveway. A dark shadow caught her attention. She reached to her left and grabbed the wood axe and slowly turned to face the intruder. She lowered the axe as Ken stepped out of the shadows.

"Why are you here?"

"We need to talk. Where's Josiah?"

"He's at Grandma's." Kat wished she had insisted Josiah stay with her.

Ken mounted the porch steps and walked to Kat. "Give me a minute."

His face was chapped and red.

"How long you been here?" she asked, concern creeping into her voice.

"About an hour."

"You're a fool, Ken Melbourne. You could have frozen to death in this cold."

"You're worth it."

"Right." Kat unlocked the door. "The clock's ticking."

BC pounced from his hiding place behind the door.

Kat took a well-practiced leap to her left. "Missed," she said as she walked in and threw her coat over the arm of the chair.

Ken swung his leg behind him before it became a scratching post. He bent down and in a swift motion captured the cat and picked him up. BC growled and raised a paw. He caught Ken's scent, placed the paw gently on Ken's chest and nudged his chin.

"Never have to worry about you. This is the best watch cat anyone could ask for."

Kat motioned to the couch and sat in the chair facing him. BC cuddled into Ken's lap.

"I love you, Kat."

Anger flooded her. "How dare you say that!"

She came out of the chair, walked to the door and opened it. "You love yourself, Ken. We've been through this. Please leave."

"I have thought about you every day I've been away."

"Nice. Actions speak a lot louder or haven't you heard? Besides, we came to an understanding before you left. I do not want to *live* with a man. I want a husband. Old-fashioned but true."

"I still say we need to get to know each other. Living together assures that."

"Living together assures that two people are together and separate. It's really easy to leave, no messy divorce, no fuss. I don't want that. It's easy enough to abandon those you love when that big commitment is made—you know the M word." Kat thought back on her childhood—her mother walked out on Kat and her father when Kat was young. The pain was still fresh in her heart.

"I'll think about it. I am just concerned we'd be making a big mistake."

"A mistake?" She shot a wounded look at Ken.

"I don't want to hurt you."

"Too late. You already took care of that when you walked away before."

"I left with the understanding we would take some time to cool off and think about us—rationally. We did have some very intense, very quick feelings. You know as well as I that it was probably due to facing death. Same as shipwreck victims or guys going off to war."

"Really? Then why are you here? You already have your answer." Ken cringed. That had not come out right.

"I'm trying to say, I thought my feelings would change once I left. But they haven't. I still love you. But, marriage … ? We haven't even spent a full month with each other."

"You were ready for me to uproot everything and live with you—and we didn't know each other a full month. I think your libido's running your brain. I didn't say we had to get married today. We can get to know each other and not live together."

Her phone rang. She looked at the number and didn't recognize it.

"Hello."

"Hey, Kat, this is Brandon." Kat's heart sank.

"Oh, hello. I'm so sorry I missed our meeting today. Something came up. It was a little crazy."

"I wondered. How about tomorrow?" Kat looked at Ken.

"Don't think I can. But I will be coming by the library tomorrow afternoon, how about I bring you an espresso from Jo's?"

Ken had figured out who was on the other end. His jaw flexed. He scooped up BC, placed him on the couch and walked out the door.

"Got to go, Brandon. See you tomorrow."

Kat ran to the door but stopped short of screaming, "Come back!" She pulled back the living room curtain instead. A familiar heartache overcame her as she watched Ken walk across the road and toward the path to town. She grabbed BC, buried her head in his rich black fur and wept.

———

Ken power-walked down Kat's drive and to the road. He entertained the idea of turning back, thought better of it and continued up the path to town. He had to walk off the rage that filled his mind the instant he realized that librarian was on the other end of the phone. *How could you be so nice to that guy?* The urge to punch McGill until his face was bloody almost seemed logical. *Calm down, cowboy.* He told himself. *He's not your battle—you are. Get honest here.*

"I'm not giving up. I don't give up." He climbed the narrow path. A strong shot of bourbon was the one thing he wanted above anything else right now. He plowed past the ravine and into town.

He walked up and down Main but had no luck locating a bar. He stopped in front of the Ravens Cove Inn and walked into the reception area. He looked at his watch. *Too late to call Andersen.* He looked at the sign on the counter which read, "Ring bell for twenty-four service." He rang the bell. A sleepy-eyed attendant appeared out of the back room.

Rubbing his eyes, the fifty-something man looked up and focused on Ken. He was in striped maroon, grey and white bottoms and a white t-shirt. His silver hair rimmed a large bald spot and glinted in the lobby light.

"What can I do for you, Mr. Melbourne?"

"Is there a place a man can get a drink in this town?"

The astonished look from the still sleepy owner told Ken that the sign had not been meant for this type of information in the middle of the night. "Our only bar is around the corner. Take Main toward the police station and turn left at the first street you come to. Take a right on Poplar. Keep walking and you'll find it. Good night, sir." The man stalked back through the doorway.

Ken followed the directions to the bar. He was going to drown his troubles tonight. Not his normal MO but tonight he wasn't his normal self. Limbo and the craziness of the town were taking their toll. He wasn't really an FBI agent right now, and he was in love with someone who was being courted by a librarian of all things. *At least he has a job*, Ken thought. That brought his spirits even lower and the drink called more loudly.

Poplar Street was black. The buildings that lined the small road were deserted and in a bad state of disrepair. His senses came to alert as he made his way toward the only light on the street. A small neon sign blinked, "The Watering Hole" and "Open" alternately. He walked to the lights and through the flimsy blackened glass door. The place was dead.

"What can I get you?" a tall, dark blond man asked.

"Bourbon, straight. Make it a double."

"Well, you are looking to get away from it all, now aren't you?" The bartender pulled a bottle off the back shelf.

Ken stared into the dark gold liquid before picking it up and taking a hesitant sip. The bourbon burned his throat. Not the highest quality but palatable.

This evening had turned mighty ugly in every way. He muscles still ached from the battle in Old Town. Their bullets were useless against those horrid creatures.

"Gnomes." He said into the brown liquid.

"Pardon?"

Ken looked up at the bartender. "Nothing."

"Want another?"

"Sure."

Those yellow eyes filled his mind. Large, intelligent ones. He and Bart had circled, back to back. That's when something happened. The little monsters were coming in for the kill. Gun chamber empty, Ken swung the firearm and missed. Small hands grabbed his calf and he fell to one knee, face to face with the stinking beak nose of the creature. He could have believed he was imagining all of this except the hot and strong breath issuing from its mouth made it clear he was in a fight for his life. He swung again and caught the creature in the neck. It shrieked, fell backward and flew back at him. The gun was ripped from his hand. Somehow, he managed to grab the flashlight from his belt. He flipped it around to use it as a club and hit the on button in the process. When he raised his right arm the light hit one of the creature's eyes. It screamed and covered its face.

"You see that?"

"You bet I did." Bart threw down the gun and grabbed his flashlight. He turned it on and swung the flashlight so the beam caught the other two square in the eyes. They shrieked and ran for the darkness of the trees. The remaining four came at Ken.

They followed their comrades when the blue light struck.

Bart and Ken stayed back to back, circling the area with the flashlights. They kept them up as they separated and backed out of the clearing and out of the courtyard toward the street. Once there, they both turned, jogged to the truck, slammed the doors and locked them in unison.

"Okay, we're fighting a myth again." Bart turned to Ken.

"I'm darn tired of fighting things that don't exist but do exist."

"Made no sense just then, pal. But, I get what you're saying. Ditto."

Ken's breath was still ragged from the adrenaline pulsing through him. He felt his heart rate begin to drop as he concentrated on slow, easy breaths.

"I saw them watching us just now."

"Yeah, they moved to the edge of the clearing. I was sure they were going to come after us."

"Why didn't they?"

"Light is not their friend?"

"Not true. They didn't have any problem with the spots in the courtyard."

"It's the LEDs in the flashlights. What's different about them?"

"They last longer is all I know. But they are more intense light."

"Who cares—they worked."

"So, why didn't they follow us out?"

"I really don't know and I don't care. But maybe for some reason they can't leave the houses?"

"Maybe. Or maybe something has to tell them to."

"I just thank God they didn't. And why did they come after us anyway? Iconoclast wouldn't show his hand unless he thinks he can win."

"What demon thinks it's going to lose?"

Bart and Ken sat in silence. Defeat and fear came close. Visions of a night not so long ago flew into Bart's vision. The helplessness returned.

Ken couldn't stop thinking about how he had lost his credibility when he couldn't explain the serial killings in logical terms. And now it was happening again. He grew angry, then sullen. Self-pity raised its ugly voice whispering to him about how everything was unfair, and he didn't deserve to be treated this way. His heart sank.

Bart ventured in a shaky, almost indiscernible, voice. "In the name of Jesus, be gone." Ken shot a disgusted glance in his direction. "Not you, too."

Bart felt rather sheepish but noticed he felt lighter. "Got a better idea?"

"No." The reality of a spirit world, a world he had been grateful not to know about, smacked him right between the eyes. He had believed at the ravine but buried that belief when he returned to work. It didn't fit in his world and with his goals.

"I feel like a real idiot. Be gone, in Jesus' name," he said halfheartedly. The self-pity, weariness, and regret left as fast as they had come.

Bart could see the attitude change with the glint that had reappeared in Ken's eyes.

"Looking better, brother."

Bart dropped Ken at the hotel. He'd felt so good he couldn't sleep. So somehow he'd gotten the bright idea to walk to Kat's and have that conversation he'd long meant to have. And the rest was history.

"So, here I am, staring at an empty glass." He plinked the glass onto the bar.

"Want another?"

"Yeah, why not." A third glass appeared. As sometimes happened when he had a couple of drinks in him, Ken became a little more talkative.

"Hey."

"Drink okay?"

"Drink—yeah, its fine. I just have a question."

"Don't know as I have an answer, but shoot."

"Have you ever run into anything, well, anything you can't explain?"

"Like what?" The bartender's wary look told Ken a lot. He didn't care; just wanted to know.

"Well, like strange, small, and nasty animals that walk on two feet."

The barkeep stared in unbelief at the question.

"Is this some weird joke or trick?"

"Not meant to be."

"Did Larry send you in to give me a hard time?"

"I don't know a Larry—not in Ravens Cove, anyway." He looked at the name sewn into the man's shirt, "Kal."

"How'd you know my name?" Ken pointed at the shirt.

Kal relaxed. "Oh."

"These are real questions. Not a joke."

Kal looked around the bar. No one had come in and the place was empty except for him and Ken. He came around the bar and sat down on the stool.

"Why you asking?"

"Because I saw something like that tonight. In fact, several somethings and they tried to kill me and my friend, that's why."

"Where'd you see them?"

"At Old Town."

Kal became thoughtful. "I thought I saw something. It was a

few days back, though. It was at Old Town."

"Do you know what it is?"

"Yeah, it's a Kumrande."

"What's that?"

"You aren't from this area of the world, huh?"

"Not hardly."

"Well anyone who is can tell you there are many creatures that man has not seen and that exist. The Kumrande is one. There's other things, too—they have names for them all over the world like nymphs or fairies or goblins or …"

"Goblins?"

"That's what it looked like to you?"

"If anything matched a goblin description that would be it." Ken couldn't believe he was carrying on this conversation in the same routine way he would discuss the most recent baseball statistics.

"They can look like several different things, but that's their true shape. If you saw one in its true form, you should be dead."

"I almost was but they seem to have an aversion to LED lights."

Kal raised his eyebrows. Ken pulled his flashlight out of his belt and clicked it on. "LED lights." He clicked it back off.

"Well, isn't that something." Kal looked at Ken again.

"Listen, friend, they aren't done with you. When you see them, it's because they have come to take you to their underground world—for a Kumrande picnic. They like humans. So you better not travel at night. You're safe during the day but then again, we are in a dark time for Alaska."

"That's not too comforting."

"If they are here right now, someone or something has bidden them here. They are kinda like the spirit world's zombies—no souls. Suppose to obey the evil ones."

"Can you kill them?"

"Don't know. When I saw one the other day, I only saw a dark shadow but the shape could only be a Kumrande–itsy man with cloven feet. That's the way my mom described it."

Ken was still trying to deny this could be happening—again. But he wasn't going to alienate this man who had given him more information in ten minutes than it took to get out of Bart in days.

Ken laid his money on the bar. "Thanks, Kal. You be careful, too."

"Thanks, man. Come back anytime."

Ken left the bar and walked just a little faster than normal until he reached the inn. He sneaked up the stairs so he didn't disturb the manager for the second time that evening, undressed and was asleep before his head hit the pillow.

Kat cried for an hour after Ken left. Once the tears subsided, she got up, walked into her small bathroom and washed her face. She threw cold water over closed eyelids to reduce the swelling that was an inevitable side effect of her tears. By tomorrow morning, she'd probably look like marshmallows had been stuffed under her eyes.

Kat sought comfort under her old tattered quilt. She stared at the wall across from her bed. Her body screamed for sleep but her brain yelled to be heard. BC jumped up and curled into the middle of her back. The body heat, coupled with BC'S deep, rhythmic purr sent Kat into the previously elusive slumber. A periodic scratching brought Kat up from the sleepy depths. The sound seemed to be in her room.

BC sat statue-straight at the end of the bed, tail swishing, staring intently at the window. She pushed back the covers and was greeted by the chill of a house she loved to keep at sixty-two degrees. She grabbed a throw from the bottom of the bed and wrapped it around her shoulders. A bare cotoneaster bush screeched against the glass as it moved in the night wind.

"I knew I should have cut that thing back last fall." She plopped back on her pillow, snuggled under the quilt and tried to go back to sleep. The scratching started again. BC leaped to the floor and focused on the braided rug between the bed and window. Kat concentrated on the same spot and—for a moment—was sure she saw something, too. BC growled and pounced on nothing.

"You having bad dreams, cat?" She flicked on the light and walked around to where BC was sitting, although his attention was now on the wall beside the window. Something caught her eye and Kat bent over and scrutinized the old braided rug. A small, wet patch was evident.

"BC, really, can't you get to the box?" Kat walked off in disgust and grabbed the roll of paper towels from the kitchen. She sopped up the liquid. It was clear. She gave it a tentative sniff. It had no smell. She touched it. It was cold and a small piece of ice melted under the warmth of her finger. A shiver started up her spine and traveled at lightning speed to the base of her neck. She grabbed her phone.

"Someone's been in my house." Her voice shook. She held the phone in a two-handed death grip to keep it steady.

Bart didn't question her. "Stay on the phone. I have to put mine down to grab my coat. But if something happens you yell at the top of your lungs, hear me?"

Kat nodded.

"*You hear me?*"

"Yes, yes, sorry."

His truck slid to a halt in her driveway. He jumped out, still in his old grey sweat suit that doubled as pajamas. His hair stood up and out in all directions, naturally curly like hers. He bounded up the stairs.

"You said you didn't see the intruder."

Kat shook her head from side to side.

"Then how do you know someone was here?"

She led Bart to the bedroom, over to the rug and pointed at the slight, wet spot that had begun to dry.

Bart crouched down and touched it. The small circular outline was still darker than the dry rug.

He stood up. "You sure you didn't drop some ice on your way inside sometime today?"

"I haven't been to the window or that side of the bed all day. So, I don't know how ice would get there."

"BC?"

"He doesn't have outdoor privileges when it gets this cold."

"You heard scratching?"

"Yeah, I thought it was the bush outside the window. And, it *was* rubbing on the window. But then I was sure the sound was closer and BC seemed to be tracking something. It almost sounded like scuffling across the floor, when I think about it. Anyway, I turned on the light and didn't see anyone. But then I went over to check and there was this wet spot. That's when I called you."

Bart checked his wrist and realized he had forgotten his watch. He looked at the clock over Kat's sink. Five o'clock.

"I'm sorry for calling you out here. I could have sworn there was someone in my room. You go on home and I'll see you in a couple of hours."

"Nothing doing. You grab some clothes and that cat. You can stay at my house."

"That's not necessary, really."

"With what's going on around here, I believe it's more than necessary. I had a pretty weird night last night. This makes it even weirder." Bart told Kat about the run-in he and Ken had with the two-footed creatures.

"You're kidding, right? You just want to scare me like when we were kids so I'll do what you tell me, right?"

"I wish. I wasn't going to tell you this but it seems necessary now."

"We went to see Mrs. Tellamoot last night and …"

"We?"

"Grandma, Paul, and Josiah went with me."

"She didn't want to tell us at first but she did. Her people believe the buildings in Old Town were responsible for all those deaths a century ago. They talked about some white man who brought a new religion to the village and some evil Native girl who married him. To make a long story short, they opened a portal of some kind to the spirit world and everyone that was in the village died except a small hunting party who returned to find them."

"Relevance, here?"

"She also talked about these little people that worked for the evil ones and were like slaves to them. And about a white wolf turned warrior that fought demons and won and buried the dead to boot. Then—you're gonna love this one—it shot into the sky like a blue streak. Sound familiar?"

"I'll say. Get your stuff and that darn cat. You're coming with me. I need to find Melbourne then we'll get to the office."

"I can stay right here."

"He's involved and you know it. You call Gram and Paul. Looks like we are back together for a reason."

Kat knew he was right. She didn't want to believe it. But she grabbed a change of clothes and they were on the road, BC tucked under her arm and then in her lap.

Large, yellow eyes watched the taillights recede. "Nihilist won't like this, Mandor."

"I almost had her; that infernal animal of hers wouldn't obey me. Why?"

"That animal is in a household that is protected by the Great One."

"We need to meet with our fellows and we need to find a way to get them before they discover the plan."

They galloped on their small goat feet toward the path and quickly disappeared.

Chapter 10
Retribution

A demanding beep brought Ken out of his alcohol-induced sleep. He fumbled for the cell phone.

"Yo," he croaked. His mouth was so dry he was sure someone had stuffed cotton in it while he slept.

As Bart began to explain everything, he sat on the edge of the bed and in spite of a pounding headache was coming around fast.

When Bart got to the part that someone or maybe something had broken into Kat's, adrenaline washed any remaining fog from his mind.

"I'll meet you at Jo's in twenty minutes."

Ken was on his second cup of very strong coffee when Bart walked in. His bloodshot eyes met Bart's tired but clear ones.

"Where'd you end up last night?"

"At the only bar in town."

"Since when are you a drinking man?"

"Since I got back to this forsaken place."

"We like you, too."

Ken broke the silence. "The bartender shared an interesting bit of trivia with me. Seems he'd seen one of those creatures, well the shadow of one of those creatures, a couple of days before we had our run-in."

"You don't say?"

"I do say. Anyway, he had a name for it—a Kumbayee or something like that."

"A Kumrande."

"That's it. And how do you know? I get really ticked that I can learn more from a stranger in this town than I can from someone I consider a friend."

"Sorry, just taught to keep my mouth shut. And, I wasn't sure that's what it was. Needed to do a little more research before I named it. Less than twenty-four hours ago, I thought it was a myth."

"Whatever. It seems we are not supposed to be alive and it seems those things are going to try again until we are the blue-plate special."

Bart closed his eyes and put his thumb and forefinger on the bridge of his nose. "I really miss plain old run-of-the-mill police work."

"I hear you, brother."

"I don't know who or what has brought this into the town. Kat visited Mrs. Tellamoot. Bernice told her these are portals the demons are coming through and that someone had to invite them in."

"That'd explain the bleeding wall."

"I liked your first idea better. Anyway, we have to find out who is doing it and find some weird book named *The Book of Fallen Angels* to put a stop to this thing."

"Where do we start?"

"Kat's going to the archives at the library today—in fact, she should be getting there pretty soon. She's gonna get the names of those who lived in the village. Someone has to be connected to that place."

Ken's face tightened as he remembered Kat's honey-sweet tone when she talked to the librarian. He did not like the idea of her going within a city block of that library—actually, that librarian. "You sure that Brandon guy isn't the problem here?"

"Just because he has an eye on Kat doesn't mean he's a demon worshipper—you need to get that jealousy under control."

A slight flush crossed Ken's face. "I admit I'm jealous but I don't know anything about the guy either. I'm always suspicious of someone I don't know."

"He answered the ad. He lived in the bigger city of Clayton about twenty miles south of here. He showed up late last November, interviewed and as he was the only applicant and qualified, the council snapped him up. From what he's said, there was nothing for him in Clayton. He moved here."

"Sounds reasonable."

"Yeah, it does. But when I say it out loud, I realize no one called any references on him. And when he was asked about his ancestry, as everyone is because that's what counts around here, he was vague and said he was a Heinz fifty-seven and gave a short laugh. Odd for someone who says he has lived here a good portion of his life."

"Maybe I should ask him a few questions."

"Maybe you shouldn't. I'll stop by and talk to him later." Bart grabbed his coat and hat.

"First, we need to get to Grandma's—you still have a tongue lashing ahead—long overdue I might add—but I wouldn't drag you into the lion's den right now except the pastor and Josiah want to talk. Kat will join us right after her library jaunt."

"I'll meet you there. I forgot something at the inn and need to call the office."

Bart eyed Ken. "You'd be smart to avoid the library on your way to Gram's."

"Probably."

"Don't say I didn't warn you."

———

Kat made it to her hair appointment with a minute to spare. The shop was dark. Kat cupped her hands to her face and peeked through the glass. Cassie wasn't inside. Icy fingers of the cold breeze worked their way through Kat's outerwear. She paced back and forth in front of the shop in an effort to stay warm. Twenty minutes later, she ripped a blank deposit form out of her checkbook, scribbled a quick note, and slid it under the salon door. *So much for showing Melbourne what he's missing.* She ran her fingers through the uneven strands and headed back up Main.

Kat ducked into Jo's, ordered and was out the door in a flash. She saw Ken standing up and drawing on his coat and hid in the alley beside the bakery until he disappeared into the Ravens Cove Inn. She crossed the street and was at the library in a couple of minutes.

Kat's footsteps announced her arrival as they echoed off the tall, stone walls. Brandon's head came up from behind the information counter.

Kat extended the coffee to him. "Again, I'm sorry to have missed our appointment." She could not bring herself to say date.

"Apology accepted." Brandon reached for the piping hot liquid and took a sip. He flashed a charming smile.

Kat smiled back. "I have some quick research to do. Can you direct me to the Alaska archives?"

Brandon pointed left. "At the very back of the room along the wall. You want some help?"

"No, I'll find what I need. I'll let you know, though, if I run into trouble."

Kat hurried into the large room. Small tables were in a tidy row and flanked on two sides by towering bookshelves. Tall slits of windows let in a muted north light. Banker's lamps, some with amber shades, some with green ones, lit the center of the tables. The room beckoned Kat to sit and spend the cold afternoon reading.

If only. Kat made her way to the back. Old journals lined a four-shelf, waist-high bookcase that ran the length of the wall. She flipped through the publications and took the one entitled, *Clans of the Early Twentieth Century.*

Gathering two or three books that looked promising, she plopped on the floor in front of the shelves and perused the journals. She located a ledger for the Forgotten Place and, just as Mrs. Tellamoot had said, the names were listed in neat penmanship and alphabetically. A scribble of black ink on the bottom of the page noted the names had been translated.

"Interesting."

"What's so interesting?" Kat jumped and turned. She blinked and rubbed her eyes. Gary Wenfred smiled down at Kat.

"Your dead." Was all she could squeak out.

Gary patted up and down his sides. "Don't feel dead." He thrust a hand down at her. "Touch me."

Kat continued to stare into Gary's eyes.

"I said, touch me!"

Kat stuck her hand out and touched his hand. She drew it back as if touching hot fire. "You're cold." His skin felt like it had been in a freezer.

"It is winter."

Kat willed herself to be calm. "Just looking at these old journals. They have quite a bit of history and bring back some memories of my grandmother's stories."

Gary came closer and bent uncomfortably close to Kat's left shoulder. "The Forgotten Place?"

"Yes. Since it's a part of our history now, I wanted to understand what it was like." *I'm talking to a dead man, for Pete's sake.*

"There are books and stories on it, you know. Much more interesting than a bunch of names in a journal."

"I like names. They are important to my family and to me." She held the book tight. At this point she was almost pinned between the shelf and Gary.

Gary sensed her discomfort. His smile broadened. He pushed his knee into her back in a much too familiar way. The pressure caused her to want to scream.

"Excuse me, *Mr. Wenfred.* I need to stand up."

"I like you this way." His voice went low and hoarse.

"I don't." She put her legs against the bookshelf and pushed. Wenfred lost his footing which gave Kat the opportunity to jump up and turn around. Her face was flushed and her emerald green eyes flashed "Warning, warning, incoming" at him. He didn't take notice of that, either, and moved in closer.

Kat smiled at him just as she doubled a fist and punched him in the gut. Gary was taken off guard by Kat's strength. He doubled over, then looked up at her, fury and vengeance in his eyes.

"There's no one out front." A voice boomed through the silence.

Gary twirled right into Kenneth Melbourne and disappeared. Ken grabbed for the mist and succeeded in giving himself a huge hug.

Relief flooded Kat when she saw Ken. She had been sure Gary was going to beat her or worse. She had given her best punch but wasn't sure she could have beaten him in an all-out fight.

"What the hell was that?"

"Gary Wenfred."

Ken stared in disbelief at Kat. She held up a hand. "I know, he's dead. But, he was here." Her eyes said, *I dare you to call me crazy.*

Ken noted the flashing eyes. He pointed at the document with his chin. "What you got?"

"Something I need to get a copy of." She walked toward the front desk, stopped and turned. "Thanks." She smiled up at Ken.

Ken grinned. "Glad to be of service."

Kat looked into his eyes and seeing the smile and warmth couldn't help but feel she was safe and home. A loud groan broke the moment. Kat rushed to the counter.

"Brandon! Are you okay?"

Ken came up fast behind her. Brandon lay on the floor, rubbing the back of his head.

"What happened, McGill?"

"Don't know. I turned to get something from the back cart and the next thing I knew, I was seeing you. I must have slipped."

Ken helped Brandon to his feet. "You want to see a doctor?"

"Don't think so. Just a bump on my hard head. I think I'll be fine."

"You sure, Brandon? I can get Doc Billings here in a minute." Kat said, concern lacing her voice.

"I'm sure." He smiled warmly at her.

"I'm going to get some copies before I leave. If you change your mind ..."

"I won't but thanks." Brandon sat down and started logging more magazines.

Kat walked to the copier; Ken followed.

"You don't need to stay. I'm fine."

"I'm not leaving until you get out of this place. I don't care what you say." He took her hands. "I don't believe what I saw but I know you were fighting somebody and I don't know where that somebody went." He scanned the library. There was no one else but the three of them in the place.

Kat went silent and copied the ledger of names. She threw her shoulders back and walked toward the desk and paid for the copies.

"Hope you can go for that cup of coffee soon."

"I'm really busy lately Brandon. Don't know when I'll get a chance."

"Well, call if something changes." Brandon threw an angry look at Ken.

"I will. Thanks for your help."

Ken walked beside her until they were at the bottom of the grey, concrete steps. "Thanks again." She took two steps then turned, "Why did you end up at the library, anyway?"

Ken walked over, placed his hands on her shoulders and looked deep into her eyes. "I came here today because I knew you were going to be here. I couldn't stand knowing that you might have another, umm, interest in your life."

"You came because you don't want me but you sure don't want someone else to have me. That's just great." She narrowed her eyes in disgust and tried to jerk free. He held her just a little firmer.

"Listen to me. Yes, I was jealous. Yes, I don't want anyone else to have you. But if I really thought it was all over between us, I'd leave and never look back. But it isn't. I know it; you know it. I love you."

"You said that before."

"I did and I meant it. I am so sorry I hurt you. I had to get away and think. Things happened too fast and I knew I wanted you in my life but I just couldn't commit to marriage. It never seems to be a pretty end, at least for my associates in my profession."

"What can I say, we are still back to where we were, but thanks for giving me the information so I can understand why you said the things you did before you left."

"No, I'm not back to where we were. I am clearer than ever that you belong in my life. When I saw you and you were in trouble, all the feelings rushed back. I don't ever want to long to hear your voice or drink in your amazing eyes. Please marry me, Kat."

The shock ran through her like a jolt of electricity. "Do what?"

"Marry me." It was with a strong, confident voice he said it the second time. He had shocked himself the first time it came out. But he was sure now, more sure than anything he had been about in his life.

These were the words Kat had longed to hear and now that she had, fear was running rampant. Instead of jumping into his arms, all she could think of was to get away.

"Let me go, please." She pulled back. He held firm.

"Let me go, now, Ken." She pulled harder. He held firmer.

The anger came into her eyes and she relaxed. So did he. She lifted her arms and pushed with all she had. He lost his footing on the icy sidewalk and started to fall backward. He grabbed her and she went down with him.

"Oomp. Feels like old times." He smiled at her, still holding her arms. She smacked his chest with one hand then used it to push off.

"Not so fast." He grabbed her and gave her a quick kiss on the mouth. She stopped and looked at him. She leaned over and kissed him hard, then pushed off.

"I'll marry you. Can I go now?" He released her. She jumped up and smiled mischievously down at him. "Need a hand?"

He pushed up to his feet and grabbed her shoulders. "Really?"

"Really, you big dolt. We'll work out the details later. Right now I need to get to Grandma's and go over this list with her and the others."

"Can't we at least celebrate—some time alone, maybe at your place?" He looked at her with a twinkling hope in his eyes.

"Not that kind of celebrating. We aren't going to celebrate in that way until we are married."

Disappointment descended over Ken's features like the final curtain in a play.

"Oh, for goodness sake, you are such a baby." She smacked him again—on the arm this time. "I'm old-fashioned and happen to believe in waiting until we are married." She confronted his disappointment with a firm look.

"Okay, so a cup of coffee, then?"

"One to go and you have a deal."

They crossed the street and walked into Jo's. Ken grabbed a straw, tore off the top and blew. The paper landed on the sparkling counter.

Jo closed the cash register. "Want a few more straws or can I get you something to go with the one you just claimed?"

"A mocha and a ..." Kat looked to her side and then down. Ken was on his knee.

"Get up!" A rosy flush crept up Kat's neck. "Get up!" she hissed. "You're making a scene."

Ignoring her heightened discomfort and the instantaneous quiet, Ken stayed on one knee. He held up a paper ring.

"Katrina Agnes Tovslosky, will you marry me?" He lifted his arm and the ring.

"We're waiting here," Jo said from behind the counter.

Kat looked at Jo, then at Ken, a foolish lopsided grin on his face, still holding the paper ring toward her. She shook her head, a smile of resignation on her face.

"Yes, you big idiot, I'll marry you." She held out her left ring finger until Ken slipped it on.

He stood up and she kissed him hard on the lips.

Applause broke out around the room.

"I always said you were a pushover." Wendy stood behind Kat, arms crossed and her right foot tapping.

"You always have said that. Guess you're right."

Wendy gave Kat a disapproving look. Then her face broke into a wide smile. She threw her arms around Kat with enough force to push her into the counter.

Wendy turned disapproving eyes to Ken. "She could have done better, you know. You high tale it out of Kat's life again and you will definitely be answering to me."

Before she could say another word, Ken grabbed her and gave her a big hug. "I love you, too."

Wendy recovered and gave him a sheepish smile, then went straight-faced. "I mean it, Melbourne."

"I know you do. I'm not planning on messing it up this time."

"Good. Well, I need to go let everyone know."

"Well, hope you didn't want it to be a secret engagement," Kat said as she watched Wendy duck into the store next to Jo's.

"I don't want it to be. Otherwise, I'd have proposed in the woods."

"These are on me." Jo beamed as she placed the mocha and a latte laced with cinnamon on the counter. Ken looked at her, surprised she remembered.

"Don't look so startled, Mr. Melbourne, it's what I do."

He shrugged. Her memory seemed wasted in this small town. He and Kat left hand in hand, leaning close. Kat's heart was soaring and her joy was hard to contain. She sobered.

"Grandma is still upset, you know."

"I know."

"I should have asked before I said yes."

"We'll go ask her now. I've got to get her lecture over with anyway. No time like the present."

Kat wrapped her arms around Ken's waist. Ken put his arm around her and they walked north on Main just enjoying the time together, not needing to say a thing.

Brandon McGill watched them from the library window. A look of determination settled over his handsome features.

"Okay, Ken, the game is on. May the best man win."

By the time Kat and Ken reached Grandma Bricken's tidy house, they were giggling and messing around like teenagers. Ken grabbed Kat on each side and dug his fingers into her ribs. She wiggled out, almost slipping on the stoop. He grabbed her, held her close for a moment, and then let go.

"Better get this over with."

"I've got your back if you get into real trouble."

Ken shot a rankling look at Kat. "I think I can handle myself with your Grandma."

Kat smiled. "We'll see, tough guy, we'll see."

She opened the door, gave Ken a quick kiss on the cheek and disappeared into the house. The smell of onions and meat greeted her.

"That you, precious one?" Alese Bricken called from the kitchen.

"Yep, Gram, and you have a visitor."

Gram came out of the kitchen wiping her hands down her apron. Her radiant smile turned into a menacing frown.

"I see." She turned back to the kitchen.

Ken planted his feet in the entry, feeling less welcome than he'd been on his first visit. "Maybe I'd better go."

"What happened to, 'I think I can handle myself?'" Kat grabbed his shoulders and turned him to face her. "It's now or never. If you leave, you have no chance of winning her back."

"I'd rather get a tooth pulled." Ken turned back around but made no move toward the kitchen.

Kat whispered into his broad shoulders, "I've got your back, Tough Guy" then snickered into his shirt. Ken stiffened and walked in.

Grandma's back was to him. She pushed a heaping mound of vegetables into a pot of stew.

Josiah looked up and smiled. "Well, look what the Kat dragged in."

"Funny, Mr. Williams, very funny." Ken lingered at the kitchen door. He took a hesitant step toward the large, welcoming table.

Alese Bricken whirled around. The rapid movement sent him back into the doorway.

"How dare you not call to even let us know you were alive, Kenneth Melbourne. How dare you! You were part of my heart. I thought I was part of yours. You not only broke her heart, which was sin enough, you broke mine." She whirled back to the stove, a slight sniff the only indication of her sadness.

Remorse and guilt flooded Ken. "I'm sorry, Mrs. Bricken."

She stirred with frenzy and stayed silent.

"I am truly sorry."

She laid the spoon on the counter and turned back around. Sad and unforgiving eyes locked onto his remorseful blue ones.

"Sorry doesn't fix everything. I wish it did." The hurt was evident in her soft tone. "When I take someone into my heart, as I did you, and then I am as rejected as I was by you, I am not able to easily forgive or forget."

Kat watched the exchange. She strolled to the cabinet and retrieved two coffee cups when the dialogue came to a very loud pause. Ken and Grandma were looking into each other's eyes. Kat returned to the table and set the cups in front of two empty chairs.

Josiah reached over and squeezed her hand. He graced her with a tender smile and broke the silence. "Then Peter came to Jesus and asked, *Lord, how many times shall I forgive my brother when he sins against me? Up to seven times?* Jesus answered, *I tell you, not seven times but seventy times seven.*"

Alese's straight back relaxed. She wiped her hands, came to the table and sat down. Kat grabbed another cup and set it before her grandmother. Alese motioned Ken to sit. He took a chair directly across from her.

"Josiah is right. I forgot that truth. I am sorry I did not accept your apology, I do now. I am still hurt but I will pray for deliverance."

"I didn't know that I was so important to you. I thought if Kat and I weren't together, then I shouldn't contact you, either."

"You were wrong." Grandma searched Kenneth's face until he was squirming like a kid. "But, I believe you. We won't speak of it again."

Kat's eyes sparkled above a relaxed smile. Ken smiled back at her. Her look was one of deep love and respect. *Why do I want and need that from you, my KittyKat?*

Kat remembered the paper she had in her coat pocket. She kissed Ken on the cheek, jumped up and trotted into the entry hall to retrieve it.

"Hey. Where you been?"

"Some of us have to work. You seen Melbourne?" Bart was not sure he wanted to hear the answer.

"In here."

Bart looked at Kat. She smiled. He looked at her finger as she held the coat with her left hand and rummaged through the pocket until she found the paper.

"Started paper jewelry as a sideline? I realize Ravens Cove's boring in February but I didn't think I'd ever see you stoop this low." A smile played on his lips.

Kat looked down then gave him a sheepish grin. "Ken made it."

Bart's eyebrows shot up. "Ken Melbourne made it?"

She walked to Bart and gave him a big bear hug, stood back and whispered, "we're engaged." She threw her hand over Bart's mouth right before he yelled.

"Shhh. I haven't told Gram yet."

"I can't let you out of my sight for a minute."

"You should have heard Wendy at Jo's."

"Now that's romantic, a proposal at Jo's."

"Pretty romantic—and he spared no expense." She wiggled left hand fingers to highlight the paper band.

"We better get the duct tape if you're going to keep that expensive thing on much longer." They laughed and headed to the kitchen. Kat placed the papers in the middle of the table and Grandma took them. She started to read aloud.

A more sinister type of planning meeting was taking place in Old Town. A dark fog seeped under the walls then settled in the mansion's attic. A red light within the fog throbbed on and off like an old hotel sign. A dark figure was outlined with each pulse of light. Four small, cloven-hoofed beings faced the black, angry mist.

"You had the men and they got away. You were in that horrid child of God's bedroom and you couldn't take her," a voice boomed from within.

The Kumrandes stood stock-still and silent.

"Answer!"

"They had lights. Blue lights that pierced our eyes and made us blind," Nihilist answered.

"The animal of that woman would not obey and challenged me."

"You are cowards. There are still three more portals to open. I don't care how, but you find and destroy the old man and the rest of those who are a threat to our plan. And do not fail this time!" Atramentous exhaled in the Kumrandes' direction; a gale-force wind picked them up and blew them in balls toward the door. The door flew open by itself and they tumbled down the attic stairs and the stairs of the mansion.

Kal the bartender saw four small, grey balls blow through the old house's door, down the steps and into the courtyard. The door blew shut with a loud bang. He watched as the four balls unwound themselves and stood up. He realized what he was seeing and turned to run. It was too late. They ran him down and pulled him to the skull rock, pushed, and it opened. They dragged the unconscious man into the depths below.

A few short hours later, the body lay in front of the cannery. The chest was open and so was his throat. He began to deflate like a balloon as his insides disintegrated. Maggots wiggled out from his chest and neck, covering him like a sick winter coat. The portal in the cannery had burst into the upstairs office with such force, it blew out the glass windows separating the office from the hallway in front.

This portal's light did not pulse. It was a steady, sick yellow. Gambogian walked through the opening and smiled. "It's good to be back."

"It is indeed." Caitiff, the small shadow figure, walked out behind him.

"You find out what the Six knows. I'm going to locate Iconoclast's lost friend."

Caitiff dove into the floorboards to the underground and traveled toward Ravens Cove. Gambogian set off to find a small church and the man who chose to minister from it.

———

Reverend Lucas stood at the podium in the new home church that the city council had gifted to him after some of Ravens Cove's finest citizens had burned down his old one. His notes for the Wednesday service lay before him.

"Come home for some dinner." Tanya called from the back of the church.

"Not hungry."

"You need to eat. Come home, just for thirty minutes."

Paul looked up at his beautiful blessing of a wife and nodded. He walked down the rough steps that led to the podium and took her hand. They continued out the small door and down the steps.

He felt a sharp pain, released Tanya's hand and grabbed his left arm. The pain turned to a stinging throb.

"What's wrong?"

"Feels like something bit me." Another sharp pain hit his right arm. The sting became an unrelenting fire. He grabbed it. Weakness overcame him and he dropped to the icy ground.

Tanya clutched his arm, draped it around her shoulders and lifted him off the ground. She walked him to the church steps. Paul yelled and doubled over from an invisible punch. He perceived a sick, yellow light glowing from his shirt, then it was gone. Tanya tried to get him to sit on the steps. He refused.

Gambogian screamed into her mind, "You're next, daughter of Eden."

Gambogian's ochre aura grew dim. Weakness overtook him. He had not calculated the loss of strength from opening the ingress. "We're not finished yet," he screeched and flew to the cannery.

"Get me into the church."

Tanya threw Paul's right arm over her shoulders. She leaned him against the church door, holding him steady with her body and struggled with the knob until she heard the click of the latch. The door opened and they both fell through. Paul stayed on the floor.

He tried to get up and fell back to the floor. "Sorry, sweetheart, can't manage my muscles." His words slurred and his eyes were half-closed.

"I'll call Doc Billings." Tanya ran for the door mentally kicking herself for not insisting on getting a phone put in the church.

"Get Grandma Bricken." Paul's voice whispered after her.

"You need a doctor."

"I need the Great Physician, not Doc Billings." He pulled up his shirt and a large scratch materialized. As Tanya watched, more scratches appeared and turned a fiery red.

"Oh no." Panic laced her voice.

"Call Grandma."

She nodded and ran. She loped across snowdrifts, threw open the front door, ran to the kitchen phone and dialed.

"Please be there. Please."

The phone trilled at Alese Bricken's home. Grandma was concentrating so hard on the ledger Kat had brought from the library, she had blocked out anything happening around her.

Kat smiled at Ken, rose and walked to the small table. "Good evening," she answered.

"Kat?"

"Yes."

"This is Tanya Lucas. Something's happened to Paul. He's asking for Grandma Bricken."

"Is he ill?"

"He's in the small church. He is in great pain and asked me to call Alese."

"Not to state the obvious, but have you called Doc Billings?"

"He wants Grandma. I saw the wounds that came out of nowhere mind you. This is a demonic attack."

Of course it is. We couldn't just have a run of the mill illness in Ravens Cove. What good would that be?

"Hold on."

Kat walked to the kitchen door.

"Tanya Lucas needs to talk to you, Grandma."

Grandma looked at Kat. "Excuse me?"

"Paul's wife is asking for you. It's urgent."

A minute later Grandma put her head back in the kitchen door. "I need to get to the church."

The small troop stood in unison.

"I was hoping you'd say that."

———

Paul lay on the floor of the church.

Tanya looked at Alese Bricken through wet eyes. "He lost consciousness before I got back here." Tanya ran her hand over Paul's feverish cheek. She dipped a rag into a bucket of water and placed it on his forehead. Paul responded with a body jerk and a sharp, ragged breath. The small group encircled Paul and linked their hands together.

"Precious Jesus, our dear brother is in agony. We ask for Your healing touch and mercy for his body, mind and soul. Restore his health, merciful Lord, as only You can. In Your powerful name." Josiah bowed his head.

Tanya's silent tears became sobs. "How could he be attacked by evil? He is a man of God. How could God allow this?"

"I don't know God's mind but I know His power," Grandma said.

"Please, precious Jesus, fight for this man. He loves you and believes in you. His will to fight has been stolen, O God. Revive his soul. Your will be done, gracious and wonderful One."

"This is not helping. He needs a doctor." Kat pulled out her cell phone and dialed.

Doc Billings arrived out of breath and disheveled.

"Sorry to get you out so late."

"My job. Now back up so I can take a look at him." Kat and Ken stepped away from Paul.

"He has a temperature of 103 and these abrasions are oozing." Billings yanked the gloves off his hands. "What happened to him? And how long has he been ill? He should have been in a hospital days ago." He frowned then looked at Tanya.

Tanya hung her head. "You wouldn't believe me if I explained."

Ken looked at his watch then cleared his throat. "To answer your question, he's had this disease for about an hour."

"Maybe that's your sick idea of a joke. It would have taken much longer for this to be so advanced."

Doc grabbed a syringe and a gold liquid from his bag. "This stuff will help if we are not too late. We need to get him to the hospital in Clayton." He shot the liquid into Paul's arm.

"This was a demonic attack, why didn't he respond to prayer?" Tanya Lucas covered her face and wept.

"Madam, this is a staph infection and an aggressive one at that. This man is going to die if we don't get him to a hospital. Now, help me get him into the car."

A soft voice sighed past Kat's ear, *pray. Now.* The fear of embarrassment yelled, *don't do it! You'll be labeled a fanatic!* The soothing tone of the first speaker murmured encouragement. She put an arm on Doc's. He looked down at her.

"You too?"

"Just give me a minute, then take him," she said, feeling so foolish and yet unable to not pray.

"Dear Jesus," she started in a halting voice, "I know I don't have the faith of so many I know and love. It just isn't who I am. Still, if you are there, I am begging you to save this man. He loves You faithfully and proves it every day. Please make him well. In Jesus' name. Amen." She mumbled the final part, anger filling her being toward the God that would let this happen to this kind messenger of His word.

"Feel better now?"

"Not really."

Doc's eyebrows shot up. He shrugged. "Help me move this man, time counts." Ken, Bart, Josiah, and Doc each grabbed an arm or leg and lifted. The heat of the infection radiated through Paul's clothing. It was hard to carry him. He felt like he'd burn through the gloves they wore.

Well that was sure worthless, not to mention demeaning. Thanks for nothing.

Paul moaned and his eyes opened. He looked to his left and saw Ken. He looked to his right and saw Bart.

"What are you guys doing? Put me down."

"You're sick. We need to get you to the hospital."

"I think I can walk myself. Have since I was ten months. Put me down."

"He's delirious. Keep walking."

"I'm not delirious. Put me down." Paul yanked one arm free.

Doc nodded and they lowered him to the floor. Confusion darkened Doctor Billings' features when Paul sat up.

"I've never seen an antibiotic work that fast." He rubbed his chin and stared at Paul.

Paul shot a smile to Doc before he headed to a standing position.

"Whoa, friend, you are very ill. Not such a good idea." Ken pressed down on Paul's shoulder.

Paul gave Ken a "How stupid do you think I am" look and pushed up off the floor. He stood and stayed upright.

"So now you can walk to the car for the ride to the hospital. Good thing. You're a bit heavy when you're out cold." Bart quipped, trying to buy time to make sense out of what was happening.

"I feel great."

The doctor walked back to Paul and snatched his shirt up.

"What do you think you're doing?"

"Does this look great?"

Paul looked down and saw a few streaks of pink up the middle of his abdomen.

The doctor looked at Paul and then at the rest of them. "What's going on here? This man was at death's door."

"Seemed like it." Josiah backed away from Paul and smiled at Doctor Billings.

"If I hadn't seen it with my own eyes, I'd say you had pulled a nasty trick on me."

"Would I have been involved in such a trick?" Alese stepped in front of Billings.

"I would have no reason to believe you would, Mrs. Bricken. I'm going home now." Doc ran his hands through his disheveled mop of hair.

"You okay, Doc?"

"Just need rest. I'll be back to look at you tomorrow, pastor."

"We can talk then."

"Yeah, we'll talk then." He walked to the door and out into the night.

Paul looked at the others. "Thanks for coming."

"Welcome. What happened?" Josiah was the voice for the small group.

"I was mugged—by an invisible assailant."

"Who?"

"Don't know. But when the last pain hit my stomach, I saw, just for an instant, an ochre yellow light hanging over my shirt."

Josiah, who had been saying a silent prayer of thanks for Paul's recovery, shot his head in Paul's direction.

"You know it?"

"I know it," Josiah said firmly. "That horrid color belongs to one of Iconoclast's demons. I had the honor of meeting him in person, right before Iconoclast tried to eat me for dinner. He is called Gambogian and is one of Iconoclast's eight."

Bart let the reality of his words sink in. "So, he is really back."

"What do you mean by really back?" Tanya asked.

"I believed we had a sick copycat on our hands. I was hoping the Anchorage M.E. would confirm that. There were enough differences from Iconoclast previous attack, I was sure someone was emulating him. The last body was missing his heart and throat. But that purple and black liquid was all over him."

"When were you planning on letting us in on this bit of news? After one of us dies?" Tanya's voice held a threatening edge.

"I wouldn't let that happen."

"Really? My husband's illness says different."

"Enough!" Grandma Bricken scolded Bart and Tanya before the interchange erupted into an all-out screaming match. "These brutes would love us to fight. Divide and conquer is one the most tried and true tactics in any battle. Who do you think perfected it?"

"I know, I know. If you've told me that once, you've told me a thousand times." Bart gave his great-aunt an impatient look.

"And I'll keep saying it until I get it through that thick skull of yours." They locked eyes. Bart broke contact first.

"Truce." Bart looked at Alese.

"Truce." She pulled Bart to her.

"Not to interrupt a Kodak moment here, but we need to find out how Iconoclast found a way to return to Ravens Cove."

"It began with Old Town. Let's start there." Kat snatched her coat from the floor.

Ken caught her hand. "Not at night. Bart and I found out what can happen out there at night."

"The Kumrande," Grandma said decisively.

"How did you know? Another dream?"

Grandma nodded.

"And, it gets crazier and crazier." Kat shook her head and looked in the direction of Old Town. "Hey, tell me you see what I'm seeing."

"That can't be good." Bart watched as a black fog rose, exploded into a mushroom cloud and then descended like grave clothes over the buildings. A murderous shriek issued from a wispy shape that shot out of the mist and flew toward the ravine.

Chapter 11
Near Completion

Gambogian had not anticipated weakness. The attack on the man of God had taken so much from him, Caitiff was given the job of finding Pet. He sped to Ravens Ravine to search for the missing demon.

The old hag tree shook as Caitiff came close. A sickly grin exposed jagged carnivore teeth that protruded outward from his ebony face. His leathery hand touched a snarled limb. "Soon, friend, soon."

A dull burst of yellow light dropped like stars from the tree before it turned deathly grey.

"Those vile mortals have taken the energy from us all. Our revenge is near." Caitiff headed down the path. Nihilist blocked his way.

"You are not welcome here. Iconoclast promised this land to the Kumrande."

"I belong anywhere I am directed to go by the Commander."

Nihilist and his tribe drew their swords and rushed forward. In a rapid move, Caitiff cut through the air with his four-inch claws and dissected the Kumrande on Nihilist's right. The small being fell to the ground; a look of surprise contorted his dying face.

"I will pass and take my chances with Iconoclast. I believe he would appreciate my killing all of you—as you are becoming more of a nuisance than a help."

"We shall see." Nihilist, begrudging this weak demon's victory, stepped aside. His warriors did the same. Caitiff unfurled and snapped emaciated wings to the side. He took flight. Bony trees, carbon copies of the one at the opening to the ravine, lined the path's walls. Each gave an imperceptible shake when he passed. Caitiff nodded his head side to side. He came to a burn mark in the path.

"A place of holy fire." Caitiff flapped faster. Any demon perished if he even touched such a place by accident.

He reached the bottom of the path and landed in front of the rock wall that now separated the footway from the ravine floor. He walked from one side of the boulder to the other, scouring the ravine path as he went.

He growled, then shrieked. No answer.

"Pet, you loathsome shapeshifter, come out. I have no time for your tricks! I know you escaped the return to the Abyss. I did not. But, I am back. And, your master is at the door. Come out. Iconoclast commands it."

A bush rustled, Caitiff walked to it. Nothing. Another bush rustled on the far side of the ravine. Caitiff stomped to the other side and looked. Still nothing.

He heard a mischievous laugh, this time coming from a few feet up the ravine wall. He scoured the area and caught a brief glint of lavender. A small vine trembled.

Caitiff pushed off with his strong back haunches and took flight. He pounced on the vine in one move and held it with ease as it wrestled in his grip.

"Iconoclast needs you and Gambogian needs you, too."

The vine's dull brown shade faded and a black and purple mist took the form of a one-footed being.

"Why would Gambogian need me? He's a strong demon."

"Gambogian has been weakened in an attack on that self-righteous preacher. He is recovering but not soon enough. He needs you to form the trio with Iconoclast."

"Iconoclast has been banished to the abyss."

"There is an ingress. Why else would I be here?" *And why do we put up with your ignorance?* Caitiff thought.

Purple and black pulsed as Pet considered the risks. He was not complete without his fellow demons but the abyss was a horrible fate. The hatred over defeat at the hands of those inconsequential bags of bone and dust won out in the end.

"I have missed the hunt so I will come. But I must choose a form so I am not vulnerable."

"Might you hurry this somewhat?" Caitiff loathed this little pip-squeak's need to show off at any opportunity. He hated it even more that he had no choice but to be a captive audience— if he came back without Pet, he would be shackled in the abyss at the hand of Iconoclast.

A wicked smile crossed Pet's misty features. As Caitiff watched, Pet's purple and black form condensed until it was an inch in diameter and round. His small claw popped out from the middle of the sphere. He bent it into a V and it disappeared into the other side of the ball, forming a hanger. When he was done he was a black, translucent, and miniature shape of a glass fishing ball, iridescent purple swirling in five different directions to the top claw disguised as a hook.

"Thank the trees." He wouldn't admit it, but even Caitiff was impressed by the small being's creativity. He picked up the ornate ball and flew to Old Town.

The small troop, minus Paul Lucas who chose to rest, settled at the familiar meeting place of grandma's kitchen table. Bart arrived late. He had stopped by his house and retrieved BC at Kat's request.

Wendy Hareling breezed into the kitchen. "Alright, something really odd's going on here and I think you guys know what it is."

All eyes focused on Wendy. Kat weighed the options and what truth, if any, she could tell her. Wendy could easily whip the townspeople into frenzy with just a sliver of information.

"What makes you say that—other than the fact that you are bored beyond belief and need to stir things up?"

Wendy glared at Kat. "I just ran into Brandon McGill. He was flying down the library stairs, like the place was on fire. Then," Wendy looked at Kat, then Grandma, "then I saw two trails of black, like a wild-looking fog, come up beside him. One on either side. If I was a swearing woman—and I'm not," she said to keep Grandma from launching into her tirade on swearing, "I would swear that they took the form of two men and began talking to him. He looked pretty shook up."

Kat set her coffee cup down with a thud. "And, you expect us to believe you why?"

"I would never make others think I'm a loon to get information."

Kat lifted her eyes, hooded beneath her lids, letting Wendy know she didn't believe her.

"Okay, I don't have much pride when it comes to getting a good story. But, this time, I'm telling you what I saw."

Visions of a night not so long ago swam before Josiah. A night full of murder and violence. A night that had almost taken the lives and souls of those sitting at the table and the whole of Ravens Cove.

"Tell me what these beings looked like again."

"They were mists, solid and dense—like the thickest fog I've ever seen."

"How'd you get away without being seen?"

"Pure luck? I was almost in front of the library when Brandon ran down the steps. He turned right. If he'd turned left, he'd have run smack into me. I still don't know how he missed me, though. That's the first time in my life I've felt invisible."

"Okay. Go on."

"Anyway, these mists got more and more solid. They took on the shapes of men. As the shapes grew more visible, they placed hands under Brandon's elbows and slowed him down. It was the freakiest thing I ever saw."

"The question is why you could see them. They should not have been visible to the human eye—most human eyes, anyway." Grandma pondered this.

"I know what I saw."

"I believe you." Kat remembered the lights that had mesmerized her not so long ago, and talking to an animated rock. She remembered seeing a huge, fiery blue man. She patted Wendy's hand and smiled. "Welcome to my world."

"You believe me?"

"Oh yes."

"Thank goodness." Wendy grabbed the stepstool by the stove and dragged it to the table. "That was just the icing on the cake. I was walking past Willowbend Circle earlier and I saw lights flicker from Old Town. I stopped to get a better look but the buildings were dark. I started back for Main when a weird noise brought me back to the town. Imagine my surprise when I saw these weird three-foot tall animals, walking on two legs dragging something big over to that icky skull rock. There's some kind of hole underneath that rock—did you know that?"

Bart leaned over the table and looked Wendy in the eye. "Two-legged creatures. You're sure?"

"Oh, yeah. Those ugly little things are hard to forget because they were giggling—what animal giggles? She shuddered. "It was a deadly sound."

"Wonder what they were dragging?" Bart looked at Ken.

"You know I don't scare easily."

"No—I'm the scaredycat. You're just a Nosy Nellie."

Wendy shot a sizzling look to Kat. "I'll forget you said that—for now."

"You two never change. Save the character barbs for another time, will you?"

"Is tomorrow good for you?" Kat looked at Wendy.

"I'll need to check my calendar." They burst into laughter at the same time.

"Look guys, I don't know what's happening but I'm scared to walk the streets of Ravens Cove for the first time in my life. I really don't want to go back out tonight—she looked at her watch. It was approaching two—"this morning."

"No one needs to be going anywhere right now. I have plenty of room. You girls take the sewing room upstairs. Bart and Ken can take the couch and floor in the living room. Josiah knows where he sleeps." Grandma stood up. The white band on Kat's finger caught her eye.

"Why are you wearing a paper band?"

Kat looked at her hand and her heart sunk. She had forgotten to tell Grandma before Grandma found out on her own.

"Isn't it great that she and Ken are engaged? Isn't that the craziest thing!" Wendy blurted out.

Kat's eyes opened wide, her mouth went into a straight line. "Thanks so much," she mouthed at Wendy then grabbed Grandma Bricken's hands.

"I meant to tell you earlier. Then then the pastor got ill and Wendy showed up. I am so sorry."

Grandma looked at Josiah. He smiled and shrugged. She looked at Kat.

"That is not a proper ring."

"It's the best I could do at the time."

"He proposed at Jo's. Isn't this sweet?" Wendy said hoping to help.

"Not really." Grandma got up and left the room. Kat rose to go after her. Josiah grabbed her wrist.

"Let her go, Kat. She needs a minute."

Kat sat back down and leaned into Ken for comfort.

"I, for one, think this is great news," said Wendy. "I'm going after her."

Wendy walked to the kitchen doorway just as Grandma Bricken was coming back. She had a small, grass basket in her hand. Deep red and hunt green patterns snaked through the natural grass container. Grandma set the basket in front of Ken. He gave her a questioning look.

"Open it."

Kat's heart had started to race. She wasn't sure what Grandma Bricken was doing. She was afraid it was a ritual of disownment or something.

Ken opened the small basket, looked inside, and pulled a black felt package from within. A broad smile straightened the frown of a moment before. He handed the fabric to Kat. Nested in the middle was a small gold band, with a tiny diamond glinting at her. Tears filled her eyes. She ran to her grandmother and threw her arms around her neck.

"You aren't going to disown me?"

Grandma hugged Kat close. "Why would you ever think such a thing? You are my blood. I will never disown you. Your mother ran off and your father was killed. I know you are waiting for anyone you love to do the same thing. I will never do that to you." Grandma said this as much for Ken's benefit and understanding as for Kat. She pushed Kat back so she could look her in the eye.

"Do you believe me?" Kat sniffed and nodded.

"This was my engagement ring. It was my mother's before that."

"I never knew you had it." Wendy had handed a tissue to Kat while she was in the process of blowing her own nose. She grabbed another and dried her eyes.

"There was no reason for you to know until now. Kenneth, put that ring on her finger and make this right."

Kat walked over and sat down next to the man she had fallen in love with such a short time ago.

Ken removed the paper ring and set it aside.

"I'm going to miss that on your finger."

The delicate gold ring was a perfect fit. Kat admired the ring through wet eyes and watched the tiny diamond sparkle in the kitchen light.

"It's perfect." She ran to her grandmother and threw her arms around her again. "I love you."

Grandma Bricken smiled, tears in her eyes too, and patted Kat's back. "Be happy child of my heart."

"Don't you keep a bottle of elderberry wine around here?"

"As a matter of fact I do—mostly for medicinal purposes, of course."

"Of course." The group chorused.

Grandma poured cordial glasses of wine. "To the child of my

heart and to the love of hers. May your life together be a journey blessed in times of joy and even more so in times of sadness."

"Here, here." Bart raised his glass to Kat, then Ken and drank the cordial in one gulp.

———

"To the release of Iconoclast and our fellow fighters." Atramentous raised a black chalice and sipped the thick red liquid it contained. Gambogian, Caitiff, Bruit, Trepaner, Prevaricator, Venenose and Profligacy raised their chalices.

"To the next sacrifice that will bring our number to completion. Complete before and complete again." Gambogian threw back his opaque neck and tossed the blood down.

In unison they raised their cups and chanted. "To the end of our confinement. To the release of Iconoclast. To the taking of Ravens Cove."

Chapter 12
A Piece of Heaven and a Taste of Hell

By the time the small troop were up and dressed, the smells from the kitchen were irresistible. A plate of reindeer sausage and a plate of eggs sat in the middle of the table. Sourdough toast and orange juice completed a meal fit for royalty.

The group gathered at the table. "Thank you God. Your provision is always abundant. Bless this food and let it nourish our bodies as Your word nourishes our souls. In Jesus' name. Amen."

They laid out a plan over breakfast. Bart and Ken would drop Kat at the office on their way to Old Town. Wendy, Grandma and Josiah would return to Mrs. Tellamoot's. Phone calls were to be at intervals of every thirty minutes.

An icy Inlet wind greeted them as they left the warm house. Heavy laden clouds promised snow before day's end.

After watching Kat go through the police station door, Bart and Ken headed to Old Town. The dark fog had lifted but the place was disconcertingly silent.

"We don't have many birds in the winter but we still have chickadees and nuthatches. They are usually flitting around somewhere." Bart's stomach grew uneasy.

"Let's get this done and get out of here as soon as we can."

Ken looked at the structures. "I can't shake the feeling that we're being watched."

"Me either." They moved toward the skull rock and examined the stone.

Ken gave it a push. It didn't budge. Bart joined him and they both pushed. It still didn't budge.

"I'll get a crowbar." Bart moved away from the stone and walked toward the old cannery.

"Wrong way …" Ken caught sight of a large mound in front of the cannery and straight-lined it to the building.

The sight would have made stronger men retch. A bag of mush lay under thousands of wriggling larvae. Bart breathed an angry sigh then took his phone from his pocket.

Doc Billings pulled up, looking as tired as Bart felt. The concern lined his face as he grabbed his black bag and came around the Audi.

He viewed the body, not even bothering to bend over.

"I want to know how these bodies are ending up here and in such a state of decomp. Someone should have been missed before this." He scratched his head, put on his gloves and went to work.

"Speak to me." Bart said into his phone. His eyes stayed on Doc Billings and the corpse.

"Anchorage M.E. called about the first and actually the second bodies. You got the case numbers?"

"Doc Billings called me with them earlier."

"Also got a call from Jack Calphor at the troopers."

"What'd Jack say?"

"The excavator arm might have been tampered with."

"Might have been?"

"Says his findings aren't conclusive."

"Why?"

"It's a clean break. There were no tale-tail marks that would indicate sabotage."

"Then the metal must have been defective."

"He tested it. The integrity of the metal was not comprised—his wording not mine."

"That all he said?"

"Yes. Except he'd send the official report tomorrow."

"Thanks." Bart disconnected, went through the list of speed dial numbers and punched the one labeled A.M.E. Bart identified himself and rattled a string of numbers into the phone. His brow furrowed as he listened to the report.

"Thanks." He hung up and looked at Ken.

"Same signs as the last murders—sulfur and some weird herbal mixture not from Alaska. But this time, and it was confirmed, the heart was literally ripped from the chest—the M.E.'s words—and the throat had been ripped open too. All the signs of an animal killing, except they'd never seen a predator in Alaska leave that kind of mark. They got a call in to an expert on animal attacks. They'll get back to us."

"Like small, weird Kumrande teeth, maybe?"

"I didn't feel the urge to tell the M.E. about the battle for our lives with creatures that don't exist. How about you?"

"Oh, no. I've lost enough credibility." Ken thought back to one of his last conversation with his chief.

"You should talk to someone about those hallucinations," Chief Andy Binning said. And, this wasn't the first time Binning had urged Ken to see a shrink. To make matters worse, he'd been labeled "Fox" by his peers, and asked on one occasion if they should open an X –Files division in Anchorage.

"Let's take a look at the cannery. Seems that one is our new crime scene." Bart stopped at the outlines where the bodies of Gary and Johnny Campo, now confirmed, had lain. The body of the newest victim had just been removed. "There's a pattern, I just can't quite put it together."

"Me either." Ken looked at the three white outlines. Each outline pointed to a building. They sat equidistant from each other all with the heads pointed to the doors of the buildings.

"You know what else? There has been a murder a night. I don't like that pattern either." Bart thought back to October and the deaths that had occurred each night then, too. Grandma had said there would be five deaths and then Ravens Cove would fall to the darkness. Bad enough he wanted and needed to stop the killings. Now he realized the town was on a high speed collision course with destruction and he didn't know how to stop it. A sense of urgency made Bart restless.

"We got to move, Ken. And we got to move now." We're out of time." They disappeared inside the cannery.

Wendy dropped Grandma Bricken and Josiah at Mrs. Tellamoot's.

"I'll be back to get you in an hour." Wendy was not inclined to listen in on the crazy legends. She had shaken herself earlier this morning, as light approached, and decided her imagination had been running wild. The others still had craziness going on and she needed to get away to keep her head clear.

Grandma waved as Wendy drove off. She turned and knocked.

"Didn't expect to see you so soon, Alese."

"We have a list of the victims. I don't recognize any of the names, thought you could give us some insight."

Mrs. Tellamoot retrieved her reading glasses and motioned them to a small three-seat table.

"Most of these names are still used in the clan." Something is missing, though." She removed her glasses and looked at Alese Bricken. "The names of the white settlers are missing. And, some of the Native names, too."

"How do you know that?"

"My mother believed in memorizing the legends and tales of our people. Said memory couldn't be burned up in a fire. I'm a little old now so I've lost the names. But I remember the count. It was fifty-one. There are only forty-five names here. There were two pages—you only have one."

"That's all Kat found at the library archives."

"Then it's been misplaced. Give me a minute to think." She stood up and walked into the tiny, dark kitchen. She gazed out the window into the healthy, green spruce that gave the small area color, but also blocked the light of the winter's day.

"Two of the names of the white settlers are easy to remember—Oliver Podratshrell was one of the white settlers. Marta, adopted into our clan as a young girl, became Oliver Podratshrell's wife."

Grandma Bricken wrote the names in a small notebook she had brought with her. A car horn announced Wendy had returned as promised. Thanks, Bernice."

Bernice handed her the list of names. "You need to find that other piece of paper."

"I'll let Bart know. If anyone can locate it, he will."

———

Kat had just finished the initial report when the brass bell clanged to announce Wendy's arrival.

"Grandma and the old guy are back at her house."

"His name is Josiah."

"Whatever. Time for a break?"

"Well, I really wanted to see that dog at Doctor Douglas' office."

223

"I'm always game for a trip to the vet—particularly that vet."
Wendy had had a crush on Douglas for years.

"I should let him know how you feel."

"You should keep your mouth closed."

"Wendy loves Carl, Wendy loves Carl." Kat sang in a childish melody.

"I don't anything of the sort. I just think he's attractive …
And smart, and funny."

"That's the closest thing to love I've ever heard come out of
your mouth."

"Just because you're in love doesn't mean the whole world is.
Good grief, Kat," Wendy said in disgust and headed out the door.

Kat flipped over the "back in an hour" sign that also had
Bart's cell number on it for emergencies, and locked the door.
A few flakes floated to the sidewalk. "Looks like the snow the
weather guy promised has arrived."

"Woopee."

Nyna was at the front counter when they arrived.

"Hey, haven't seen you in eons," she said to Wendy.

"Let's get a drink sometime. And, let's get this one to come,
too." Wendy pointed her thumb in Kat's direction.

Kat never enjoyed girls' night out. She had not ever enjoyed
what Wendy called "Sharking." When Wendy went out it was
to find a friend for the evening—of the male persuasion.

"Better not count on me."

"Yes. She's spoken for now."

Nyna looked at Kat's left finger and saw the gold ring. "Congratulations. Who is the lucky man?"

"That FBI guy."

"Good for you, Kat. Invite me to the wedding. I want to
catch the bouquet."

"You're already invited."

Nyna's eyes sparkled. "Have a date yet."

"Not yet."

"You came about that animal, huh?"

"How's he doing?"

"I better let Carl tell you." Nyna disappeared behind the back office door.

"I wasn't expecting you today." Carl Douglas walked through the swinging door and grabbed Kat's hand. "I definitely wasn't expecting you today, Ms. Hareling. You've made a good day even better." He gave Wendy a warm smile.

Carl likes Wendy, Carl likes Wendy, Kat sang in her head. *Sure seems to be a lot of that love thing in the air or maybe I have a heightened awareness.*

"That canine is going to make it. And, more amazingly, that animal has been nothing but gentle since he started to heal and come around. Want to take a look?"

Kat nodded and followed him to the kennels in back.

The white wolf stood up and focused gold eyes on the newcomers. His ears went back and his tail started to go from side to side in rapid motion.

"He's as cute as any puppy I've ever seen." Kat walked over and offered her hand. He sniffed and pawed at the kennel door.

"You okay with a little one on one?"

"You bet."

Douglas flipped the latch. The canine bounded out and put both paws squarely on Wendy. She gave him a gentle push on the chest. "Down, big guy."

He trotted to Kat next, sat on his muscular haunches, and looked into her eyes. She smiled, bent down and scratched his head. "He's amazing. How old?"

"A year and a half, if that."

"Got a home for him?"

Carl Douglas laughed. "Twenty-four hours ago I thought he was a goner. Placing him was the farthest thing from my mind."

"What do you think about Mrs. Tellamoot?"

"I like the idea but don't get your hopes up. I tried to put an abandoned lab with her and she'd have no part of it. Told me there was no dog this side of heaven could replace old Benny."

"She hasn't seen this one. Is he strong enough to travel?"

He smiled when he realized where Kat was going with this. "Most times, I'd say no. But this guy is an exception. I think that could be arranged."

Kat looked at Wendy. "Will you take me and this one for a ride?" Kat knew the last thing Wendy wanted in her pristine vehicle was a wolf. *Banking on your need to look good to Douglas. Don't let me down, Winsome.*

"Of course." Wendy's voice could have put most people into a sugar coma. "Let's go."

Douglas grabbed a lead and collar. "Bring him back in a couple of hours."

Kat laughed when the white dog started prancing and pulling on the leash. "Obviously knows walks."WC, as she had dubbed him, yanked her forward and out the door.

"You're as manipulator."

"If need be."

WC waited for Kat to open the passenger door. She motioned to the back. "There's not enough room for both of us in that bucket seat. She flipped her seat forward. WC jumped in and moved to the middle of the backseat.

"Please make yourself at home." Wendy shook her head and got behind the wheel. "Mrs. Tellamoot's it is."

They pulled up in front of the small cabin. Kat yanked the front seat forward and WC flew out before she could grab the lead. "Hey. Stop." She pursued him to the edge of the woods. She was dumbfounded when he veered and turned back. He galloped to the front door, sat down and whimpered. He pawed at the front door and whimpered again.

"Benny?" Mrs. Tellamoot knew it wasn't Benny but couldn't help herself. She opened the door. WC stood on his hind legs, slapped a paw on her either shoulder and licked Bernice's face.

Kat ran to the porch and caught hold of the lead. "Down. So sorry, Mrs. Tellamoot."

WC dropped obediently to the ground but never took his eyes off Mrs. Tellamoot. His lips parted in what Kat swore was a grin.

Mrs. Tellamoot's eyes filled with tears. They made glistening tracks down her cheeks as she looked at the amber-eyed creature before her.

"You've come back." She bent down and threw her arms around the white dog and buried her head in the thick fur of his neck.

Wendy whispered in Kat's ear, "think we should let them have some time alone."

Kat doubled her fist and hammered Wendy's arm. "Stop it."

Mrs. Tellamoot looked up at Kat. "How did you know?"

"I didn't. Just thought you must be lonely without Benny and this poor guy's an orphan."

"I'll take him." Bernice caught hold of the leash. Kat held on. "Doctor Douglas made me promise to bring him back to the clinic. He's been very ill—they almost lost him."

"Pshaw. This dog needs love, not a stinky old hospital. Come in." She dropped the lead and so did Kat. The dog followed them in, walked to the rug in front of the stone fireplace, circled twice and lay down in a ball. His eyes never left Mrs. Tellamoot. She motioned Kat into the kitchen and handed her the phone.

"How is that dog acting?"

"Content. He won't take his eyes off her."

"Tell Mrs. Tellamoot to keep him tonight. I'll bring some food out on my way home. She's agreed I can come see him tomorrow early before I go into the office. If he's still doing well, he can stay and she can finish his nursing."

"Great."

Kat hung up and turned to Bernice. "He stays here."

Mrs. Tellamoot threw her arms around Kat's neck. "I can never repay you this miracle. My home is always yours—and Alese's." She turned and smiled at Wendy, "and also yours."

Wendy's brow wrinkled. "Thanks?"

"Did you know I went to school with your momma?"

"No. Mom never talked about you."

Sadness clouded Bernice's eyes. "How silly of me. Of course, she wouldn't have. Long before you came into this world, she was my best friend. Then we had a stupid fight about … something I don't remember. I always thought we'd make it right someday. She passed before that someday came."

"You weren't at the funeral."

"I grieved and honored her here." Bernice placed her hand over her heart. "I still do."

Tears sprang into Wendy's eyes before she could control them. "No one speaks of my mother anymore."

"There are not many of our clan around anymore. But I am here and your mother is still in my heart." Mrs. Tellamoot touched Wendy's cheek. "You look like her."

Wendy took Mrs. Tellamoot's hand and smiled. "I will honor your words in my heart."

"Come tomorrow for lunch, then. I will tell you stories that will make you laugh and cry. We can make it a tradition."

"I think I'd like that. Tomorrow it is."

Kat was surprised by the relief and gratitude that flooded her. Wendy had grown so hard after her mother's death. Kat couldn't remember the last time Wendy had cried. Her gratitude both humbled her and softened her heart toward the God that allowed her to watch Him heal her friend's soul.

———

Mayor Orthell arrived at Old Town just as Bart and Ken were coming out of it.

"What is happening, sheriff?"

"I'd say we have a serial killer on our hands, mayor." Bart wasn't going into what he and Ken knew to be true. He was sure it was all the proof the mayor would need to get him thrown out of his job.

"Mayor, you don't look so good."

"I don't feel so good."

"If you know something about this, now's as good a time as any to come clean."

"Not now. Meet me tonight around ten at my house. I have something to show you."

The mayor hurried through the courtyard and into the log cabin.

"Tonight at ten it is."

"The man's involved. You know that."

"Yeah, but I don't know how he's involved. I've known Tommy for a long time. He's a flake, he's a politician and he is a real pain in my backside, but he's not a murderer."

"Accomplice, then."

"I guess, just makes no sense."

"Since you seem dead-set against taking the mayor in for

questioning, I think we should get to the ravine before the snow makes it impossible to find that path.

"You guys seem to be very serious here." Brandon McGill had appeared out of, it seemed, thin air. Bart wondered how long he'd been listening. Ken turned and felt an overwhelming urge to grab the man and beat him.

"We're here on police business. How about you?"

"I'm the librarian and, due to circumstances beyond my control, a little shorthanded." He focused on the yellow tape and body outlines in front of three buildings. "I was planning on taking some pictures of Old Town for the archives. But this was not quite the look I was hoping for."

"It should be back to normal soon. How about I call you?"

Brandon continued to stare at the outlines.

"Is there something else?"

Brandon raised raisin black eyes to Ken. Hatred crossed the blackness before Brandon got it in check. "Just wondering if I could stick around. This should be added to the archives."

"How about you don't and say you did. This is a crime scene, not some lurid story for posterity. I would expect that from the news guys, not a librarian." Bart turned and faced McGill, planted his feet and put his hand over the flashlight.

"I think you're wrong and this should be documented. It's important to remind our citizens that a small town doesn't always equal a safe town. Call me when I can take those pictures." He turned and walked toward Main.

"Another satisfied customer," Bart said.

Angry blue-grey clouds had replaced the soft gray ones of the morning, threatening to turn the lightly falling snow into a blizzard. As if to confirm it, the wind picked up and the snow flew sideways.

"If we're going to get to the ravine, now's the time," Ken said.

"Need to run by the office for a rope and some supplies."

The police station was as warm inside as the day had turned cold without. Kat's voice added to the sheltered feeling of the place. "You're welcome. Let me know how Benny's doing." She hung up. "Hi."

"Benny's dead. Or has he come back, too?"

"Nothing so dramatic. Mrs. Tellamoot thinks that the white dog is Benny reincarnated. Who am I to argue? So, she calls it Benny." Kat shrugged.

Bart let out a tired sigh. "You shouldn't encourage this, Kat. That dog could still be dangerous. How did she end up with him, anyway?" He held up both hands. "Wait, you don't have to answer that. All this supernatural gobbledygook is making me psychic, I'm sure. You took that beast out there, didn't you? How'd you get Doc to agree?"

"I walked in and saw it. That is the gentlest animal I've ever seen. Doc agrees. He thinks the infection and lack of food and water made him aggressive."

"Then you and Douglas are both insane."

Kat glared up at Bart. "And you're a big jerk." She turned back to the typing, tired of her cousin's cynicism.

Ken walked through the door at the end of the conversation. The tension still hung in the air like a dirty fog. Kat's eyes shot up. She just glared at Ken.

"Should I walk out and come back in again?" He turned toward the door. Kat relaxed.

"No, just having a disagreement with my dear cousin here about animal behavior."

"That white dog?"

"Yep." Bart was behind Kat and he rolled his eyes upward in a frustrated motion.

"Well, tell me about that later, since that snow is getting heavier by the minute and we need to get to the ravine before there's no more daylight."

"You going to the ravine? Not without me." Kat jumped up and grabbed her coat.

"Thanks a lot," Bart mouthed from behind Kat.

Bart grabbed the rope. Kat was already sitting in the center of the bench seat in the truck by the time he got in.

"We need to make a stop before we go to the ravine. Seems Kal didn't show up last night for his shift at the Watering Hole. His girlfriend's saying she hadn't seen him since around five. He'd said something to her about the Kumrande and stopping by the Old Town before he went to work."

"Looks like the ravine trip is off."

"Just delayed." Bart looked at the snow. "We got to get there today. The deeper this snow gets, the harder it's going to be to find that path."

"Maybe we should go get Josiah. He knows where the path is."

"I really don't want to bring any more of us out than have to come out tonight."

"No, you're just a stubborn jerk and want to find it by yourself—heaven forbid you'd ask anyone for directions."

"She's right, you know."

Bart shot Ken a scathing look.

"Not about the jerk part, but the need for directions part."

"Fine, let's go get the old guy right after the bar trip."

The Open sign was unlit. Bart tried the door.

"Barbara Manchester said she'd meet me here." Concern laced his voice.

He doubled his fist and banged on the metal door frame. Barbara answered and let Bart, Ken, and Kat in. The smell of cigarettes and old beer accosted Kat's nose. It wrinkled involuntarily in response.

The bar owner pointed to a petite, blonde-haired woman at the bar.

"That's Kal's girlfriend. She showed up a couple of hours ago. After we talked, I thought we'd better let you know."

Bart walked to the blonde. "Kimberly, isn't it?" She nodded. It was obvious from the red eyes she'd been crying for quite a while. She picked up a napkin and blotted her nose.

"I won't keep you long. Did you and Kal have a fight?"

"No. He kissed me goodbye and said he was heading here after Old Town. I told him not to go there!" She broke into fresh sobs.

Bart willed himself to be calm and compassionate. "The only other question I have is what was Kal wearing the last time you saw him?"

"His norm—plain black T-shirt and blue jeans. He kept a clean work shirt here at the bar." Kenneth joined Bart, leaving Kat and Barbara chatting by the door.

"Alright, Kimberly. That's all for now." Bart motioned Barbara over. "She's in no shape to be by herself. The girl broke into uncontrollable sobs over the one question I asked."

"I'll keep her here with me. Let me know if you find him."

"That's what the corpse had on," Ken said, once they were out of earshot.

"Yep. I think we just identified our John Doe." Sadness and defeat laced Bart's words.

"We'll stop this." Kat responded as if she could hear his thoughts. "I promise, Bart. We'll stop this."

"Too late for some."

"Yes, it is. But, you can't muddle in it or we will lose. Come

on, focus on the here and now so we can end this before someone else dies."

Bart straightened. "What do we know about Kal and his in-
volvement here?"

"I met him last night. He was a wealth of information on
those weird creatures that attacked us. He said he'd seen their
shadows. Can't believe he was foolish enough to go back."

"I do." Bart flipped his notebook open and wrote Kal's name
next to John Doe, then flipped it shut.

They drove in silence to Grandma Bricken's. Kat had called
ahead to make sure Josiah was willing to go to the ravine. He
was standing on the porch, bundled in the old coat and boots
Kat had first seen him in.

"We got to do something about that outfit." She smiled at him.
"You look like an escapee from the second-hand store's trash bin."

"If we get through this siege, I'll take you with me to get a new
one. Gentlemen—and lady—time is much shorter than I thought."

"Why would you say that?" Ken asked. Josiah had not been
privy to any of the most recent occurrences at Old Town.

"Let's just say a little birdie told me, rather showed me, some
not-too-pleasant visions. Iconoclast's army is assembling." He
looked at Bart and Ken, "but you knew that already didn't you?"

"What aren't you guys telling us?" Kat pulled forward on
the bench seat from the tiny back well of the truck. She had
been chosen for this honored position, as she was the shortest
of the group.

"We don't know anything for sure. Just have a lot of similari-
ties between this case and the murders last fall," Bart said.

"It is a certainty."

"What other explanation is there, Bart? Have you found an
explanation for the Kumrande, too?"

Bart and Ken sat silent, both knowing they had no explanation for the small, nasty creatures.

"Does Grandma know?"

"Indeed. She knows we only have a few hours."

They had arrived at the ravine. The snow wasn't letting up. The increasing wind sent stinging flakes onto any exposed skin. They stopped and walked past the ravine path. The hag tree guard caught Kat's attention. She walked to it and touched it. It shivered.

"Bart ... Ken ..."

"What?"

"That thing moved."

"It's windy. Of course it moved."

"It shivered."

Ken walked up to Kat and looked at the tree. He reached a hand out and gave it a slight flick with his finger. It shivered again. By this time the small group surrounded the tree to scrutinize it more closely.

"That is a very bad omen, as it were." Josiah remarked. "If it is showing signs of unnatural life, it has been awoken by someone or something." Josiah leaned over and stared at the old path.

"There are tiny footprints, numerous footprints." He walked toward the path. Ken grabbed his arm.

"Not a good idea. If those are what we think they are, you are walking into certain death."

"It is still light. I can hurry. I am drawn but do not know why."

"Then we all go—except you, KittyKat. You go to the truck."

"I don't think so, FBI. I'm not going to be a sitting duck. You guys are stuck with me."

"Light's fading. We go now or not at all." Bart urged.

They took the path in pairs, holding onto the scrub and alders lining the trail. A few feet in they stopped. A small, ugly skeleton lay at their feet. It had been slashed in two.

"Blood's still evident. Something sure picked this thing clean."

"Look at the feet."

"I know those feet. What killed it?"

"*What* is the correct term. If that is a Kumrande, it wasn't killed by a man. Only a demon can destroy them—and God's angels."

"I'm hoping for the latter."

They stepped over the small lower half of the being and continued to the end of the path. The rock stood as strong as ever. They scoured the floor.

"This is a waste of time."

"Not so much." Josiah walked to the left wall beside the boulder and touched it. A purple and black liquid dripped from the rock.

"Look familiar?"

"Unfortunately, it does." The smell of sulfur and decay was still in the air, faint though it was.

"But why here and what does it mean?"

"Don't know. But I do know it is Iconoclast's mark."

Kat walked up and looked at the purple and black, tinged in an ochre yellow. "That's the mark of Pet. I thought that thing had died!" Fear gripped her and she wished she'd stayed at Grandma's. She cursed her need to be a part of things and not just let them lie. They were all staring at her, waiting for an explanation.

"I know those colors. I was entranced by them, remember? I know that thing's smell. Can't you feel the evil? It's odd that evil has its own feeling, isn't it? That sensation is the one I had when I was deceived by that horrid little rock and that smell is its smell."

"Let's assume you are right. Then where is it?"

"It's not here anymore. I know it. I think it was in the ravine all the time. It must have gotten on this side of the doorway."

"It hid in plain sight." Bart said. Everyone's eyes turned to him.

"My grandma told my mom about these demons that specialize in shapeshifting. It was easy to trick people into hell." He felt foolish. He shrugged. "Just saying."

"This is very dangerous. If Pet has returned to Iconoclast, well, their power will be complete."

They climbed back up the ravine path, turned right and skirted the large chasm that opened onto the ravine floor.

It was getting dark as they approached a tiny, almost invisible path. "I'll go first." Bart tied the rope off to an alder branch that looked like it would hold. Ken held the rope just in case.

Ten minutes later he heard, "All clear."

Ken sent Kat down, then Josiah. He checked the woods around the path. The Kumrande were here once, who was to say they'd left. Satisfied he was alone, he started down the rope.

"This one can die now." Nihilist came out of his hiding place, unsheathed his razor claw and sawed the rope. Ken was fifteen feet above the ravine when he felt the rope give.

He grabbed at bushes and small plants, hoping for anything to break his fall.

Kat had been watching for him to come down and screamed when she saw him tumbling toward the ravine floor.

"God help him," Josiah said.

Ken hit an outcropping of rock and bounced to the left. He grabbed a tree, much larger than all the rest. This one held. He managed to snag a branch with his right hand.

"Let go." Kat yelled. He did and dropped to the ravine floor. His legs buckled and he fell to the ground.

"That was close."

"What happened?"

"The rope was fine one minute and went slack the next. I guess it must have rubbed on something enough to make a weak spot and break."

Bart yanked the rope down from above. "This rope has been cut." He held it out to Ken.

"I double checked the woods before I came down. I was alone."

"You're alright. That's what matters." Kat squeezed Ken's hand.

"Anyone know where that tree came from? Crazy as it seems, I would swear it reached for me before I ever saw it. And, then I thought for a moment that it wrapped its branch around my hand, not the other way around."

"Trauma does play tricks on the mind."

"More likely, God answers prayer." Josiah said with a big smile.

"It's out and out hot down here." Kat unzipped her coat. "It must be a good sixty degrees warmer." The smell of fresh air tickled Kat's nose. She could not find a source or a breeze. It was as if she'd walked into different world.

"I think it is a taste of heaven." Josiah remarked.

"Where's the light coming from?" They looked around and could see no reason for the ravine floor to be glowing, but it was. They could see as clearly as if it were day.

They walked to the gurgling stream and a small bush full of ripe red berries. The rest of the ravine was green.

"I don't understand it but sure enough, you could have lived here. There's no wind, there's not even any snow getting in here. It's melting before it reaches the bottom."

Josiah walked to the wall he had slept near for those months.

"There is something new. It was not here before." He pointed at an etching. "It's a directive."

"Find the *Book of Fallen Angels.*"

"I wonder if someone wants us to find that book Mrs. Tellamoot talked about." Kat said, humor her best defense when confused.

"Seems so." Next to it were written the words *Podratshrell* and *Orthell.*

"*Podratshrell* was one of the names on the ledger from the Forgotten Place. *Orthell* wasn't mentioned at all."

Josiah knelt down and started writing in the loose dirt. He played with various ways the letters could go together.

Ken walked over and crouched down beside Josiah. "What if we do this?"

They all watched as he erased the *p, d, a, s* and *r.*

"That spells Orthell," Kat whispered.

"His family must have changed its name. That name Podratshrell had a large "S" next to it with a symbol that Mrs. Tellamoot says means one that has caused great harm.

"I knew I should have questioned him when I had the chance. We had better get back to town. I need to find that man and find out what he's done. By the way, you're off the hook, Josiah. You are no longer my prime suspect."

Good to know, Agent Melbourne."

Brandon McGill came out of the forest right after Ken and Bart left Old Town. He headed into Old Town and directly to the outlines.

"Amazing. In a horrible sort of way." He snapped a picture then walked to the log cabin.

Brandon located the mayor. He was kneeling in front of a dark wood stool, a deep red candle set in the center.

"What are you doing?"

"You must leave. You are in danger." He hurried over and began yanking on Brandon's arm. Brandon jerked his arm free.

"Danger from what, mayor? Do you know who is committing these murders? You do, don't you?"

"It is my fault. You must leave now. There will be another murder soon. I can do nothing to stop it now."

"I thought you were a more rational man." Brandon moved toward the small table and extinguished the still burning candle.

"No, no. As long as it is lit, there is safety."

"I don't want safety." Brandon turned to Orthell, a sneer of pure evil on his face. His black eyes had gone even blacker. His face contorted until Brandon's features were present but they looked like a see-through mask. Underneath the mask flesh and black swirled. Mayor Orthell backed toward the door, holding up his hands and shaking his head.

"Where is the book?"

"I don't know what you are talking about."

"Where is the book of my ancestors; my brothers." The voice was actually two voices. Brandon's was present but a lower, deeper one joined it. He walked toward the mayor. His voice changed again. This one the mayor knew.

"Do as I say and all will be well." It was the voice that had called him with instructions on the Old Town and the one that had sent money to fund the project.

"You? You are the benefactor of Old Town?"

"You did well, Tommy. You built it all to my specifications. I am pleased. The quartz in the courtyard, the arrangement of the buildings, the precious skull. All as I instructed. I am pleased. And, now your task is complete."

The wall behind the small table began to glow. Tommy Orthell's eyes widened as the glow grew brighter and became a large, round circle of neon gold, rimmed in lava-red. He saw two beings materialize outside of the light.

"Oh no." He turned and ran for the stairs. Brandon grabbed him and threw him to Venenose and Bruit. "Here's the sixth victim."

"Sixth! We only know of four."

"You are fools! Do you not know your commander when you see him?"

Brandon McGill's image melted away and Iconoclast stood glaring at his captains.

"How, O great one? This was unknown to us."

"How else? He came to me. He begged for revenge. I gave him his wish and, so, he had to give himself to me." The dagger teeth showed through the stretched black lips. "They never realize that they are signing their own death warrants. It is good these beings never learn."

By this time the mayor was screaming nonstop.

"Silence that thing." Venenose grabbed Mayor Orthell's neck and twisted. It cracked. The Mayor went silent. Iconoclast went over and ate his fill of the last of the terror and the brain that so empowered him.

"Now throw it out so the Kumrande can have their fill."

"Where are the others?"

"They came through the portals from the other buildings and await your instructions."

"Where's Pet?"

"He's with Gambogian and Caitiff."

"Bring him to me."

Venenose bowed and went back through the portal. He appeared a short time later with the small, iridescent ball. It began to pulse and hum.

Venenose placed Pet in Iconoclast's hand. The clawed fingers curled around the ball.

241

"What about the others? They have not had the portal opened yet."

"We will need another victim before our dwellings are complete and the last portal is opened. It is time to introduce the citizens of Ravens Cove to their new home—and new masters."

He opened his hand, "Soon, Pet, soon."

Bart dropped Kat and Josiah back at Grandma's before he and Ken made their way down Main to the mayor's house.

"He isn't home yet," A worried Mrs. Orthell told the sheriff. "I expected him hours ago."

"Did he say where he was going?"

"Just Old Town and then home for dinner."

"Maybe he had an appointment he forgot to mention. Did you look at his calendar?"

"No. He doesn't like anyone to snoop. Now I wish I had."

"Can we take a look around his study?"

"Oh, I don't know. He gets so mad."

"I'll take full responsibility."

Mrs. Orthell nodded. "But please hurry."

Bart located the calendar, rounded the desk and sat in one of the guest chairs. He flipped through the schedule. "Nothing here." He placed it on the edge of the desk. It fell and a loose piece of paper floated to the floor.

"Looks like we found the second page of that list." Bart scanned it. "Look at this." He pointed to two of the names.

"Conner and McGill. They were part of the village. And they were related."

"Why would the mayor want to hide those names?"

"Don't know. Think we have a few questions for Mr. McGill, too."

Bart checked his watch. "Library's closed. I know where he lives, though."

"Just love a small town." An insincere tone laced Ken's words.

A worried Maureen Orthell stood outside the study. "Well?"

"Doesn't look like he had any late appointments. We'll go check out a few places and get back with you."

They arrived at Brandon's. The lights were on. Bart knocked. He tried the doorknob. It opened.

Ken looked at Bart.

"Wellness check." Bart answered and walked in.

The entry was immaculate, gleaming wood floors led past a long narrow staircase to the upper floor and a hallway broke off to the side and led to the kitchen.

"Nice digs."

"This is Anita Conner's old house. Explains how McGill came to get it so soon after he got to Ravens Cove. Must have been in the family."

They went to the kitchen. The sink held two dishes. A cold coffeepot sat by the stove.

"McGill, you here?" Bart yelled up to the second floor.

They went to the basement.

"This does not bode well."

"You are the master of understatement."

Ken walked forward into the room. There had been a violent struggle. Several books were thrown around the area. A small kettle sat on a cold, electric burner. In the middle of the floor, surrounded by a granular substance, was a five-pointed star.

"That's what the body formation was mimicking." Bart pointed to the star.

"You're right. But what does one have to do with the other?"

"This one's probably a leftover from Anita."

"It looks fresher than that. There's no dust near it or in the star for that matter."

243

"I'm calling Lucas. He knows about this stuff." Bart dialed, talked for a minute, then hung up.

"He's coming right over."

They continued to investigate. There were various odd-looking candles, half burnt sitting around the room.

"Found something." Right outside the circle and in the shadows of the far wall was a small puddle of blood and a button.

"I've got my stuff in the truck. I'll be right back." Bart darted up the stairs.

Ken opened the small kettle and looked inside. A brown, thick liquid had coagulated on the bottom.

Two sets of footsteps came back down the basement stairs. Paul Lucas held out his hand to Ken.

"Congratulations again." Ken gave him a smile, having forgotten the joy he had been feeling only a few short hours ago.

Paul spotted the star. His demeanor went all business and very serious. "I pray the blood of Jesus over this house and us. That's a protection Pentagram. Whoever made it, believed they needed protection from something that was here or coming here. Did you find any evidence of sacrifice?"

"There's some weird substance in that pot." Ken took a vial from Bart's forensic kit that was filled with a clear liquid. He dipped the swab in the congealed liquid and put it in the tube. It turned purple. "There's human blood present."

Bart had been retrieving the button and was sampling the blood on the floor. He stood up and walked to Ken and looked at the lavender color on the swab.

"That's a big yes," Bart said.

Paul looked around and to the books on the floor. "These are books of spells and incantations." One lay undisturbed to the far left of the pot.

"This one is open to a spell that is meant to call in a demon. How is it that people so easily turn to the protection of a thing they know is evil and yet they rebuke the living, true God? Can you tell me that?"

Bart laid a hand on Paul's shoulder. "I don't know. I wish I knew what made people do what they do to each other." He patted Paul's shoulder.

"I don't know who this blood belongs to, but if it is Brandon's, then we are looking for another corpse."

"Didn't Wendy see him with some odd figures last night?"

"So she said. She is the drama queen, so I wasn't taking her too seriously."

"Maybe we should now."

"Maybe."

"Let's get back to the mayor's and see if he's shown up yet."

Chapter 13
Doomsday Comes to the Cove

Mrs. Orthell greeted them. The hope left her eyes when Bart said they had not seen the mayor.

"Tommy said if he wasn't home by ten, to make sure I gave you this." She stuck out her hand. Bart took an envelope, opened it and began to read in silence.

We have had our differences, sheriff, but I've always believed you put the welfare of Ravens Cove and its citizens above anything else. I respect you because of that.

If you are reading this, then I did not make our appointment. I am more than likely dead and I want to explain what is happening. I did not commit the murders but I made a way for that to happen. I blamed you and the others so close to you for the downfall of the Congregational Alliance and wanted vengeance. That vengeance has now turned on me. I do not know how to stop what I have started. Ask my wife to open the wall safe and hand you the book that is in it. It may help you. God speed and I pray for His forgiveness. And yours.

Bart handed the letter to Ken.

"Your husband asked that you open the wall safe. That note says there is a book in it and he wants me to have it." Maureen stared at Bart, confused.

Bart did not want Mrs. Orthell to read or hear the part that her husband thought he was dead. But he knew she wasn't going to let them into the safe unless she was sure it was directed by Tommy himself. Bart handed her the handwritten letter. She read the note, handed it back to Bart and walked to the picture behind Orthell's desk. It opened and revealed a small safe. She deftly turned the combination lock, removed the book from the safe and handed it to Bart.

"*The Book of Fallen Angels,*" he read aloud. "Thank you. I don't know where Tommy is, but I'll find him."

"Let's go to the last place we saw him." They headed toward Old Town.

Ken dialed. Bart gave him a questioning look.

"Told Kat I'd meet her at Grandma's. Looks like we'll be late."

"Hello," Grandma answered.

"She's right here. Hold on."

"Going to be late. Mayor Orthell hasn't been home."

"Paul and Tanya stopped by. Paul told me about Brandon's house."

"Yeah. We're looking for Brandon, too."

"I don't think you should go to Old Town. Not from what Josiah and Grandma are saying."

"What are they saying?"

"Well, Josiah's saying something about openings to the other world and Iconoclast. Grandma is saying that the town has been set up to attract something like that."

"We'll be fine. See you in a bit."

"Hey, Kat." He caught her before she hung up.

"Yeah."

"Does your grandmother have any information on the *Book of Fallen Angels?*"

"Don't know. Let me check." She returned a moment later.

"Bernice Tellamoot talked about that with the legend she was discussing with us. Grandma's clan was not aware of that book. Mrs. Tellamoot was. You want me to call her?"

"Would you? And ask her what she knows about how this book plays into these recent disappearances and Old Town."

Kat returned to the table. "Bart and Ken are on their way to Old Town."

"That is not a good idea. Didn't you tell them?"

"I did. But, the mayor and Brandon McGill have gone missing and that's where they think the mayor is."

The phone rang again.

"Oh, I hope they changed their minds." Grandma bustled off to the hall.

"Oh, I'm sorry to hear that. Uh huh. I'll get Kat." She went to the kitchen.

"Mrs. Tellamoot is on the phone. She says Benny's missing. She tried Wendy and Doc Douglas and didn't know who else to call."

"What next?"

"Kat, he's still not feeling good. He took off like a shot toward town. Can you see if you can find him?"

"I don't have a car."

"I do." Paul said from the doorway.

"Pastor Lucas says he'll drive me around. I'll go looking and call you as soon as I know anything."

"Please hurry." Mrs. Tellamoot was in tears.

"I'll get Wendy and have her come be with you, okay?"

"Thank you."

Kat called Wendy's phone number. She answered on the first ring. "What's up KittyKat?" Kat explained the situation to Wendy.

"I'll come get you."

"No, I think Bernice needs you to be with her. Pastor said he'd help me look for Benny."

"I'm going right over. Call when you know anything."

Her cell chirped again. "Oh for goodness sake."

"Hello." She sounded pretty angry.

"Doctor Douglas here. I got a call about that white dog."

"Benny."

"Right. Anyway, I'm just coming into town from Clayton. I'll keep an eye out."

"We're on our way to do the same."

"Can Bart get out and scout, too?"

"He's on his way to Old Town on police business."

"Too bad. Well, I'll try to meet you in the middle, as they say."

Ken and Bart arrived to a dark and misty Old Town. The blue LED lights bounced off the fog. They spotted the mayor's corpse in front of the log cabin.

"Just like the others."

They looked around. The place looked the same but then it didn't. Dark shapes and forms glinted through the mist.

"This does not bode well."

"Stop saying that."

Bart gave Ken a quick smile, "Well, it doesn't."

"Been taking vocabulary lessons and you're stuck on that sentence, right?"

The attack came from behind. The Kumrande, two per man, yanked their legs out of under them, sending flashlights skidding across the snow-covered ice.

"Break their legs!"

"Iconoclast ordered they be left whole." Nihilist and the other three flipped Ken over and laid him down. Two of them held their dagger claws to his neck. Ken watched the one called Nihilist step on a stone near the skull rock. The rock slid open, an entry to a tunnel below. Ken thrashed from side to side.

A sharp sting and Ken lost his strength.

"Do that again and I'll break your legs. And I'll make sure you feel every bone snap." Ken calmed.

"Iconoclast wants this one first." The Kumrande dragged Bart to the opening.

Ken pulled one hand free. He felt heavy pressure on his right knee. "I'm so happy you don't heed warnings." Nihilist held Ken's knee in place and bent the lower half of his leg outward. Ken screamed. A growl was the only warning Nihilist got before a white blur lunged and dropped him to the ground. It pulled the Kumrande off Ken, flinging them across the courtyard. The remaining Kumrande dropped Bart and charged the intruder. The white dog yelped. A crimson stain saturated the ivory fur.

Bart pushed off the ice and ran for the flashlights. The Kumrande bolted after him. Benny recovered and leaped in front of the pursuers, bared his teeth and lunged. The Kumrande screamed as teeth clamped into flesh. Bart pointed the flashlight at the oncoming horde. The screams intensified and they galloped into the cover of the forest.

The white dog lay down whimpering and panting. Bart shone the light on him then Ken.

Bart balanced the flashlight in one hand and the cell in the other. He first dialed Doc Billings, then Doc Douglas. Doc Billings agreed to pick up Ken. Bart dropped Benny at the vet's and called Kat.

"I found the dog."

"Oh that's wonderful news. I'll let Mrs. Tellamoot know."

"Kat ..."

"Yes."

"Ken's hurt."

Terror gripped Kat. "How hurt?"

"He's got a bad cut, but more, he is feverish and unconscious. The dog's hurt too."

"Where's Ken?"

"Doc Billings took him to the office."

"I'll be there in five minutes." The phone went dead.

Mrs. Tellamoot and Wendy arrived at Doc Douglas' ten minutes after Bart. The prognosis wasn't good.

"That dog has a raging infection— again. Are you sure that wound just happened?"

"I'm sure. My friend is in the same condition."

"You're telling me you were attacked by those animals that left the hoof prints?"

"I'm telling you we were attacked by some type of part human thing that left those hoof prints. And, don't look at me that way. I know how it sounds *and* I know what I saw. Both Melbourne and the dog passed out within minutes after the attack."

"I'll start this dog on more antibiotics. I have never seen such a miraculous recovery as he had within the last two days. I hope he can do it again." Doc turned to Mrs. Tellamoot. "I'll call you when I know something."

"I'm staying."

"There is nothing you can do for him right now."

"I'm staying anyway."

"I'm staying with you, Bernice."

Bernice Tellamoot smiled up at Wendy. "I'd appreciate that."

Nyna came through the door. "Wendy said there's an emergency. What can I do to help?"

Douglas pointed to Benny.

"I'll get him prepped for the drip." She headed toward the supply room.

"Thanks for the cookies. They were delicious." Bart yelled after her. She turned and beamed at him, then hurried toward the back.

She really is a looker, Bart thought.

"I'm going to check on Melbourne. Call me when you know about that dog." He turned to Mrs. Tellamoot. "He saved our lives, you know."

Bernice patted his hand. "I didn't know but I'm glad." She went back to watching Benny.

Bart said his goodbyes and headed to Doc Billings.

Kat was sitting by Ken. So was Paul Lucas. Kat got up and went to Bart.

She tilted her head in Paul's direction. "He's been praying pretty much nonstop since we got here."

"How is he?"

"Better than he should be, from what Doc says. The fever's breaking and his breathing has become more normal. He still hasn't regained consciousness, though."

Bart walked to Ken. His hair was soaked. He had dark circles under his eyes and pallor under the deep flush from the fever. *Don't you die on me. Don't you dare die on me.* Bart realized Ken was the closest thing he had for a friend. They understood each other.

The front door creaked open.

"I'll go." Bart walked to the waiting room and returned a short time later, followed by Grandma and Josiah.

"Bad news travels fast," Bart said.

Kat ran to her grandmother, a small child once again falling into her arms. Grandma patted Kat and walked to Ken and the pastor.

Josiah joined them. A look of anger took the place of his calm expression.

"What evil did this?" he demanded, looking at Paul.

Paul shook his head. "I don't know."

"It was those nasty creatures they call the Kumrande—you know, the ones we all thought were folklore." Bart looked at Grandma Bricken.

"Mrs. Tellamoot did talk about a white settler from the Forgotten Place who practiced an odd religion. One of the parts of that religion had to do with elements of nature."

"These Kumrande are a part of that religion?"

"Seems possible." Alese answered.

"Tell me what they look like," Josiah said.

"Small, sharp-featured faces. Grey. Yellow, reflective eyes. Wrinkled."

"You're describing what the Europeans call gnomes. What the Irish call leprechauns."

"News to me. I only knew them by Kumrande." Bart was writing in his notebook.

"These creatures are brought out by someone who worships evil ones. They are creatures subject to the will of demons."

"Gnomes are said to use poison to subdue a victim. Maybe the Kumrande's do the same." Kat smiled sheepishly at Bart.

"How do you know that?"

"I read a lot. Thought it was fiction at the time."

Doc Billings had been listening. "When he got here, he woke up and couldn't make a coherent sentence. He would try to name something and the word came out totally different than what he was trying to say. When I asked him about the pain, he motioned to his head and stomach. I'll be right back."

Doc returned with a book of poisonous plants common to Southcentral Alaska. He thumbed through. "I knew the symptoms sounded familiar." He read in silence. "Yep. Those are the symptoms. It's Baneberry poisoning."

"How is it treated?" Kat asked.

"It should wear off. The fever's what threw me—it's not part of baneberry poisoning. But everything else is a perfect match."

"How about the dog?" Bart was feeling a loyalty to the animal that saved his life.

"The dog should come out of it even quicker. I'm more concerned about these deep wounds because they look infected. But, as long as Ken responds to the antibiotics, he'll be good as new. I better call Douglas."

Doc Billings returned. "Douglas is taking care of Benny. The biggest concern with him is appetite. Sometimes they lose it and then you lose the animal from dehydration and starvation instead of the poison."

"So, why would anyone use baneberries to poison someone if it doesn't kill them?" Bart asked.

"Baneberries are nasty little buggers. They will incapacitate an individual for quite a while. Lucky you weren't hit by it, too." He hung a small IV bag next to a larger one that was hooked into Ken's arm. "This one has the antibiotic; the other one will help with the electrolytes and keep them balanced. He's lost a lot of fluid. Threw up a few times and sweating like a sauna client. I've given him an antihistamine just in case. It will help negate any allergic reaction. Now, we wait."

"We are going up to the vet's office. We may be the older generation but we can help, too. We'll find out what else Mrs.

Tellamoot knows about that book." Josiah and Alese walked out together into the driving snowstorm.

"There's nothing more you can do right now."

Kat pulled a chair up to the examining table where Ken lay. It was obvious she wasn't leaving.

"Call me if anything changes." Billings left the room.

Brandon McGill stood at the upper floor window of the old house, a look of rage contorting the handsome face. Atramentous and Gambogian stood on either side of him.

"I thought that dog had been taken care of," he hissed.

"He was almost dead. Our friends had driven him to the point of insanity. He had bitten himself enough to start an infection. We do not know how or why he became healthy again."

"Send Prevaricator and Trepaner. They must stop that dog."

"Done."

Iconoclast looked out onto the courtyard and smiled. The skull had begun to change color. It had deepened from a sand to a red clay brown. It wouldn't be long now. He looked at the abandoned corpse in front of the cabin and smiled wider. "Fools think they can change their minds." He shivered knowing if the mayor had been wise enough to call on Jesus, Iconoclast would have been up against a formidable foe. He threw the thought of defeat from his mind and returned to the task at hand. He grinned as he saw people begin to mill around the old square. It had begun. They were coming to him.

Grandma and Josiah walked into the vet's reception area.

"Good morning, Mrs. Bricken and …?"

Josiah held his hat in his hand and bent slightly at the waist. "Josiah Williams."

"What can I do for you?"

"Is Mrs. Tellamoot still here?"

"She is. Won't leave that dog."

"How is Benny?"

"Remarkably well. Eyes are open. Sitting up. The wound is deep but looks like it will heal. Just need him to eat."

"Oh, that is good news." Grandma Bricken knew it would break Mrs. Tellamoot's heart, again, if she lost this one, too.

"Do you think we can see her?"

"Sure. Come with me."

Mrs. Tellamoot stood up and smiled when she saw Josiah and Grandma. Benny was standing and wagging his tail. He pawed the kennel door.

"Doc says he needs to stay put for a little while. I think Benny disagrees." She laughed.

"Bernice, do you have any specific information about that *Book of Fallen Angels*?"

Her face paled. She dropped into the chair beside Benny and put her hand through the kennel bars to pet him for comfort. "Why do you ask?"

"Seems Mayor Orthell had it and now Bart's got it. The mayor indicated it had something to do with the murders around here."

Bernice's eyes shot to Alese's. "If that's true, Ravens Cove is about to meet the same fate as the Forgotten Place. I thought it was odd to bring all those old buildings here 'as a tourist draw' like the mayor said. There is only one way to stop it. That is to call on the holy angels of God to fight for us."

"We have prayed, Bernice. It doesn't seem to be working." Josiah shot Alese an alarmed look.

"I know that Jesus hears us. I just don't know why this is happening and why He won't stop it." Alese sighed and sat down.

"That book not only brings back the demons and elementals, it brings back the strongest of all the evil foes—right under Satan, that is. And, as you know, our battle is not with flesh and blood, Alese."

"Then what are we supposed to do?"

"I think the evil foe knows his battle for the souls of men is with God. But people, arrogant as we are, think we can fight that battle for God. Maybe God wants us to know for a fact that He is the only one that can fight this battle. Not us," Josiah said.

Mrs. Tellamoot look at Alese Bricken. "The Forgotten Place was all but destroyed. There were some, in the hunting party, that survived, as you know. My grandmother told me there was a man of God, who joined them that day. He had come as a missionary and wanted to learn the ways of the people. The story goes, and no one could confirm it, that when he saw the destruction, he fell on his knees, cried out to the Lord to fight, and went into the village. They said they heard footsteps like an army above their heads. The next thing was the tale by the Native saying he had sneaked back to the village and saw the death and the angel that was fighting."

"I can't believe my own arrogance," Josiah said. "I have been acting as if I was calling on God. I was calling on God and expecting myself to fight this evil myself. I am a fool."

"I am, too. I have been doing the same thing." They looked around and saw Paul Lucas behind them.

"Kat told me you were here. There is an odd thing happening in the town right now. A gathering at the Old Town. People are going there like they are on a mission or in a trance."

"It is the beginning of the end. That is what happened in the Forgotten Place before the slaughter. All the people came out and stood in the town center. No one understood why they didn't run or hide. Now I know why. The deceit has been woven over them."

"I know where I need to go." Paul walked toward the door. It was getting light. The snow had stopped but the sky still hung with deep grey clouds not sure it was finished dumping its load.

"Not without us, Paul. You'd be a fool."

"I've been called worse in the name of my Lord."

"Lord," Josiah began, "help us. We have sinned against You. We have forgotten we are weak and cannot fight any battle without You. Please, God, help us. Please fight for us. In Jesus' name. Amen."

Paul sighed. "Pride is such a deceitful thing—the heart of man laps it up like water."

"Agreed. Let's go."

"We need to tell Kat and Bart."

They walked into the small medical clinic. Bart was all smiles, as was Kat. Kenneth came out from the back.

"Ah, the small family has reassembled."

"We are not the only ones in a reunion. We need to get to Old Town. Your illness has been a diversion as much as a close encounter with death. It has given Iconoclast time to assemble his comrades and to grow stronger," Alese Bricken said.

Ken went for the door.

"Wait a minute. You aren't going anywhere," Kat said.

"I am going somewhere. I feel fine."

"Kat, he needs to go, we all do. There is a crowd gathering at Old Town. There is a slaughter about to occur."

"He's been so sick." She looked into Ken's eyes, pleading with him not to go.

"I'm fine. And I have you." He lifted her chin and kissed her gently.

"Why do we have to do this? Why?" she screamed. "Hasn't God put enough on us already?"

They stood and looked at her. She wiped an angry tear from her right eye.

"Guess not. Let's go." She stormed toward the door.

They arrived at Old Town. The old skull was maroon and its eyes were glowing with a light of their own. Two people were dead in front of the old hotel. Others were standing in front of the skull, like waiting their turn on a carnival ride. Brandon McGill stood behind the skull, greeting each one. Bart lurched forward to get to them.

"Stop. You can't do this, Bart. Haven't you learned that yet?"

"I can't stand here and watch a massacre."

"We aren't here to watch a massacre. We're here to ask forgiveness and pray. Why do you think we weren't affected by the odd call of the demons?"

"I am the sheriff. I am supposed to protect these people. What do you want me to do?"

"Wait on the Lord."

The sky started turning red. "Iconoclast is definitely here." Kat was pointing to the red smoke. They watched as the smoke rose higher and people drew closer to their doom.

"Do you accept me as your king?" Bart heard McGill saying. He looked closer. Brandon McGill's face wasn't right. It kept contorting like the skin didn't fit quite right.

"Do you see that?" He pointed to Brandon. Ken looked where Bart was pointing and watched.

"Yeah, that's just wrong."

"I do not believe that is Brandon McGill we are seeing. It's a demon. I've seen it before when I was in the ravine. Lord, reveal the truth of this being. Please God make it reveal its true form. In Your name, Jesus. Amen."

At the "Amen" the small troop watched as Brandon McGill's

façade dissipated and what stood in its place was an enormous black being. Its chest was four feet across. Its skin was black leather and molded to its rib cage like armor. The claws glinted in the growing darkness. In its hand was a small purple and black ornament. Each person wanted to touch that ornament.

"What is that?" Kat asked. Something niggled her subconscious. "I know that thing."

"Dreaming maybe?"

"I don't know." Then she was sure she perceived a low, melancholy melody. "Hear that?"

"I do," Josiah said, "it sounds familiar."

"That's the tune I heard when you were in the ravine!"

"That's the rock thing. That's Pet!" Kat said loudly. Too loudly. She got the attention of the thing at the rock.

Several people had touched Pet. Dried blood was evident on either their left or right hands.

"We have visitors, O friends. Please help me to get rid of them."

Those people turned and started toward the small group.

"Wendy!" Kat screamed and lunged forward.

Ken grabbed her. "She can't hear you, Kat. She's not Wendy right now."

Paul fell to his knees and cried out. "God, help us and help our town. I do not understand why Ravens Cove is so important in the battle between You and evil. But it is. I can only call on You because Your son died for me and made the way to You. God save us."

The mob was on them. Bart and Ken had pulled guns and pointed them at the people. One of the mob screamed. A Kumrande had grabbed him from behind, to be the next sacrifice to Iconoclast.

The mob stopped for a moment, almost broken from the

trance. The small group ran across the street into the trees. The crowd stopped at the edge of Old Town, unable or unwilling to leave. Wendy and some others went back to the skull and stood in line again. The rest made a barrier at the entrance to Old Town.

Wendy was next at the Rock. Kat watched in horror as the lighted eyes glowed brighter and the beak mouth opened. Wendy stepped forward. A blur of white flew through the human wall and ran to the skull.

"How the heck did that dog get out again?" Doc Douglas came running up behind them and stopped. Fear gripped him as he watched what was going on in Old Town.

"God help us." A surprise to all, he ran forward and fell to his knees right in front of the mob.

He held up his hands. "God of my fathers, God of Abraham, Isaac, and Jacob, I beg you to hear me. You fought for my ancestors in the days of old. You fight for your children today. Please renew Your wonders now, O God. Please. Save us for Your sake. In Y'shua's mighty name, send your warriors. Amen."

"Who's Y'shua?" Bart asked Grandma in a whisper.

"That is the name of our Lord and God, Jesus Christ. That is His name in Hebrew."

What sounded like a mighty clap of thunder came through the air. So loud the ground shook and trees quivered.

"What's that sound?" Kat asked Ken. Ken shrugged. He was intent on watching Doc Douglas, who had gone prone on the ground and was not moving. The mob in front of him had tried to reach him but couldn't.

"I hear footsteps, lots of them. Up there." Kat looked up but saw nothing.

"So do I."

Prevaricator and Trepaner went to work, spreading lies and deceit. It was the demon's only hope.

"Not true," Trepaner whispered in Kat's ear. "You're overwrought, maybe even insane."

"I think I'm just a little cracked right now." Kat said to Ken.

Ken looked at her. He'd never heard her waver on what she knew she saw. He was sure he saw something dark behind Kat. A sickly black aura. He had seen this before.

"Paul. Here. Now." Paul Lucas walked to Ken and Kat. "Do you see that?"

"Be gone in the name of Jesus, you evil being." Trepaneer flew toward the Old Town center like he was a baseball and had just been used to hit a home run. The black being fell at the rock center.

Iconoclast growled. "We are not done, man of God. You have lost." He grabbed Wendy and they watched in horror as the skull began to slide to the side, mouth still open.

"No!" Kat ran forward before they could catch her. She stopped a few feet in front of the human wall.

Iconoclast had forgotten Benny in the hubbub. Benny grabbed the evil being and bit down. It screamed. He released Iconoclast and tugged on Wendy's jeans, dragging her a short distance from the hole. Pet fell to the ground and Iconoclast grabbed him back up before the dog could get it.

Iconoclast reached for Benny and caught him. The dog writhed and snapped at his hand. "I suppose Dacoit would like some dog, too." Iconoclast laughed as he took Benny to the skull and lowered Benny to the mouth.

A bolt of lightning broke through the gathering darkness and struck the skull-rock in the center of the head. The lightning ricocheted and hit Iconoclast in the arm. He dropped Benny.

Benny snapped at him one more time before he ran back to Wendy. Wendy was unconscious. He started licking her face.

Mrs. Orthell screamed profanities and insults at the small troop, accusing them of killing her Tommy. Accusing the sheriff of not doing his job and telling them all how she'd enjoy murdering each and every one of them. Kat took off and broke through the human shield. She hit Mrs. Orthell like a linebacker and ran to Wendy and Benny. She grabbed Wendy and tried to pick her up but she was deadweight. The others followed her in and ran to her. They were surrounded by the mob.

"You are all we needed to make this bloodbath complete. I can always depend on mortals to be the fools they were created to be." Iconoclast came forward. "Now we can truly feast."

"You first. I still hunger for that lost sweetness you would provide in your death." He grabbed Kat. Benny lunged and Iconoclast kicked out and caught the dog in the stomach. Benny flew to the other side of the courtyard.

"Y'shua please help!" The disembodied march resumed. The forest trees vibrated to the increasing clamor of the rhythmic beat.

The sun's light tore through the overcast town. A golden staircase appeared, one misty step at a time, and hovered several feet above Old Town. Dots of silver light took on the form of glowing men, dressed in bronze breastplates. Each held a polished sword. Rainbows of light shot to the ground each time a sword reflected the sun's light. Benny's gold eyes focused on the warriors. He jumped toward the opening to heaven, wagged his tail and barked a loud greeting.

"Thank you, O merciful One." Doc Douglas fell prone on the ground.

The angel's leader lifted his sword to the heavens and the

doorway disappeared. He advanced into the courtyard. The glowing army followed.

"Iconoclast drew a graphite-colored saber and held it high. "We will not bow to you or your God!" The demon militia fanned out from behind Iconoclast.

"So it has been ordained." The lead angel's sword sung as it sliced the air.

Iconoclast's wings snapped out and he took flight. The lead angel met him in midair. Iconoclast's eight took to the skies and were met by the awaiting army. The skies rumbled with the thunder of war. Banshee shrieks followed a melodic, metallic hum.

The small troop of human warriors ran to Doctor Douglas and helped him to his feet. As soon as he was upright, he took off for the courtyard, looped his arm around Wendy and pulled her into the street.

"Where did you come from?—not that I minded the short winter romp." Wendy smiled at the vet.

The clamor above them grew louder. Wendy threw her hands over her ears and looked up. "Odd time of year for thunder."

Kat snorted a laugh and threw her arm around Wendy's shoulders. "Sure is, Winsome. You got here late. Just keep watching."

Kat resisted the urge to duck and cover when Trapaneer plummeted to the earth, a foul-smelling mist in his wake. He landed outside the Old Town sign and dissolved into the sidewalk.

Tears filled Kat's eyes when a glowing being shot toward the ground, sparked then evaporated against the blue sky.

Grandma gave her a quick squeeze. "They don't die, sweet one."

"I know. Just made me sad to see one of the good guys go down in flames."

Iconoclast somersaulted to the ground in front of Dacoit and touched his blade to the skull-rock. The graphite caught fire.

The commanding angel swooped low and landed between the small cabin and the boulder.

Iconoclast sprang from the ground, glowing embers trailing his sword. "Be gone from my home." He dove at the angel swinging the flaming blade. The golden broadsword met Iconoclast's weapon in midair.

"Be gone *to* your home." The lead angel held his sword to the sky. A streak of lightening met he weapon. Blue sparks danced down the shaft to the curved handle. They fell to the ground opening a bright hole in the courtyard. He pointed the sword at Iconoclast. Iconoclast shot to the top of the old house. A line of blue fire broke left and up. It looped back on itself and fell over the demon. The misty rope pulled Iconoclast forward until he hovered over the fire. The opaque rope disintegrated and Iconoclast fell into the hole. A blinding fountain of white vapor shot out of the chasm. When the light waned, the angelic beings and the demons were gone.

"I am really starting to doubt my sanity," Kat said.

"We all saw it. Stop doubting just because you can't touch it, smell or see it," Josiah said, "and you'll be fine."

"I believe that is the definition of faith." Alese walked up smiling.

Mrs. Tellamoot jogged into their midst. "There you are." Benny came running to her, jumped up and licked her face until her laughter filled the courtyard. Doctor Douglas joined them.

"Thank you."

"For what?"

"For intervening on behalf of Ravens Cove—and us."

"Those bodies are gone," Bart remarked. "There were two bodies in front of the old house. Or am I losing it?"

"Buried by the angels, just like the story," Mrs. Tellamoot said.

Even Orthell's body had disappeared. "He was taken and buried, too. God's mercy is unfathomable."

The small troop thanked God for salvation. A group of townspeople had stayed behind.

"We don't know how we got here," Mrs. Orthell said.

"We do but you may find it hard to believe," Paul told her.

"Why don't we go to my house, Maureen? We'll explain to you."

Maureen Orthell smiled at Alese Bricken. "I'd like that."

Epilogue
Of Cats and Dogs

Bart and Ken returned to Brandon's house. They were surprised to find his body in the basement. He lay outside the protective circle, both wrists slit.

"Suicide, I think." Sadness overtook Bart. "What a waste of life and soul."

Ken nodded. "Brother, I don't know why we were spared again but I know I believe now."

"Me too."

They said a prayer over the body and called Dr. Billings for what they hoped was the last time in this capacity.

They got in Bart's old truck and went to Grandma's.

The laughter that greeted them was like a breath of fresh air. The heaviness of the murders and evil that had almost destroyed Ravens Cove lifted.

Time to heal, rest, and celebrate life. Ken heard in his head. It seemed Bart heard the same thing.

Grandma's house was overflowing with the townspeople. The feeling of joy and the sound of laughter grew.

"I've taken too much for granted in my life, Bart, and thought I had nothing but time. I'm changing that, today." Ken noticed that Nyna was standing in the hallway watching Bart and Ken come in. Her eyes stayed on Bart.

"I think you should take that advice, too." He motioned with his head toward Nyna. Bart saw her and smiled.

"Think you're right, good friend, think it's time to start living for today. Who knows what could happen tomorrow." Bart walked to Nyna and took the extra coffee she had been holding.

Kat ran and threw her arms around Ken. A familiar sting hit his leg. "Ouch. BC you have to stop doing that." He picked him up and cradled the cat like a football. Benny came running out of the kitchen and sat in front of Ken. A low growl issued from BC. His tail swished back and forth and his hair started to stand on end.

Benny gave BC a wary look and went back into the kitchen. BC relaxed and cuddled close into Ken's arms.

Ken put his other arm around Kat's waist and gave her a squeeze. "I'm thinking we should run off together. How about you?"

"After the ceremony." She smiled.

He leaned down and kissed her gently on the mouth. "Then how about we plan a real party—a wedding reception right here in Ravens Cove?"

"I'd like that. I'd like that a lot." She smiled up at him. BC walked off Ken's arm and into Kat's and started to purr, emerald green eyes looking into Kat's of the same color.

"I think Black Cat agrees, too."

"Good thing. I don't need any more scars from that critter."

"Let's find the group and the pastor and get this party planned."

"I already have the party planned." Wendy had come up behind them, listening in as she was adept at doing.

"Of course you do, Winsome." Kat grabbed a handful of auburn curls and tugged.

"It's what I do, KittyKat. It's what I do."

Grandma was watching the interaction from the kitchen doorway. These were the times she cherished. All was right with her family and all was right with her world.

Josiah walked up to her. "Should we tell them?"

"Not now. Let them celebrate and enjoy. There's time enough to prepare for the next battle." Grandma slipped her arm through Josiah's. He gave her hand a squeeze and a pat.

"And we will be ready for that time." Josiah said. "Until then, let's do some celebrating ourselves." He grabbed Alese Bricken around the waist and swung her into the hall and to her adored family.

The End

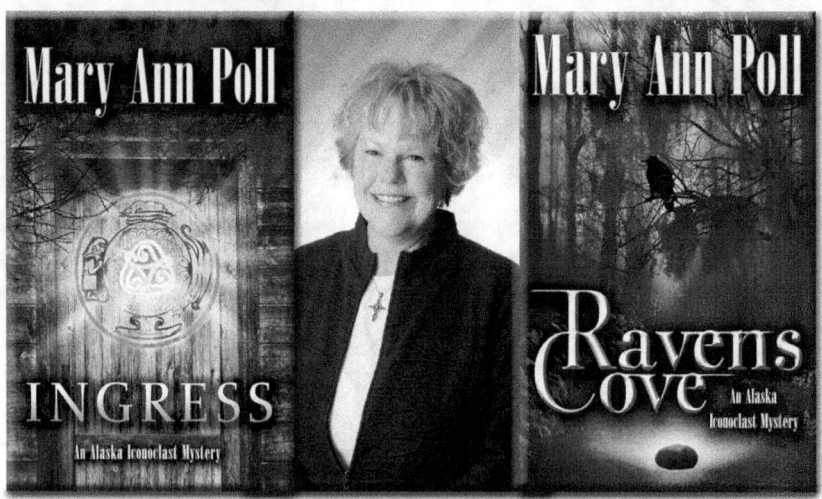

To contact Mary Ann for book signings or to arrange for her
to be a guest speaker for your group, call or email:
Phone: (907) 240-0375 ••• mapoll@gci.net

Use this Coupon to Order Additional Copies

Please ship to:

First Name _____ Last Name _____

Address _____

City _____ State _____ Zip _____

Phone Number _____ email _____

			Quantity	Total
Orders shipped via Air Mail the day they are received.	Ravens Cove	$17.95 each	_____	$ _____
	Ingress	$17.95 each	_____	$ _____
	Shipping and Handling No S and H with purchase	3.00 each		$ _____
	of two books or more.	**Grand Total**		$ _____

Credit Card Number _____ ❏ VISA

Expiration Date _____ Signature _____ ❏ MC

Publication Consultants

8370 Eleusis Drive, Anchorage, Alaska 99502
phone: (907) 349-2424 • fax: (907) 349-2426
www.publicationconsultants.com — email: books@publicationconsultants.com